SHE WAS ENCHANTING ALL RIGHT.

And when Willis had ordered her to stop embarrassing him in front of the dean and the rest of the faculty, Anathae just wouldn't listen. Then he told her to vanish and that's exactly what she did. Willis didn't know where she'd gone and he didn't care. At least not until someone sidled up to him and asked him in what topless bar he'd picked up his lady demon.

Opening his mouth to reply, Willis heard himself responding in a voice that sounded very much like Anathae's breathy soprano, "French kiss a Nile crocodile!"

Willis's eyes grew wide. *Good grief*, he thought, *she's possessed me . . . !*

Great Science Fiction from SIGNET

A PERSONAL DEMON

David Bischoff, Rich Brown, and Linda Richardson writing as Michael F. X. Milhaus

With an Afterword by Ted White

Ⓞ

A SIGNET BOOK

NEW AMERICAN LIBRARY

PUBLISHED BY
THE NEW AMERICAN LIBRARY
OF CANADA LIMITED

NAL BOOKS ARE AVAILABLE AT QUANTITY DISCOUNTS WHEN USED
TO PROMOTE PRODUCTS OR SERVICES. FOR INFORMATION PLEASE
WRITE TO PREMIUM MARKETING DIVISION, NEW AMERICAN LIBRARY,
1633 BROADWAY, NEW YORK, NEW YORK 10019.

The novel A PERSONAL DEMON is based on a series of magazine stories
written under the pseudonym Michael F. X. Milhaus and appearing in the
following issues of *Fantastic*: "A Personal Demon"—February, 1976; "In a
Pig's Eye"—May, 1976; "With Good Intentions"—September, 1977; "A
Trick of the Tail"—December, 1977; and "Where Angels Fear to Tread"
—April, 1978. In that form, they are copyright © 1975, 1976, 1977, and
1978 by Ultimate Publications, Inc.

First Printing, September, 1985

2   3   4   5   6   7   8   9

SIGNET TRADEMARK REG. U.S. PAT. OFF. AND FOREIGN COUNTRIES
REGISTERED TRADEMARK—MARCA REGISTRADA
HECHO EN WINNIPEG, CANADA

SIGNET, SIGNET CLASSIC, MENTOR, PLUME, MERIDIAN
AND NAL BOOKS are published in Canada by The New American
Library of Canada, Limited, 81 Mack Avenue, Scarborough,
Ontario, Canada M1L 1M8
PRINTED IN CANADA
COVER PRINTED IN U.S.A.

TO THE VICIOUS CIRCLE

PART ONE

1

Put on your disbelief suspenders, dear reader, as Coleridge might invite, and make yourself welcome outside this cozy little apartment near Powhattan University, that arcade of academia tucked away in the ivy-covered ivory-white pseudo-Greek buildings in the heartland of New England.

Powhattan—"old P.U." to friends and enemies alike—was a yawningly normal institution of higher education, or at least it was until the fateful night of Professor Willis Baxter's faculty party. . . .

Come. Let's peer in and see how it all began.

Willis Baxter, Professor of Medieval Literature, arose from his near-drunken slouch on the couch and, with five Irish whiskeys in him and the somewhat encouraging voices of otherwise bored partygoers behind him, repaired to his study for the elements he needed to conjure up a demon.

It was, he felt, the least he could do to help alleviate the boredom which was beginning to settle on the partygoers like an unwanted and ragged cloak. They were dutifully in attendance at the insistence of Dean Cromwell Smith, as was Willis himself—although, in truth, since the party was being held (at the "request" of the dean) in Willis's garden apartment, it was also somewhat more than that. Willis was only glad his upstairs neighbors were not at home, since the partygoers made up in loudness what the party itself lacked in interest.

"What's this hubbub all about?" the dean was demanding,

having squired the party's wealthy guest of honor, Norman Rockhurst, into the crowded dining room. Hot to trot with the rich man's tax-deductible charity allocations, the dean had devoted the entire evening to attempting to toady to the man—with no apparent success as yet.

"Baxter frequently tries it when he's sloshed," explained Larry Hawthorne, Professor of Renaissance Literature, as he lumbered to his size-fourteen feet and groped about in his jacket pocket.

"Tries what?" Rockhurst asked.

Hawthorne pulled out a Ronson, relit his evening's cigar for the fourth time, and blew out an acrid stream of smoke.

"With some people, it's lampshades," he said, bellying up to the dean and the wealthy contractor. "They down a few drinks over their limit—with Baxter, it's two—then don a lampshade, dance about, and come on to the ladies. But Baxter's more original—when *he* gets drunk, he tries to summon up demons from the netherworld."

"Ridiculous!" pooh-poohed the millionaire.

"Demons? Balderdash!" echoed the dean—who was precisely the sort of person who would say "Balderdash!" even in this day and age.

"Of course, it's all in fun," chimed in Gertrude Twill, the dean's secretary and office manager.

Gertrude, against Willis's wishes, had chosen to wear a very short dress to the party—the kind of dress that tends to draw male attention to nyloned legs. Although her legs were not drawing much attention, it must be admitted they were indeed her most attractive feature.

It was sometimes bandied about—usually with accompanying snickers—that Gertrude might be Willis's one and only "girlfriend." In truth, they had dated for eight years—and at times the professor wondered what he saw in her. He would think, briefly, of her soft lips; then, involuntarily rubbing his mouth, less briefly of her braces. Most of the time, favoring a martyrlike disposition which had been drilled into him by the Catholic catechism of his youth, he accepted the inconvenience without questioning the therapeutic value of perpetually wired teeth which made kissing somewhat reminiscent of the Spanish Inquisition.

"Well, conjuring, though!" Rockhurst said, suddenly struck. "I suppose a few magic tricks might liven up this party a bit."

"They just might," agreed the dean.

Professor Baxter returned at this moment with a purple-and-red-striped bag with "Macy's" emblazoned on its sides. At a small space he had cleared in the center of the room, he dropped the bag to the floor and, with a certain uncharacteristic flair, requested another Irish whiskey to fortify himself. Gertrude supplied the sacred potion, which Willis slurped down in one quick gulp. He rubbed a hand over his plain, long-nosed features. A hush fell over the crowd as the dimmed lights cast odd shadows across their expectant faces, and even Larry Hawthorne was quietly intent as he puffed his cigar, the smoke of which hung like incense in the air.

Willis stood silently a moment, as if preparing himself for the ritual—while, in truth, he was praising the Irish for inventing so sassy a whiskey. Abruptly he began to mutter the *Desiderata* in Latin.

"All right, Baxter," Hawthorne said derisively, "precisely *which* demon are you thinking of inviting to join us in these festivities?"

"What the *devil* difference does it make?" asked Rockhurst, smiling broadly at his own quick wit. Dean Smith laughed uproariously, and, as he cast a stern eye over the partygoers (university employees, all), so did everyone else in the room.

Hawthorne explained, "I really don't believe in this business, but I've read a little about the stuff—and it's *supposed* to make a difference. The demon must be summoned by his or her True Name. One of the most respected scholars in the field of demonology, Raymond de la Farte, theorized in his most recent book that the reason it's nearly impossible to invoke a demon in this day and age is simply that most of them have been consigned to Hell forever."

Observing that his knowledge of the obscure had, for once, aroused interest rather than ennui in his listeners, Hawthorne took the cigar from his mouth, struck a pose he often affected in the classroom, and continued: "You see, when someone tries to summon a demon and *fails*, the ritual requires him to consign the soul of that demon to Hell forever—otherwise, it's believed, the demon can use that entryway to our world at some later date and, without someone there to control it, wreak all sorts of havoc.''

"I guess that makes sense," Rockhurst said.

"Yes, but can you believe this sort of thing?" Hawthorne asked, dropping his pose as he turned to the millionaire.

Rockhurst made no answer, so Hawthorne resumed both his pose and lecture: "De la Farte suggested that demons, while endowed with magical powers, might not be able to be in two places at the same time. That is, if indeed there was some 'limit' to their magic, it might be such a thing as this. An interesting possibility. Because, you see, de la Farte demonstrated that, with what was once a considerably more widespread interest in demonology and what with the number of demons being finite, the chances are quite high that most of them would have been summoned by two or more conjurers at or near the same time. The best-known demons certainly, the lesser-known demons almost as certainly.''

He paused to note that he had indeed captured the attention of several other partygoers. Not wishing to lose their interest, he continued, "Thus, while one demonologist might succeed in summoning a demon, if another tried to get the same demon while it was doing something for the first, he would fail in the attempt—since the demon wouldn't be there to be called. And, by the requirements of the ritual, the one who failed would have to consign that demon to the netherworld forever. When the demon returned to Hades, after doing the bidding of the successful magician, it would thereafter be unable to leave Hell by virtue of the second conjurer's ritual and therefore could never be successfully summoned again.''

Willis, who was busily working with his tools—drawing a pentagram with Silly String, laying out a star within the pentagram with drink straws and swizzle sticks—could hardly contain his amusement at Hawthorne's words.

For you see, dear reader, although Professor Willis Baxter's most daring in-person feat to date had been when he had fondled Gertrude's elbow at a local drive-in movie, he also led something of a secret life. And it was one of his most closely guarded secrets that he *was* Raymond de la Farte. The good professor reveled in his confidential study much as a fire-and-brimstone preacher might in a private pornography collection.

Hawthorne, turning to indicate his rival with a slight nod, went on: "So if Professor Baxter here hopes to be successful, he'll have to use the True Name of some obscure or lesser-known demon who, one presumes, might not have suffered such a fate."

Willis started to ask, "What's your mother's name?"—but then reconsidered as he remembered Hawthorne's short temper and long reach. He substituted, "What would you suggest, Larry—should I consult the Yellow Pages, under 'Demons, Unlisted'?"

"Well," said Hawthorne helpfully, "there's the new Wilheim, *Minor Demons of Egypt*."

"Haven't seen it yet," Willis admitted.

"It has a few obscure names in it, I believe. How about Ptenagh? A sort of Pan, I think."

"Obscure? Hardly!" Willis scoffed. "Pembroke. *Solomon in Egypt. 1934*."

"How about his daughter, Anathae?"

"Daughter?"

Hawthorne brightened, preened at what so clearly demonstrated both his own obscure knowledge and his rival's ignorance. "Yes. Anathae. Half demon, half human."

"All right," Willis said. "It'll do."

Rockhurst, obviously a bit tired of all the talk, suddenly grinned and asked, "When do we get to the good part? You know, virgin's blood and all that? More important, where do we get the volunteers?"

Willis glanced briefly at Gertrude—but decided it was better not to broach a potentially touchy subject in front of everyone. Instead, he said, "We'll have to make do with mine," and pricked his finger with a pin.

Then he raised his hands—slightly bloody finger and all—for silence.

He was determined to try his best to make the ritual look impressive—since, despite his scholarly interest in the subject, no matter what demon he decided to call nor how inebriated he became, he did not expect the summoning to work. For, indeed, he had no belief in these things; it was the correctness of the form, the proper incantations, the very antiquity of the ritual itself which appealed to the scholar in him and therefore held his interest.

As he lowered his hands in a curving gesture, a hush settled over the company.

When all was quiet, Willis's fingers began to twitch like a squid's tentacles and he started to incant the appropriate phrases in guttural Franconian—to capture the soul of the meaning, and also to mask its more than slightly obscene content.

A fevered zeal—which some may have believed only to be the effects of the alcohol—suffused his face with a red tint, and his guests began to murmur to themselves uneasily, like a crowd watching a trapeze artist working without a net.

But as Willis stooped to light candles the circus air seemed to dissipate; the room darkened as he became stationary at the north tip of the pentagram.

The silence surrounding Willis's words was somehow ominous—it was almost *too* quiet. His discourse slipped into Old Bavarian—"*Gueliche lande cumen ger . . .*"—his arms wriggled like frightened snakes, snapped together with a flourish: ". . . *Anathae!*"

The stillness and silence which had hovered around his chant like a voiceless swallow gave way to the feel and sound of wind.

Wait a minute.

Wind?

In an inside room of the *apartment?*

Yes, the causeless breeze seemed to ruffle through Willis's rumpled hair, and even the candle-thrown shadows began a slow dance up the wall. Then he heard a tentative whisper, a feminine voice as soft as a butterfly's wing: "*In francia fui.*"

Frankish, thought Willis. *Quite frankly Frankish.*

His breathing hastened. No longer entirely aware of the people around him, Willis Baxter felt very much alone with that silken voice—which, he knew instinctively, was no joke.

"*Guaes ge dar daden?*" he whispered tremulously.

And that voice, young-girl-sweet, responded: "*Disnaui me

There was now no question that the wind was a wind; it blew full and strong and whooshed to a mighty crescendo.

Then there was a blinding flash of light, like that of a tiny nuclear explosion —and, just as suddenly, the wind stopped and the room was quite normal again.

Only . . . not quite.

For there, in the south corner of the pentagram, facing Professor Willis Baxter, stood a girl—not more than sixteen, by her features—clad only in long, tawny red hair.

2

Two tiny horns sprouted from her forehead, and a short barbed tail curled from the base of her spine just above her smooth, absolutely bare, undeniably perfectly formed derrière.

Her breasts were firm, her nipples large and creamy pink.

Her lithesome legs tapered to a pair of dainty hooves; a sprinkling of curly red hair grew up almost to her knees.

Her waist seemed almost too thin when, suddenly, it curved deliciously out to meet the well-formed curve of her delicate hips.

She angled her angelic (fallen variety, of course) and faultlessly freckled face about, surveying the people around her with curiosity. Her eyes darted like captive birds until they lighted on Willis—whereupon they turned mischievously green and she fluttered long dark eyelashes at him.

"So it was *you* who called," she breathed huskily, her voice the coo of a nightingale in heat. "Did you have anything special in mind? Or do you want me to be . . . inventive?"

Willis swallowed hard, his disbelieving eyes abulge, and stepped back—scattering a couple of the swizzle sticks which made up the pentagram. "You," he gasped, his tongue taking on the texture of a potato chip, "are Anathae?"

"None other—and yours, for so long as you may desire," she said. She curtsied with admirable grace, her slender hands outstretched as if to hold what was her entirely nonexistent dress. "Do you desire me now?"

teacher, Willis had usually been able to appreciate the

16

beauty of young women who had taken his courses without feeling any particular desire—or, if human enough to perhaps at times feel the desire, not any real need—to become intimate with any of them. But the female before him, although younger in appearance than any P.U. coed, did not (he admitted to himself) precisely inspire him with fatherly feelings.

This was in part because her voice was the epitome of seductiveness—Bo Derek rising from a foaming sea, disdaining a towel, yet with young-girl innocence glowing off her in cool, stunning waves. At the same time, her words and fiery gestures seemed to invite, if not actually beg for, frantic, clutching debauchery.

The girl-demon wiggled excitingly toward Willis, her bare breasts bobbing only slightly and her long red hair flowing behind her in the afterwake of the breeze. Willis continued to step back as he tried desperately to summon up such words, thoughts, feelings as he had used like a shield to protect himself on the rare occasion when a P.U. coed had caught more than his passing fancy—what people would say of him, how it might have an adverse effect on his career, how he should feel ashamed of having such feelings about a female obviously so much younger than himself. But he could not help but believe that, somehow, the summoning up of a demon had been, comparatively speaking, a piece of cake—at least, he couldn't easily shake the strong feeling of desire which this petite red-headed female, with so few words and movements, had sent coursing through his veins.

She followed him out of the pentagram, stepping over the breach he had caused. And then, with nimble hands, completely ignoring the partygoers around them, Anathae plucked at the top button of his shirt. She had the shirt half off and was licking her ruby lips in moist anticipation when the stunned silence of the forgotten company erupted into an excited babble.

Willis heard a squeal and noticed, peripherally, that Gertrude had fainted dead away.

"What is the *meaning* of this outrageous spectacle?" demanded the dean.

"Don't be a killjoy!" Rockhurst shouted out enthusiastically. "This is better than any show in Vegas!"

Willis had turned slowly toward the dean, hoping some explanation might occur to him before he would be called upon to open his mouth, when he felt a small hand give his pants zipper a frenzied tug.

Aghast, he looked down.

Sure enough, Anathae had his trousers halfway down, exposing his purple polka-dot underwear for the assembled multitude to see.

He said the first thing that came to mind: "Stop that and get out of here!"

Anathae withdrew her slim hands from their mad disrobing chore and pouted prettily at him.

"Later," she said, licked her lips, then winked naughtily—and, with another flash of light, she disappeared.

Given a choice in the matter, Willis would have preferred to believe she had never been there at all. But then his trousers, freed of her hands, fell all the way down to his gartered socks, and several of the faculty wives present gasped and clutched at their husbands for support.

Willis's face quivered at the redder levels of the spectrum as he made a violent attempt to resheath his bare, pale legs.

But this hasty and, indeed, decidedly frenzied action set him off balance—he teetered in the middle of the floor, wavered, stumbled forward a few wobbling steps, tripped on the manacles which had once been his trousers, and fell headfirst into the ample lap of Mrs. Hildagarde Boothbuthle, who immediately began to yelp in the contralto that was the pride of the Powhattan University Glee Club.

Willis, asprawl across her lap, tried to mumble an apology—but Mrs. Boothbuthle merely shrieked again and heaved him onto the carpet.

From this vantage point, he managed to work his trousers back over his knees by holding his legs up off the floor; he then regained his feet, pulled his pants back up over his hips, and zippered his fly.

He immediately saw, somewhat incongruously, that the dean, Rockhurst, and most of the other partygoers had turned their attention to efforts to revive Gertrude, who seemed to be noises somewhat between that of a castrated sheep's d a ship's foghorn. Only Horace and Hildagarde

Boothbuthle and Larry Hawthorne continued to regard Willis—
the two former with looks of indignation and horror, the latter
with a pitying smile.

Hawthorne sidled up to Willis.

"Well," he said conversationally, "it certainly looks as
though you may have cooked your own goose here.. Of
course, the dean probably would've named *me* head of the
department *any*way—but a stunt like this . . . Frankly, old
man, I can't begin to understand what you could've had in
mind. By the way, in what topless bar did you pick up that
delicious-looking female?"

Willis intended to say that it had not been a magic trick.
He also intended to explain, in the properly frigid tones, that
he was not in the habit of frequenting topless bars—but the
words he tried to form never reached his lips.

Instead, in their place, he found himself saying in what
sounded very much like Anathae's breathy soprano, "Eat
camel dung, eunuch! Copulate with syphilitic lepers! Suck
the rotten eggs of a vulture! French-kiss a Nile crocodile!"

Hawthorne's eyes grew wide—but no wider than those of
the distraught Willis. *Good grief*, he thought, *she's possessed
me. Well, at least it's limited to my tongue.*

Not so, lover boy, rejoined a voice in his mind—and, to his
horror, he found that his right hand with a will of its own was
folding into a fist.

"No!" he shouted, stepping back quickly so that Hawthorne would be out of reach. Nonetheless, he felt the urge to
swing.

Ah, Willis, you're no fun, he heard the demon-girl's pouting voice claim in his mind.

I've got to get out of here, he thought as much to himself
as to her, *before she makes me do something I might regret.*

Willis's shout had drawn the attention of the partygoers
back to himself. He stammered apologetically, "I'm . . . I'm
sorry. Pardon me. I'm afraid," he managed to smile, "I've
had a bit too much to drink. Please, all of you, stay. I think,
perhaps, if I got a breath of fresh air. . . ."

"Yes," Dean Smith was quick to say, "I really believe
that would be . . . advisable, to say the least, Professor."

Rockhurst, one of the few people at the party without

female accompaniment, was able to verbalize his disappointment: "Will there be a second act to your show tonight?" he asked.

"I'll be back," Willis promised.

"Good man!"

Willis turned, shuddering, trying desperately not to see the shocked, stunned, and even horrified expressions on the faces of the other members of the faculty present. They seemed to be saying that they found their previous boredom preferable to what they had witnessed, whatever *that* might have been, and they were wondering why he had not had sense enough to perceive this beforehand.

His feet seemed not to be his own as he stumbled to the hall closet, threw on his camel-hair overcoat, and attempted to propel himself in the direction of his front door.

Wait a sec, Anathae's voice sounded in his mind. *It's going to be cold out there—let's at least bring a bottle.*

No! he wanted to shout back—but found his unwilling legs propelling him toward the kitchen. He struggled against the notion even while conceding to himself that another drink certainly couldn't hurt him and just might help, and gave up the struggle when his trembling arm opened a cabinet, reached in, and snared a half-full bottle of Teacher's Scotch.

There. Now we can go, if you like.

Willis slipped the bottle into a coat pocket, and negotiated his way back toward the front room of his apartment.

Dean Smith, he noted, cast a disapproving frown at the bottle in his pocket as Willis went by but apparently did not want to interrupt what he was saying to Rockhurst.

Blushing, Willis heard the words of others hanging in the air—"disgraceful," "undignified," and even "shameful" —which he realized his guests were using in reference to what they thought had happened. Mrs. Petruccio, the chemistry professor's wife, was smiling and whispering something in her husband's ear.

Then he was out of his apartment into the chill early-January air.

He checked only to make certain that his nosy neighbor, Henrietta Bradmorton, wasn't peeking out of her apartment window, as she so often did, with her hand on the phone ready to call the police if anything she saw should displease her.

Then, slipping and sliding on the icy sidewalk, Willis made his way to his dented green Volkswagen, which, as always, was parked out front.

Leaning against it, he shook his head breathlessly, half in disbelief and half trying to clear the alcohol he had already consumed from his enfeebled brain.

3

"Okay," Willis said, his voice a whisper, "you've had your amusing bit of fun."

He drew in several bracing breaths of the cool night air. "You've probably also ruined my career," he added in a weak, tired voice. "Now kindly, if you please, get the hell out of my head!"

But, Will, it's so nice and comfy *in here! Really, you're quite extraordinary, you know—although not always in a positive way. For instance, I've just been leafing through your piles of pleasant childhood memories—*

"Out, I said!" Willis shouted. "Or would you like to hear me use an exorcism?"

"Oh, Will, you're so . . . *forceful*," she cooed. "At least, you are when you're sloshed."

He found himself staring at the nude, shivering Anathae, who had appeared seemingly out of nowhere and was now perched on the fender of his car. He wondered, inanely, if he should let her call him Will—and then, almost instinctively, he drew off his coat and put it over her shoulders.

"Thank you." She smiled. "I'm really not used to this sort of climate, you know. Nor, for that matter, to acts of kindness. You're truly a kind man, Willis. And I know precisely what kind. Screwed up—but kind."

"Am I, now?" Willis growled, pulling the Scotch from the coat pocket for added warmth. "And precisely which university in Hell gave you your degree in psychology?"

"Dear, *dear* Will," she said. She fondled his cheek with

her warm little hand—from which he drew back to take a long bracing gulp from the bottle of amber liquid.

"I was inside your head—I *know* you . . . know you as only you can know yourself," she went on in a somewhat more serious tone of voice. "And you may not realize it, but you're astoundingly different from most of the other humans who've conjured me up." Her green eyes narrowed as she reflected on this. "Most of them, you know, are full of hate and pride and the desire to impose their will on others. Really, in many respects you're quite admirable. As for the areas where you're not . . . well, I *could* take care of them, change you for the better with a few words and gestures—but they're the sort of things you'd resent, and anyway you should really work on those yourself. But, of course, I also saw some nasty hang-ups and repressed guilts cluttering up your psyche—and I could help there, especially in the psychosexual area. What you need, hon, is a little couch therapy."

She hopped down to the pavement and embraced him. Smiling brightly into his astounded face, she giggled and suggested, "Let's go behind those bushes."

Involuntarily, Willis glanced in the direction of the bushes before getting a grip on himself.

No, no, ridiculous—it simply wouldn't *do*.

He grabbed her arm, opened the door of his trusty if somewhat ancient VW, and thrust her into the passenger seat. "Don't move!" he told her in a loud but not quite angry voice.

"I won't. But isn't this car a little small for—"

He slammed the door and ran to the driver's side.

"—couch therapy? Still, I suppose we could try."

As Willis was getting into the car, Anathae was busily slithering out of his coat, her eyes glowing like fiery coals.

"Stop," he said quickly, surprising himself when his voice cracked at the edges. "You're at least *supposed* to do what I say. So listen, Anathae, you either start behaving yourself and doing that or I'll have to send you right back where you came from."

"Willis! You wouldn't!"

"Look—I have half a mind to do it anyway right now. You'd better believe I would!"

"No. You're a kind man—you wouldn't do that. You've no idea what it's like for me Down There." A tear seemed about to form on the edge of her eye, and it was all Willis could do to resist the urge to wipe it away—tenderly.

Poor child, he thought.

In an attempt to feel a little less sympathy on her behalf, Willis slurped some more of the Scotch.

"Listen," he said, "if you're a demon, I assume you must have some magical powers. Do you think you could maybe *use* some of them to whip up something for you to *wear?* I'm *cold*. I need my *coat*."

She proceeded to doff the coat again.

"No! No! For goodness' sake! What's happened already is bad enough—if Miss Bradmorton should look out her window and see me, or if a cop should pull up and find me here with a naked teenage girl in my car, that would be the end of me, my career and everything. Get some clothes on first, *then* give me my coat."

"You wouldn't *really* send me back, would you?" she asked as her hands moved busily under the coat. "You've no idea of how tormented I am Down There. Thousands of well-endowed males all around me—"

"You poor girl," sighed Willis, quite sincerely. "No wonder—"

She banged the dashboard in frustration. "And there's a damned glass barrier all around so I can't get to them!" The Volkswagen rocked with her fury.

Willis muttered, "Boy, am I in trouble!" Then he took another long lesson from his Teacher's before he asked, "Have you got any clothes on yet?"

"Yes."

"Okay. Let me have my coat."

"You really could be fun, Will, if you gave yourself half a chance," she said, removing the coat.

She was wearing a quite attractive red silk dress with a modest neckline and matching boots to cover her hooves. Her hair had assembled itself to conceal her pert little horns.

An ember, seemingly, had begun to glow in Willis, and he was uncomfortably aware that not all of it had been caused by his consumption of alcohol. He had to admit that, even fully clothed, this half-human and half-demon female was surpassingly beautiful. No, more than that; provocative and, yes—either despite or because of the fact that she seemed indecently young—desirable. And it was, he realized, in some way he could not define, something even more than the provocative desirability of a beautiful movie star or pinup.

"You like?"

"Yes," he admitted reluctantly.

Willis slipped into his coat with difficulty in the confined space, his mind ajumble, trying to find something negative about Anathae which would let him stop regarding her in quite this fashion. *Too young-looking,* he tried to tell himself, *although, of course, some older males are attracted by that. But I'm not. Besides, she's a demon—or at least part demon—and she might be bewitching me. Anyway, there's Gertrude—*

"I'm not," Anathae said.

"Not what?"

"Not using my magic to bewitch you, Willis. And as for comparing me to that dog you've got for a girlfriend—"

"Now just a minute," Willis said heatedly, "I'll not have that sort of talk about Gertrude."

"I'm not talking about her *looks*," Anathae said. "She's not much to look at, but of course that doesn't mean anything, anyway. No, Will, I'm talking about her *personality*—how it's affected your relationship with her. The thing I find hardest to understand is that you both know you don't love each other—in fact, you know when you're honest with yourself you don't even *like* her for what she's done to you. The truth of it is, you can't understand why you've let her get you in a position where she can henpeck you."

Willis found he was breathing hard. Before he could mouth his intended rejoinder—"Oh, yeah?"—Anathae went on: "You know damned well that, at some point, Miss Twill will have marriage on her mind, even though you both make each other uncomfortable, and also that you'll never know beforehand, and perhaps not even afterward, if you're compatible in bed—where you're bound to spend at least a third and maybe as much as half of your life—because she won't let you get in her pants now and might not even then. For all you know, she might be a walking, talking mannequin!'' Anathae smiled slyly. "At least you know what *I've* got is real!"

"Can't we change the subject?"

"All right. Let's talk about you." She held up a hand, and suddenly there was a long thick cigarette in it. "Want one?"

"No thanks," he said.

"As I see it, you've got a lot of potential, but no gumption." She flicked a finger, and it sprouted flame, which she used to light her cigarette. "That's like a Mack truck without wheels." She blew it out. "A hell of a lot of horsepower going nowhere in a hurry."

She sucked hungrily at her weed, held the smoke in her lovely lungs for a long moment, then blew it out in square shapes. "Nice trick, huh? You learn a few things like that when you've got a few thousand years on your hands to practice."

The headlights of a car flashed by, catching the first few flakes of a snow flurry in its beams. "Not much chance for stuff like that where I come from," she commented wryly. "Anyway, as I was saying, you need some self-assertion. I know your problems on that score, so I can sympathize. But it takes action to clean out your skull—"

"Who says I *want* to clean out my skull?"

"*I* do. Because that's what you need to get what you really want. And what you really want, modest though it is, is to be head of the university's Literature Department."

"I don't have to be told that, and anyway, I didn't give you permission to go poking around in my brain!"

"You didn't forbid me, either. What I'm saying is that I'll help you, if you really want to succeed. Now listen—"

"Hold it!" Willis said heatedly. "Let me get this straight. I call up a demon and suddenly she wants to take control of my life. And I don't even have to ask because I *know* at what price. So *you* listen, Ana." She seemed to be giving him her full attention, but he nonetheless paused for a few seconds, wetting his lips, since the alcohol was beginning to slur his speech. "I'm fully capable of meshing . . . of *messing* up my life on my own without help from you."

She chuckled, not unkindly, at his mistake and said, "That's precisely my point."

"I mean—"

"Oh, I know what you mean. Really, Willis, I do. You want to do it all on your own, rather than have the help of magic, which is quite admirable. But, as you've said, my appearance here, among other things, just might block your way. Fortunately, I'm grateful for what you've done—I would, frankly, rather be Here than There. So I'll help you get rid of those stumbling blocks. Maybe, later, I can help you in other areas where you need it, too."

Willis was truly beginning to feel the effects of the alcohol and, consequently, was starting to regret the amount he had consumed. But, he told himself, he wasn't *that* drunk. Calmly, he asked, "And what price would you charge for this little service, Ana? My soul? Sure, I grant you I want the position, even want it somewhat desperately—I have ideas on teaching that I would really like to see implemented. But thanks but no thanks—not at *that* price."

To his surprise, she giggled. "Oh, Willis, some human ideas about demons are *so* silly! I'm not *that* kind of demon. You did me a favor, getting me out of That Place—so, if you want, I'll do you a few. The first is to help you get that job you want so much—even if you *wouldn't* give your soul for it. Of course, I already knew that."

She blew a triangle of smoke in his face, causing him to cough.

Funny kind of smell, he thought.

"So let me get the lay of the land," she continued, brushing back a stray lock of hair. "Thanks mostly to what's just happened, the man most likely to get the job is Larry Hawthorne, right?"

"That's right. He's also been making passes at Gertrude lately."

"Well, unfortunately that form of dementia won't disqualify him," Anathae said. "So, it seems to me, if something happens to him, your way is clear. Of course, you wouldn't condone pushing him out the window of his high-rise apartment—"

"Heavens, no!"

"I know you wouldn't, Will. So we'll have to do it the hard way. Hey, you want a drag of this?" She proffered the half-smoked cigarette. "I'd like some of that Scotch. After all, even though I probably shouldn't have, *I* had to really work to get you to bring it out with us."

He paused only briefly, realized she had to be much older than the sixteen-year-old she appeared to be, and handed her the bottle but waved away the cigarette. "Uh-uh. No to-bacco. Alcohol's my only vice."

"If anyone knows that, Will, I do. But who said it was tobacco?"

"Do you mean it's . . ."

She shrugged. "It's all we smoke, where I come from."

"Gaahh!" Willis exclaimed.

4

This should be noted, dear reader, and noted well: As a university professor, while Willis Baxter was a bit of a nebbish in some respects, he was nonetheless well aware that a few members of the faculty (to say nothing of a substantial number of students) indulged in the smoking of Other Substances. And although he did not partake in this practice himself and made it known that he did not want it at his parties, he considered himself a tolerant man. If anything, people who indulged in his own legal vice, liquor, seemed to suffer more ill effects. And alcohol, too, had once been illegal. In any event, Willis Baxter, while at some times a bit of a Milquetoast and at others something of a bookish boob, lived in the modern day and age and was not a hypocrite. To each his own, he felt.

For that reason, it must surely follow that the "Gaahh!" which Willis exclaimed was not a "Gaahh!" of disdain or disapproval, nor even a "Gaahh!" of dismay or disbelief.

No, the "Gaahh!" which came so suddenly from Willis's lips was entirely the result of the fact that just as Anathae made her calm admission, he espied a police car patrolling his street, which caused his natural paranoia to boil over.

"Gaahh!" Willis exclaimed. He also pointed in the direction of the police car for Anathae's *éclaircissement*, adding, "If they should find me here with you, smoking one of those, I'll be sunk for good. I wish I could get out of here!"

"Anything you command, lover."

She muttered a few words and gestured. There was a faint

hissing sound, like a lizard licking his earlobe, and Professor Baxter suddenly found himself lying on his own bed on top of a heap of coats.

He blinked his eyes in surprise. Anathae, he saw, stood in near darkness by the bed.

"What happened?" he asked her.

"You said you'd prefer to leave. I assumed you wanted to come back here."

"And you—"

"Fly me, I'm Anathae."

She had the whiskey bottle in her hand and took a sip. "That's part of Hell, too—watching American television."

She set the bottle aside and hopped onto the bed to snuggle up to Willis.

"So, lover. Time for Project Manmaker. I'm your instructor, Miss Bliss, and I *love* to make men. The first lesson is self-confidence—if you don't love yourself and show that you do, people will assume you're not even worth liking. You've already got all the *ideas* you need to get that job—but they won't help you if they stay locked up in your head because your lack of confidence won't let you bring them out. You have to believe in them and in yourself; *then* when you tell them to Dean Smith, *he*'ll believe in them too—"

At that moment, however, Larry Hawthorne stumbled in. His slurred "Shorry" made Willis aware that Hawthorne had also, as the saying goes, put away a few.

But upon seeing whom he had interrupted, Hawthorne did a double take and exclaimed, "Profesher Baxshter! And the little magic-trick lady! How'dja get here without coming through the front door?" He glanced at the window, but since Willis had, somewhat earlier, tried to open it to let the evening's cigarette and cigar smoke out and failed, the window having recently been painted over, Hawthorne knew they could not have entered that way.

In his mind, Willis heard Anathae's voice saying, *We'll get back to our project later.*

Slipping off the bed, Anathae moved toward the Professor of Renaissance Literature. "Aren't you," she asked, with just a touch of awe in her voice, "Professor Lawrence *J.* Hawthorne?"

Hawthorne seemed a trifle taken aback; he was indeed Lawrence J. Hawthorne but was unaware of any other Lawrence Hawthorne to explain Anathae's emphasis on his middle initial. "Why, yes. Willis, if you're not too drunk, introduce your colleague to this stunning girl."

"Miss Anny Bliss, Professor Hawthorne," purred Anathae, offering her delicate hand to him. "You teach Renaissance literature at the university, don't you?"

Hawthorne beamed, made a noticeable effort to overcome his condition, bowed over her hand, and slobbered on it in what was obviously intended to be a debonair kiss. "Most pleasant to meet you, I'm sure," he said in a notably deepened voice as he smoothed back his tangly black forest of hair. "Can I, perhaps, get you something to drink?"

Willis, who was now well into feeling the effects of his own alcoholic consumption, was on the verge of pointing out that she was much too young to drink when Anathae said to Hawthorne, "Certainly!"

She slipped the length of her arm under Hawthorne's flabby biceps. "Oh, goodness, I never expected to meet a teacher of *literature* with such muscles," she oozed. "I bet you're just *so* strong!"

Her mouth made a cute little O, and Willis could see that Hawthorne, who had started to melt when she'd introduced herself, was beginning to get a little gooey around the edges. "Professor Baxter *promised* to introduce me to you if I came to his party," Anathae continued as she turned Hawthorne and began to propel him out of the bedroom.

If the statement was obvious flattery, the unlikelihood of his rival making any such promise being in itself suspicious, Hawthorne did not deign to mention it. He said, "You've . . . heard of me?"

"Oh," Anathae said as they went out the door, "hasn't *every*one?"

Willis, numb from his drinking, had a sinking feeling as he watched them leave. The events of the recent past, particularly the past hour, were muddled, to say the least, but despite what she'd "said" in his mind just before getting off the bed, Willis wasn't entirely sure what was going on.

So, as he did so often when faced with one of life's

problems, he grabbed the deserted bottle and started drinking—and thinking—with a vengeance.

He found the tone of his thoughts shaped by the alcohol—first relaxed, then depressed.

She's right, he thought. *Told me I need gumption. But "guts" woulda been a better word. That's what I am—spineless. Can't cut it as a professor, much less a department head. Hell, can't even keep the attention of a nymphomaniac demon I've summoned up myself—and that's saying something!*

His last thought, perhaps because of the contrast, made him think of Gertrude.

Unfortunately, he had to admit, Anathae was right there, too. He certainly didn't *like* what Gertrude had made of their relationship—and she didn't seem to like or respect him for having allowed her to do it. He'd known this, deep down, but now that it was out in the open for him to examine and think about, the realization gave him no relief. If anything, it only made him feel guilty.

How can I be such a louse? Just because Gertrude's not as pretty as Anathae?

Few women, he reflected, *could* be as beautiful, as soft, as warm, as desirable, as . . . *Stop it, Willis. Get control of yourself.* And, anyway, hadn't that very same beautiful-softwarmdesirable Anathae just left on the arm of his archenemy? And what if Gertrude *didn't* really feel anything for him? And so what if Gertrude *did* henpeck him? Wasn't it true that Gert at least had marriage in mind? Goodness gracious, if what Anathae had told him was true, that meant Gertrude was willing to spend the rest of her life with him, even though the events of their relationship had made it obvious that they felt relatively little real affection for each other, even though he was a faithless bum. Didn't that count for *some*thing?

Didn't that really make *him* the villain and Gert his victim?

"Anathae was right!" he proclaimed as he got to his feet to confront himself in the mirror—albeit wobbling more than a little. He waggled an admonitory finger under the nose of his image. "Even if it'd be *wrong* just to dump poor ol' Gert, you cad, you gotta ashert yersherf if you wanna get this job. Let 'em know that ol' crumbum Willis Baxter got some *guts* 'n' ain't afraid to speak out when he got ideas. Ideas that'll rev-o-loosh-en-eyes education at stinky ol' P.U.''

He pushed himself away from his dresser and tilted toward the door.

Once into his living room, he saw the party had thinned down considerably in his absence. Professor Rosenheim sat on the couch, staring ahead glassily at nothing in particular, with Mrs. Petruccio's head on his shoulder. Mrs. Petruccio was asleep.

The only other people Willis saw in the room were Dean Smith and Rockhurst. Evidently the dean had finally succeeded in figuratively nailing the rich man's shoes to the floor and was now filling his ears with plans for the new gymnasium the university would build if Rockhurst would but donate the half-million he had once said he was considering. Rockhurst wore the expression only the truly bored can properly assume, so his eyes brightened considerably as they turned from contemplating the dean's bald spot to the face of Willis Baxter.

Willis, thinking of the plan of action Anathae had proposed to him, wobbled in their direction.

"Baxter! Now there's the man of the evening, Dean." Rockhurst beamed, extending a welcoming arm to Willis.

"As I was saying, Mr. R," the dean went on without paying the slightest attention to what Rockhurst had said, "we've got some *great* plans for a swimming pool, stocked with water wings, not to mention a superb—"

"Professor Baxter, old boy," said Rockhurst, patting Willis on the back in friendly fashion, "where's the lovely lady of the party?"

"You mean Gertrude? I dunno. Lasht I saw—"

"Gertrude left in something of a huff shortly after recovering," Dean Smith inserted.

The millionaire said, "No, no. I mean your cute little red-haired 'demon.' Quite a remarkable performance the two of you put on. The dean here told me he had no idea you had such a hobby, but really, I've seen *professional* stage magicians who couldn't perform that illusion as well. Now *that's* entertainment! And in your own apartment, without apparatus, too. Tell me, did she come back with you?"

"Oh," was all Willis could say at first. Even through his alcoholic haze, he was amused; that was always the way with people—if pigs grew wings or the seas grew boiling hot, they would find some "reasonable" explanation for it all which they could believe. But realizing the millionaire was still expecting something in the way of a reply from him, Willis practiced focusing his eyeballs and analyzed, as carefully as he could, Rockhurst's most recent statement. "Anathae, you mean? She's 'round—with Larry Hawthorne, in the study, I guess."

Rockhurst laughed. "I *thought* he protested too much. He was telling me he'd only just met her."

The dean cut in sternly with, "Professor Hawthorne is a fine example of our faculty. Of course, even the *best* staffs have exceptions in quality." He eyed Willis pointedly.

"I want to go congratulate her," Rockhurst said, "after I get another drink. A fine, fine show. And, Professor Baxter, I might want your act for a little, shall we say, stag party I'm hosting next month? Now, I won't take no for an answer—and that's final. Catch you both later." Rockhurst smiled at his own adroitness in finally ditching the dean and started off in the direction of the professor's kitchen.

Dean Smith made as if to follow—but Willis grabbed him by the collar. The dean looked back at the hand holding him, then glared up at its owner. "What's the meaning of this, Baxter?"

"I want to talk to you, Shmith!"

Willis tried to match the dean's glare but had to settle for a frown accompanied by a lopsided grin. Dimly, in the back of his mind, he realized this conversation was getting off on entirely the wrong foot; firmness did *not* mean manhandling the person with whom he wished to communicate, just as confidence did not mean talking to the man as if he were some kind of grub.

"Haven't you sobered up yet, man?"

"I shert . . . certainly haf . . . have, Dean," Willis said earnestly.

"Then take your hands off me."

"Not till you hear. What I got. To say. Dean. I been at this lovely university ten whole drab years, three more than

Larry—don't you think I deserve a break today? I got ideas. I got a million of 'em. I could turn it all around. And you know I'm a brilliant scholar."

"Baxter, unhand me immediately! And go away. You don't know what you're saying!"

"But I *do!* I'm. Saying. The. Truth. God. Dammit! Dean, I'm telling you I'm the man for the job and saying what I feel for the firsht time. I desh . . . deserve to head the Literature Department. I *desire* to head up the Litrasure Department. Because *I got what it takes.*" By some astonishing exercise of heretofore dormant muscle power, Willis increased his grip on the dean's collar and managed to lift him almost an inch off the floor. *"And you'll give me the post, won't you, Dean?"*

The dean was blustering so badly only snippets of phrases squeaked through his whitening lips: ". . . never . . . you'll pay . . . drunk . . . doesn't excuse . . . gurgle! . . . in all my career . . . nonsense . . . splugh! . . . Hawthorne . . . got the job . . . if he didn't before . . . I'll get you . . . blurrgh!"

Where Willis had once seen nothing but white-hot unreasoning anger in his mind at the injustice of it all, he began to see, in its place, a dark moist mist.

He let the dean down. The dean, flapping his arms like an agitated windmill, said, "Now *this* is the outside of enough! I'm calling the police, Baxter. I'll charge you with assault! I'll fix your boat. You're through at this university, tenure or no tenure, do you hear? Through! Absolutely, finally *through.* And I'll see you in prison! I'll see you hanging from a meat hook! I'll . . . ."

However, to Willis the voice was a tiny whisper coming from miles away—and filtered through congealed lime Jell-O at that.

Willis felt himself sway back and forth.

(Or was that the room? Truth to tell, he *seemed* quite stationary.)

With each motion, he began to tick off, like a metronome, to himself, the number of drinks he must have put away that evening.

About six before the summoning—

(forward sway with a little bit of wobble)

Oh, but she's such a gorgeous, delectable, desirable thing!
"Baxter!"
—about four (or was it five?) in the car—
(sidewise tilt)
That hair! Those lips like liquid fire!
"Baxter! You just stay awake and on your feet, man! Don't pass out! You stay awake, so I can have you arrested!"
—then the rest of the bottle in the bedroom—
Those deep dark mysterious eyes in which a man might lose himself—and that quick smile in which he might find himself again!
"Baxter! I've called the police—they'll be here in a minute. Stay awake, man!"
("Tack her to the starboard side, Mr. First Mate." —"Aye, aye, Cap'n")
"Here, Baxter. Drink this coffee. Stand up straight or you'll fall on your face."
Swirling pieces of the cloudy room seemed suddenly to coalesce into Dean Smith's stern face. "Dean, Dean, Dean—you're a better man than I am, Gunga Dean!" Willis hiccoughed with pride at this demonstration of his mastery of English poetry.
And, most of all—that young, sweet, tender, oh-so-embraceable body!
"Anathae," Willis sighed. Yes, he was certain he could see her now, right before him, her clothes tight on her lithesome figure. He reached out—and hugged the dean. "Oh, Ana, Ana dearest," Willis crooned, "you're so right, so right!"
"Baxter! Get away! What do you think—there are people watching, man, and you're drunk!"
"No, Anathae, not drunk. Only high. When I think of you."
The three descending notes of the doorbell cut through his reveries and allowed him to realize who, in fact, he had been holding. Willis, noting that Professor Rosenheim was snoring on the couch, muttered, "Nobody watching, Dean—we're the only two left awake at this dull and boring excuse for a party," and tottered away.
The dean turned and walked swiftly to the door. As he did,

suddenly a commotion broke from the direction of the den in the form of a feminine laugh and a roaring masculine yell. Anathae ran into the room, looking back over her shoulder; bearing down on her, in hot pursuit, was Larry Hawthorne, grunting and groaning, his eyes wide with lust.

A very important detail, dear reader: Larry Hawthorne, Professor of Renaissance Lit, was as naked as a *Playgirl* pinup. A very improper *Playgirl* pinup.

And then, just as the dean opened the door for two burly blue-uniformed men, four crucially important things happened.

First, Anathae disappeared again.

Second, the totally naked rampaging Renaissance Lit professor, unable to break his lumbering stride, ran straight into the arms of the entering policemen—who immediately grabbed him and, without waiting for explanation, quickly began to read him his rights.

"No, wait a minute, officers, this is a mistake—" Dean Smith started to sputter.

But one of the policemen quickly assured him there was none, that in fact they had received a complaint, and a man running wildly around in the nude at a party and so obviously drunk was sufficient cause for arrest. And, with no further ado than to throw a raincoat over the professor, they began to lead the confused and shuddering Larry Hawthorne to their waiting squad car.

At first Dean Smith stood unspeaking and ashen-faced. But then he turned to say to Willis, "You may not end up in jail, Baxter, but you *are* finished at Powhattan!"

Willis wobbled unsteadily toward the voice and said, "You're quite right, Gunga, I'm drunk."

Then the third and fourth important things happened—he threw up on the dean and passed out.

5

The Green Bay Packers, equipped with special six-inch knife-sharp cleats, were conducting running practice on his head. Even as they were doing so, a wrecking crew—aided by jackhammers, chainsaws and bulldozers—was digging into the back of his throbbing skull. Mr. Clean, after using his stomach to scrub down the *Queen Mary*, had wrung it out with a steamroller and was drying it in a kiln. The entire Arabian army, in dirty sweat socks, had assembled to spread their dusty mats on his tongue and were now facing Mecca while their waiting camels expectorated in the desert that was his mouth.

Tread softly as you read this page, dear considerate reader—our hero has a hangover.

The insistent jangling of the doorbell acted like a lightning bolt to spear his already aching head.

Groaning, Professor Willis Baxter stumbled out of bed. He jumped with fright as he caught sight of a wicked-looking creature all wrinkles and mussed hair. Then he realized it was only his own reflection in the mirror and got a small, trembling measure of control over himself. "Coming! I'm coming! Please! Please stop!" he pleaded. "Merciful God in heaven, make it stop!"

Slowly, step by labored step, Willis plodded out to the front door, where he spent a minute that seemed more like an hour trying to get a grip on the knob.

It was Gertrude Twill.

"Gertrude," he said.

"You really should be ashamed of yourself, Willis Baxter," she said, pushing past him and letting the skull-shattering bright morning sunlight stream in behind her.

Willis gasped from the painful brightness and eased the door shut—but the reengaging of the lock sounded to him like a battering ram slamming into thirty feet of solid concrete.

Gertrude continued, "I really don't know why I should put up with this sort of treatment."

"But dear—" breathed Willis, trying desperately to remember precisely what she was talking about.

"But nothing!"

Willis groped his way toward the kitchen for the glass of water he was sure was needed to save his life—although, at this moment, he was not certain if even his life were worth such a Herculean effort.

Gertrude dogged his steps, trying to get him to turn around so she could put her finger under his nose, a favorite pecking position for her. Failing that, she rasped, "You were disgraceful last night! And that nude hussy!" She peered around to get a good look at his condition. "Oh, gracious, Willis! You look *sick*. Now you lie down on the couch like a good boy and I'll make you well again with some of my nice broccoli soup."

Willis spit the water he'd started to drink back into the glass at the thought of her broccoli soup—which he could barely swallow under normal conditions.

"No, no," he whimpered. "Aspirin."

"Where do you keep it?"

He settled himself slowly, carefully, onto a kitchen chair and wheezed, "Bedroom."

"Yes, dear. I'll get it. Right away." She left the kitchen but continued talking: "I suppose I'll have to forgive you, although it's not easy after all the embarrassment you've caused. Fortunately, it's nothing compared to what poor Professor Haw—"

The flow of her conversation halted abruptly.

There was a moment of total silence followed by the squeak of Gertrude's tennis shoes coming in his direction on the tile floor at a rapid clip. She stamped into the kitchen, her face beet-red.

"Oh, Willis! How could you?"

Willis looked up from his intense study of the half-full water glass he had shakily placed on the kitchen table just in time to catch her hand across his face. The force of the blow knocked him off his chair.

He stared up from the floor in bewilderment as Gertrude, gnashing her wired teeth like an angry steamshovel, picked up his water glass, dumped its contents on his head, swiveled around, and stalked out.

Willis grimaced at the explosion of the door slamming.

He gave the apartment a few minutes to stop playing its childish games and get off the merry-go-round, then allowed a few more seconds to let the tweeting birds fly out of his head. Then, resignedly, he slowly crawled into the bedroom for the aspirin—only to discover the cause of Gertrude Twill's outrage.

For there, asprawl on his bed, feet tangled in the sheets, half-opened eyes drowsy as though looking back into the recent past and pleasuring themselves in the memory of some particularly decadent but thoroughly enjoyable orgy, was Anathae—wearing precisely what she had worn when he had first summoned her.

"On, no," sighed Willis, trying to rise to his feet but slumping onto the end of his bed instead. "Oh, no," he said, truly pathetically. "I couldn't have. . . ."

Anathae's scarlet-crowned head craned up, bright eyes focusing on him. "Will!" she said, squirming over to wrap her soft bare arms around his neck and nibble his ear affectionately.

"Did I?" he mumbled, agonizing through his dim memory of the previous night. "Did we?"

"What? Oh. Did you! Did we!" She smiled and toyed with a strand of his hair. "Well, now, if you don't remember, perhaps we should start all over again."

"That does it!" screeched Willis, bolting upright over the startled demon-girl. *"That's all I'm going to take!"*

"Oh, Willis," she panted, as yet unaware of the cause of his ire, "if you could only see yourself! How your eyes sparkle and the blood courses through your veins when you're angry! I've done it!"

"You've *done it*, all right," he growled.

Fragments of the previous night's events came trickling back into his weary memory, and his feelings were a mixture of embarrassment, guilt, and anger.

He would never head the Literature Department—because of Anathae.

He had, almost certainly, lost both his teaching position and his tenure—because of Anathae.

His once fine reputation, now shattered beyond repair, would follow him wherever he might try to go—because of Anathae.

Finally, because of Anathae, he had lost Gertrude—Gertrude, who might not have been attractive, who might not have respected him, who might not have been many things, but who *had* been the only female who had ever attached herself to him in his years at the university and was the closest thing he'd ever had to a girlfriend.

Grasping Anathae by the arm, he pulled her off the bed and into the dining room without giving her a chance to stand up. The pentagram was in shambles, most of the drink straws and swizzle sticks having been crushed underfoot or shunted aside by the previous night's partygoers, but it was but the work of a moment to grab the Silly String he had left there and fill in the missing segments. Willis then dumped Anathae into the south corner of the pentagram and marched rather than walked to the north corner.

"Willis," Anathae started, "what—"

"*Ubele . . .*" he began to chant, his eyes wide with fury.

"Oh, no, Willis. Don't you remember—"

". . . *Canet minen . . .*" He tried to drown out her voice with his volume.

"I *helped* you—"

Had he bothered to look, he would have seen that she now seemed more like a frightened young girl than a demon.

"Don't send me back—"

"*Exconae chanet!*"

"We may never see each other again. And, oh, Willis, I—"

"*Insel . . . Canet!*"

"I do at least *care* for you—"

Her voice was drowned in a clap of thunder.

Willis looked down.

A wisp of smoke curled up from the center of the pentagram. Willis angrily scattered the drink straws and swizzle sticks that had remained from before with his foot.

Abruptly, the phone rang. He picked it up. "Hello!" he said gruffly into the receiver.

"Professor Baxter?"

"Yeah. Don't yell, please."

"This is Dean Smith."

"Yeah, well, if you called to confirm what you said last night, forget it. I don't want or need your stinking—"

"How would you like to be Chairman of the Arts and Science Division?" the dean interposed sweetly and quickly.

"Huh?"

"I realize you only wanted to be head of Lit—but let's face it, Professor Baxter, when you come right down to it that's really small potatoes. You not only deserve more, but President Mellon and I have been thinking for quite some time that the university should be reorganized into larger divisions."

"What about Hawthorne?"

"He spent the night in jail. For indecent exposure. Don't you remember?"

"No . . . wait. Yes! But I thought I was imagining—"

"Unfortunately not. However, President Mellon and I were able to use our influence to have the charges dropped—we pointed out that there would be no one who would come forth to make a complaint and, anyway, whatever happened, it happened on private property—and thus saved both Larry and the university from a scandal. Fortunately, I also have some influence at the local paper."

"Sorry. I was drunk."

"Yes, I'm well aware of that, but think nothing of it, m'boy. We all lose our heads sometimes . . . stomachs, too, for that matter. I'll forget last night's unpleasantness if you will, and if you'll take the position."

Still confused, Willis asked, "Why me?"

"Well, Professor, you seem to have a better grasp on human psychology than I do. Last night I thought that spectacle you presented was outrageous. Of course, I wasn't aware—as you apparently were—that Norman Rockhurst, for all his success, is still a little, shall we say, on the crude side. *He* thought it a delightful and outstanding performance.''

Willis dimly remembered.

The dean continued, ''Well, I'm a pragmatist, Willis, as I'm sure you know—and I'm not about to dispute matters of taste with a man who's willing to donate a substantial sum to the university. Rockhurst called this morning to pledge a million dollars for our gymnasium. He seems to like you, sees potential, suggested you be placed in some such position, made it clear he wants someone like you helping to run the university he's donating his money to. I must say, I don't think he could have convinced me, money or no money, had I not realized the truth of much of what you said last night—you *do* have good ideas as well as the necessary ability.''

''Dean! That's wonderful!''

''Of course, the clincher seems to have been your agreement with him.''

''Agreement?'' Willis puzzled.

''Certainly. I was there when you made it. He told you he wanted you and that girl to perform your magic act for his party. I recall he said he wouldn't take no for an answer. Seems the governor's going to be there, and Rockhurst's convinced you'll be the hit of the affair.''

Willis didn't—couldn't—answer.

''Baxter? You there, m'boy? Willis? Answer me! Baxter?''

''Yes sir,'' Willis croaked.

''It's as simple as pie. You get that young lady, perform your little magic act at his party—which, I need not point out, will be kept strictly confidential—the university will receive a cool million and you can head up the A&S Division. You'll do it, of course?''

''Of course,'' Willis replied.

''Good man.''

The dean hung up.

After a lengthy visit to the bathroom, Professor Willis Baxter began to reassemble the pentagram.

PART TWO

6

"You will *not* jump out nude at that 'stag' party, or whatever it is!"

Willis Baxter slumped into his ancient purple easy chair, worn smooth from long years of use, and pulled his hand across the dark five-o'clock stubble on his face. He looked all around the living room—everywhere but at Anathae.

It had been several weeks since he had summoned her, for the second time, just so that she could appear in the nude as part of a "magic trick" at Rockhurst's party—but in that brief period his feelings had changed. For one thing, the idea of using someone—anyone—for the purpose of furthering his career was repugnant to him, and if he had at first seen his way around this obstacle with the rationalization that Anathae "owed" it to him for the havoc she had wrought, he had lately begun to realized this excuse was somewhat shabby.

True, since he'd first called her forth from Hell, his entire life had changed. All in the space of one faculty party, he had acquired a live-in roommate who seldom took no for an answer (or at least did not acquiesce in the regular way), had himself been tentatively elevated to head the new Arts and Sciences Division, had turned a mere rival into a true enemy, and had lost an albatross of a girlfriend. But he had been quick to realized that this "havoc" had in fact been something of a mixed blessing—and it did not seem fair to one of his reasonable turn of mind to blame Anathae for the bad parts without giving her credit for some of the good.

He had waffled. He had even, at Anathae's insistence,

picked up some books on parlor magic and bought a few tricks at a magic store, since she pointed out that *if* they went, their performance should have more to it than one trick.

So now, in the early evening when the party was to be held, he was again trying to give voice to his misgivings with all the forcefulness for which she had once commended him: "You will *not* jump out nude at that 'stag' party, or whatever it is!"

"You're being ridiculous," the girl-demon replied. "If we don't show up, Rockhurst will probably be so angry he won't give that money to the university and you'll be relieved of your new position."

The rumpled professor, who could find no fault in her logic, nonetheless tried to protest: "Yes, but—"

Anathae held up her hand in counterprotest, and, somewhat dutifully, Willis lapsed into silence.

"You summoned me up again for that very reason," she said. "And besides, I'll love it! Can't you just imagine?" She pirouetted gracefully between Willis and the couch, coming to a stop directly in front of him with her hands on her hips.

The yellow mini-dress she had been wearing suddenly vanished and the pubescent lines of her body gleamed in the lamplight.

She appeared—lest you have forgotten, dear reader—to be not more than sixteen years old, or at most seventeen.

Her breasts were hard, small but fully rounded and firm, with delicate pink and flower-soft nipples; her stomach was taut and creamy smooth with a small, inward-turned navel; and her hips, although slim, nonetheless seemed full because of her eighteen-inch waist. Her tawny mane, which fell long and unruly down her back, was somewhat darker than her colcothar pubic hair, which matched that which sprinkled down her legs to her dainty cloven hooves. When she smiled and shook her head at Willis, small red horns peeped out from among her curls. Her short red tail, descending from the end of her spine, was stiff with what he had come to recognize as excitement.

"Will," she continued, her voice as smooth as butter-scotch pudding, "I suppose, since you called me here, I technically need your permission to go. So, if that's what you really want, I won't. But, honestly, I was beginning to hope that maybe you weren't quite as, well, stuffy as I first supposed. . . ." Her voice trailed off as Willis looked up at her.

His brown eyes, normally soft and anxious, glittered angrily with a jealousy he did not yet realize he felt. "I suppose you'd rather go back to Hell?" he bellowed. But then his eyes turned soft again, and he lost the advantage he might have had.

"You know I wouldn't, Will," she said softly. Anathae knelt down before him on the rug and rested her chin on his knees as her dress formed around her again. "And I hope you'll never get mad enough to send me back. You, as well as I, know the possible dangers—"

It was Willis's turn to hold up his hand, Anathae's to make no demur.

He did not need reminding that to send her back could very well mean that he might not be able to call her up again.

Willis Baxter looked down into the green fire of Anathae's eyes and sighed.

"Ana, Ana," he said, "can't you see, can't you understand that you're just a young girl whose beauty they want to exploit and use in the most vulgar way possible? After the party, there's no telling—"

He was stopped by the laughing sparkle in Anathae's eyes.

They were not, those eyes, the eyes of an innocent young girl. They were ageless, with memories of the pyramids, Peloponnesian battles, Merovingian castles, and the Hundred Years War. Looking into them, Willis briefly felt as though he'd dropped through an icy green vortex into the past—and then, just as suddenly, he was back in his garden apartment, just off campus from old P.U.

"Well, okay, scratch that," he amended. "I really shouldn't presume, given what you are, that you're incapable of taking care of yourself. It's just—"

"Come on, Will. Why don't we live a little? It's what we're here for." Her fingers began to trespass inside his pants leg.

Willis stood up and began to pace a circle between the chair and the couch. Although his shyness had abated somewhat, however much he might have liked to "live a little" right then, he also wanted to keep his head about him while he talked—and that was something he found hard to do whenever her fingers began to trespass inside his pants leg, his shyness having not abated completely. Besides, his up-stairs neighbors were at home—and he'd already suffered considerable embarrassment at their banging on their floor (his ceiling) at all the noise he and Anathae tended to make.

"Even if there were nothing wrong with it—which there is—it would be risky," he said. "I mean, if someone like Hawthorne found out about it—"

"If he knew my middle name, I wouldn't be afraid of *him*," she said, her voice haughty. "Besides, who can he tell? Not Dean Smith. The dean's agreed, for his pragmatic reasons, to turn a blind eye toward whatever happens, and, in fact, he's counting on the money which is conditional on our going. And certainly not the police—Hawthorne is out of jail on his own recognizance, thanks to the university's interven-tion and the fact that the police can't find anyone to press a complaint against him. But if they find me, he has every reason to believe I might say enough to have them toss him back in and throw away the key."

Anathae floated lightly to her feet and pulled her hair up to the apex of her head. Her eyes narrowed as she walked with exaggerated grace to the bedroom and opened the door. "Be-sides, I've been thinking that maybe what Professor Haw-thorne needs is a good lesson."

"No!" Willis said. He pulled himself up straight to his full six feet, thrust out his chin, and, with determination, fol-lowed her into the bedroom. "Please now, Ana, don't use your magic on him—the less he has reason to suspect, the better I'll feel."

Anathae's voice echoed from within the bathroom. "I thought you said you believed he might have figured out the truth about me already?"

Willis sat down on the bed's precisely laid green coverlet. He glanced at the familiar clutter on the mahogany chest-of-drawers and then at the lace underwear which festooned the night table and the closet door. A transparent nightgown lay in the middle of the floor like a throw rug.

"I can't be sure," Willis said with a croak.

He cleared his throat, forcing himself to push the images of underwear and nightgowns out of his consciousness, and began again. "I can't be sure, but he certainly *appears* to be on the right track. I don't for a moment know why he doesn't accept the magic-trick explanation like the others, but it's obvious he doesn't. He's been getting old manuscripts from the library service—the Xeroxing alone must be costing him a fortune! Technically, he's on administrative leave until the university's certain his little problem with the police has blown over. But every day, he's there in the faculty lounge, snorting at me like a disgruntled bull when he sees me looking at him and pouring over all those pages, looking for something to get back at us with—I can tell. So I don't want you doing anything that might let him know he's on the right track. He's also taken out a stack of books on demonology, including all the ones by de la Farte."

"Your pseudonym," Anathae said, her laughter echoing against the smooth tiles of the bathroom. Suddenly the shower turned on, and splashing water all but drowned out her voice. "If he only knew!"

"I don't want him to know!" Willis shouted back, as much in vehemence as from the desire to make himself heard over the water. "At lunch today he was doodling pentagrams and symbols and all sorts of weird designs all over his notebook. I sat three seats away and I could see him. I tell you, he's out to get us for what we did to him, and he won't stop at anything to do it—even calling forth a demon himself."

The shower continued to beat as loud as dropping marbles so that Anathae had to shout above the noise to be heard.

"I've already told you, Will, there's not another demon left there he can call. Well, the only other one who can still get out, whom *no* magician could ever confine, is the Boss himself—and Hawthorne would have to be both a fool and a blithering idiot to call *him*. Even *I* crouched in a corner when the Nasty One was around—gave me goosepimples."

"There's no telling what Hawthorne might be foolish enough to try," Willis replied. "I'm sure the books he's been reading all have ample warning against trying that sort of thing—but he might be angry enough not to need them."

Willis folded his hands behind his head and massaged his neck; it had been a long, hard day, and he had found the responsibilities of his new position complex and the paperwork seemingly endless. As if that were not enough, there was a matter involving four of his brightest students who were starting to go to seed, for no reason he could ascertain, and his guilty realization that if he had not spent so much of his time thinking about the problem of Larry Hawthorne, he might actually have been able to do something about it, given the coign of vantage of his new position.

But then the water was turned off in the bathroom and suddenly Anathae stepped into the bedroom, covered only by a thin cloud of steam. Her hair, darkened by water, fell in slick locks across her shoulders and between her pert droplet-covered breasts.

"Getting back to the real subject of our conversation," she said, smiling, "we have to be at the party at ten. Are we going, or not?"

Willis pursed his lips. "I have a lot of paperwork to catch up on," he said somewhat primly. "If I get caught up, we'll go. *If*!"

"If we don't, you won't have any paperwork to catch up on—Dean Smith will take that chairmanship away from you."

"The president has already announced my appointment—"

"—and he can follow it with an announcement of the appointment of your successor, Professor Lawrence J. Hawthorne. Is *that* what you want?"

Willis sighed. "No. But the more I think about it, the less I like the idea that it should all hinge on your having to do something like this."

"Dear Will, I appreciate your willingness to sacrifice all you've ever hoped for and dreamed of just to protect my 'innocence'—really, I do. I appreciate it—but I'm not going to let you do it."

Anathae sat down on his lap and stroked his cheek. "Honestly, Will, you're such a prude," she continued, the gentle laughter of her eyes indicating her humor, "you sometimes make me wonder if there's any hope for you." She batted her long lashes, nuzzled his neck with her busy lips, and started to nibble at an ear before pulling back to ask, "Well, *is* there any hope?"

"Stop it, Ana! I'm not in the mood for any foolishness! And you're getting me all wet. If you're so certain you want to go, we'll go."

"Thank you!"

"But *if* we're going to go, we'll have to leave soon. It's already rather late. We don't have time—"

"Don't worry about the time," she said.

He hoped they wouldn't make too much noise.

7

Professor Larry Hawthorne stood back and viewed, with grim satisfaction, the pentagram he had chalked on his living-room floor.

"Extreme conditions call for extreme measures," he muttered to himself, in an attempt not to feel quite so foolish about what he was doing.

Indeed, he reflected, even if he *did* feel somewhat foolish, at least he could console himself with the fact that he was not as much a fool as the others who had attended Professor Baxter's party and who had, every one of them, fallen for that ridiculous magic-trick idea to explain Anathae's sudden appearance and disappearance.

He had not, himself, tumbled to any other notion until he had had some time for sober reflection.

That had been (he shuddered to recall) after those *stupid* policemen had given him that *stupid* raincoat to wear and put him in that *stupid* "holding" cell with that *stupid* wino who had *stupidly* thrown up all over Hawthorne's still-bare feet. Oh, the humiliation! Someone, he felt, would have to pay for that—and that *stupid* Professor Willis Baxter and his *stupid* topless dancer were likely candidates for his vengeance. . . .

Even after Dean Smith and President Mellon's intervention had gotten him released (protecting both his own and the university's reputation to some extent, he reminded himself) he had continued to derive considerable pleasure from pondering just what he might be able to do to pay Willis and the girl back.

It had not occurred to him that the explanation everyone had given to those remarkable events *had to be* patent nonsense—until Professor Rosenheim had unwittingly provided the nudge necessary to set his mind aboil with speculation. Rosenheim, who had given him a wink and a smile and a nod and who had complimented him on having been "in on it" with Baxter. Rosey said he'd done well to "set things up" with the speech which had introduced Anathae. Hawthorne had accepted the unearned praise and had almost dismissed it as pure coincidence—that he'd mentioned the name of a female demon and Baxter had, all along, intended to "produce" this female. . . .

But that had made his sharp mind focus on the circumstances of her second disappearance—when she had somehow induced him to take off his clothes, right there in Baxter's apartment, and he had (no, not *really* "stupidly"—*any*one, aroused as he had been aroused, in his inebriated condition, might have done the same) run after her. She had *disappeared* into thin air just as the front door was opening and he had run into the waiting Arms of the Law.

Initially he had considered this his own drunken hallucination, but then he remembered yet another impossibility—the appearance of Baxter and that girl in the bedroom. He had *seen* Willis walk out the front door, with that ridiculous bottle of whiskey in his pocket, and he had done his own subsequent drinking in the living room. There had been *no way* Baxter or the girl could have gotten by him and into the bedroom. The bedroom window had been sealed shut.

Finally, if this had *all* been simple legerdemain, while he could surmise the purpose of her appearance out of thin air and both of her disappearances, no matter how he tried, he could not understand the purpose of their appearance in the bedroom, since he had been the only witness and it had not not contributed in any meaningful way to his own discomfort.

As a youth, Hawthorne had read widely and for a while had had a passion for Sherlock Holmes. Having eliminated the possible, the impossible had to be considered. What if Anathae was . . . Anathae?

With a growing sense of dread, he had realized that, if true, this must put an end to his plans for retribution. For whatever damage he might be able to cause Willis, he would have to pay for by contending with Anathae's magic.

But Professor Lawrence Hawthorne was not a man easily put off. If Baxter could conjure a demon, perhaps Hawthorne could do the same, and then their contest might be more equal.

So for weeks he had thrown himself into further study of demonology. He'd reluctantly accepted the de la Farte theory, after rereading it to be certain he had not misread it before, and was all but disheartened by the realization that it might take months or even years before he stumbled upon the name of a demon who might still be summoned—if, indeed, there were any such. When he'd heard, through Gertrude Twill, about the ''scandalous'' party being planned by Rockhurst and that ''that nude hussy'' would put in another appearance there, he had become frantic to obtain quick results.

Larry Hawthorne truly felt that his hand had been forced—and that there was no turning back now. He could spend a lifetime among musty volumes and still not find the name of a demon who could be summoned. Very well, then. Almost all the books he had read on the subject had warned against trying to summon the One Whom No Mortal May Everlastingly Bind, and this stricture was so stern that all but one of *them* had failed to provide the proper formula for summoning the Most Evil of All.

But that one book, by the Mad Arab, had shown the proper drawing of the pentagram as well as at least appearing to give some moderate assurance that *one* wish might be granted, at little or no peril, provided the pentagram was made properly and was never breached.

And Larry Hawthorne knew *precisely* what he wanted with his wish—to obtain some token to make Anathae powerless before him. He was certainly aware that, by all accounts, she was only a minor demon, dedicated more to mischievousness than evil, and therefore it was likely that the Boss could give him such a token. And he knew just what he'd do with it: go to Rockhurst's party—it shouldn't be that hard to get in, particularly if he arrived before Baxter and claimed to be his ''assistant.'' If whoever answered the door did not believe this, Rockhurst would certainly recognize him from the faculty party. Then he could mix with the crowd and wait for opportunity to present itself. That opportunity would depend on what Baxter and Anathae did. If they separated, Hawthorne would use the token to keep her from appearing in the pentagram—and *then,* he thought, Professor Baxter would be forced to continue, to cite the part of the ritual which would bind her to Hell on her return. With Anathae in his power, he could come back here and use this pentagram to send her back. And if he could not get Anathae alone beforehand, he could simply await her appearance in Baxter's pentagram and use the token to take over—hold her there while *he* sent her back and locked the door to Hell behind her while the helpless Baxter looked on.

And yet if this were *really* what Larry Hawthorne wanted, why, then, did he stand now, unmoving and silent, in the proper place in the pentagram he had drawn in his living room?

Was he, perhaps, considering the possible consequences?

Was he, after having gone to so much trouble, now wavering in his resolve?

But, no, that cannot be: See, now, drawing his courage about him like a cloak, how he pricks his finger with a pin and then stoops to light his candles? True, his hands may tremble a bit as he applies his Ronson to their wicks, but note how, after a slight stumble, he steps back to the proper place in the pentagram and holds himself erect, begins to read from the book in his hand.

And what's that—a wind, perhaps? And that smell? Sulphur?

8

The party Norman Rockhurst was to host for Governor Isador Asque was not, of course, to be held anywhere near the Statehouse. You can easily imagine the risks which this would entail—especially since Mrs. Asque would have looked down on such doings, had she known about them, and besides was as likely as not to burst in on the activities and make precisely the sort of fuss that keeps the more sensational national tabloids thriving.

For the party would not be strictly stag—the *guests* would be prominent males, but there would be an abundance of women on hand to provide them with precisely the kind of entertainment the prominent males of Rockhurst's acquaintance most enjoyed.

The party was, in fact, to be held at Rockhurst's fabled estate on Seneca Street in far-off Wood's Hole. The contractor had sent his missus to Boston for a weekend of shopping—an expense he could afford for his wife with far greater ease than the governor could for his.

The Rockhurst manse was one of those old, rambling Colonial structures—three stories of imposing marble and stone, with graceful pillars at the top of a stone stairway that led to the front door.

The only defect it had (if one might actually have the audacity to *call* it a defect) was that the grounds were right on the main traffic route through the town across from Martha's Vineyard. Government research work had stepped up the local economy from the old days, and there was a constant flow of cars and trucks, taxicabs and buses, sweeping right by—only a scant few hundred yards from the formerly isolated mansion.

However, a high and neatly manicured hedge bordered the grounds, shielding the premises from the sight—if not quite all the sound—of passing traffic.

Rockhurst had spared no expense in setting up the party.

Although there would be no more than fifteen guests (and an equal number of "professional" ladies for their amusement, as well as five or six people to provide other than strictly sexual entertainment), he had arranged for a buffet large enough for fifty. He had planned for special entertainment after the buffet, to be followed by a few stimulating movies, drinking, and, eventually, the ladies.

The cook had set up four large salad trays and three self-serve bars at strategic locations, as well as hors d'oeuvres, and himself attended one of two areas where hot food—succulent roasts and tender meats in tasty sauces—was available, while his most able assistant took care of the other.

The caterers had delivered the chopped liver, thin-sliced salami, corned beef, turkey, pastrami, ham, and cheese trays in good order.

The soft, exotic, and beautiful young ladies had been delivered discreetly in Cadillacs that were no different from those which had brought the guests.

Indeed, it seemed everything was in good order—except the main attraction of the evening, the special entertainment, a young lady whose nude performance Rockhurst had promised all the guests would be nothing less than sensational and whom he was counting on to get things off to their proper improper start, was still among the missing.

"Norman!" The governor's tenor voice carried easily across the crowded drawing room, even over the sounds of the British rock group on the stereo. "When's this show of yours going to get on the road?"

Rockhurst peered out into the dark-suited crowd of men in the parlor who were obscured partially by a dim haze of cigar smoke. At last he located Asque's diminutive form.

"Izzy!" Rockhurst held out his hands as Asque squeezed through the crowd and came toward him. "Actually, we're waiting for that magic strip show I promised everyone—their assistant's arrived but they haven't shown up yet."

Asque straightened the lapels of his pearl-gray suit. He was a short man of about fifty, but what he lacked in height he more than made up for in vivacity.

He was currently married to the second Mrs. Asque, had five children—the sixth on the way. The pitter-patter of little vote-getters and income-tax deductions kept him working long hard hours up at the Statehouse—and playing long hard hours after dark.

"It's a pity," Rockhurst continued, smiling, "that it has to be a *combination* magic and nude act. I mean, there used to be quite a difference between the two."

The governor bit at the industrialist's bait. "How's that?"

"Well, a magic show is a cunning array of stunts."

Asque frowned, then smirked, then laughed. " 'A cunning array of stunts.' I must remember that."

The governor looked at his watch again. "Couldn't you ask their assistant when they're coming?"

"I already did," Rockhurst said. "He said they'd be along but he didn't know when. So I left him to set up in the theater."

"Couldn't you call this girl's manager and hurry them along or something? Didn't you say you knew him?"

"No, not really," Rockhurst said. "Met the fellow—and his assistant too, although they never let on about that—at this dreadful faculty party down at Powhattan. Or at least it was dull until *she* showed up. So I made the dean an offer he couldn't refuse, in exchange for which he promised to have them both here. I really wonder what's keeping them."

The governor mouthed his cigar absently. He knew what kind of woman would appear in the nude at a party such as this one and wondered, if she turned out to be as attractive as Rockhurst said, if the pimp who'd set him up with some of those college broads could make the arrangment for him or if he'd have to do Rockhurst a favor in exchange for hers.

At that moment the door chimes sounded an elaborate scale, and Rockhurst, not waiting for his butler, stepped to the door and pulled it open.

A cold breeze flowed into the room, and standing shivering

on the doorstep were Professor Baxter and Anathae, looking for all the world as if they had just popped there out of thin air.

This was because they had, in fact, just popped there out of thin air.

Rockhurst stepped back, indicating that they should enter; when they did, Rockhurst closed the door and offered the professor his hand. "Hello, Baxter. You're late."

Willis shook hands.

"Hello, again," Willis said somewhat grudgingly. "Sorry. We came as quickly as we could."

Anathae was able to stifle her urge to chuckle at this seemingly innocuous explanation.

The millionaire turned to her and said, "You're looking just as lovely as I remember you, my dear."

Anathae fairly glowed through her freckles with delight. "Oh, do you like my dress?"

As she turned around slowly to allow its inspection, Willis blushed.

She wore what would otherwise have been a clinging full-length gown of crimson sequins—had the back not plunged down to a point just barely high enough to hide her tail and the front not fallen tightly over her breasts (while revealing she was unquestionably bare beneath), giving them a support they in no wise required. The midriff of the gown was netting, with just a scattering of sequins which did nothing to hide her perfectly formed navel and only barely stopped in time to conceal her tawny-red pubic hair.

The dress was kept together by skilled engineering and no small amount of magic.

At this display, Rockhurst, who was never at a loss for words, was at a loss for words.

But Governor Asque stepped forward to offer her his hand. "Come on in, my dear, away from the door where it's a little warmer. You must be positively freezing in that little dress."

Anathae took the governor's proffered hand, stepped farther into the foyer, and said, "You look like someone who might be willing to help me get warmed up." A smile insinuated its way across her face as she turned, beckoning to Willis. "Come on, Will. Stay near me."

The professor also stepped further into the foyer. "Just let me take off my coat," he mumbled, sizing up Asque with suspicion.

His attention was momentarily diverted when he found he was wearing a tux beneath, and his hands went instinctively to his head to discover the answer to an unasked question, in the form of a silk top hat.

Asque took full advantage of this by slipping his arm around Anathae's waist and giving her a pull in his direction. Studying the detail of her midriff and keeping his voice carefully low so that Willis would not overhear, he said, "You don't need your pimp with me around."

Anathae kept smiling but skillfully removed herself from his clutches. She was now aware, if Willis was not, of the profession of the other women at this party, and could already imagine his "I-told-you-so's." She also knew some of them were as scantily dressed as she was, and though Anathae's reasons were different from theirs, she was willing to overlook the governor's crude remark as an understandable mistake, provided he did nothing more.

For his part, the governor was perfectly accustomed to being denied from time to time—at least at first—and so did not overly brood upon her action.

Without replying to him, Anathae said, "Come on, Will. Let's get the party going."

Willis, having seen the hand leaving her hip, moved stiffly, angry because of the whispering, angry that a fifty-year-old man should have his hands on Anathae (momentarily forgetting, as it was quite easy to do, that she was herself about four thousand years old), angry again at being forced to be here.

He handed his camel-hair overcoat to a butler who had used more mundane magic to seemingly appear out of nowhere as Rockhurst stepped to the other side of the girl-demon.

Willis had to clear his throat several times to get the attention of the contractor and the governor. When at last one of Rockhurst's eyes turned toward him and Asque's head was at a forty-five degree angle to both Anathae and Willis, he decided that was about as much as he could reasonably hope for and said, "I'll have to take Ana to a room adjoining the one where we're to perform."

While it actually did not matter where Anathae went, Willis had already decided that placing her in a nearby room would give their act of magic the appearance of being part of a magic act.

"I'll be happy to escort her," Rockhurst said.

"Nonsense," the governor insisted. "I'll do it."

For the briefest of moments one could almost see, in Rockhurst's eyes, the forces of avarice beating down the forces of lust. He did not, after all, really *need* the contracts the Commonwealth gave him every year—it wouldn't be *that* hard to replace them. On the other hand, he had already spent thousands in bribes and for parties such as this one just to obtain them again, and it did not seem worthwhile to throw away all this work simply because he felt like gainsaying the governor on this point.

"Of course," Rockhurst said. Then, turning to Willis, he said, "Join me in a drink?"

Willis looked at Anathae. "You'll be all right?"

"I can handle it," she assured him.

Willis and Rockhurst walked into the parlor.

Asque followed them with his eyes, turned to Anathae, then turned back toward the parlor again—as if some previously half-registered detail about the room had at last made an indelible impression on him.

"Excuse me, I won't be but a moment," the governor said to Anathae, and, leaving her where she stood, he stepped beyond the threshold of the parlor. "Norman," he called to Rockhurst's back, "would you come here a minute?"

Rockhurst heard; he pointed Willis in the direction of one of the bars and came back to where the governor was standing.

"What is it, Izzy?" he asked.

"That girl," Asque said, not pointing but indicating with a quick movement of his eyes that he meant one of the young ladies, "is she . . . colored?"

Rockhurst turned casually to look at the woman in question, then turned back to the governor. "I don't believe so," he said. "I grant you she's dark-complected, but I know your feelings. I think she's South American."

Asque, his distaste made obvious by the curl of his lip, said, "Well, in any case, I really don't think it would be wise for any of *us* to consort with her. In fact, I think she should be removed."

"If you wish."

Rockhurst shrugged and turned about, and Asque returned to Anathae.

"Sorry," he said, trying but failing to put one of his hands on her lithe waist again. "I really have nothing against coloreds in their place, you understand. But most of them live like pigs. This one, I think, should be taught a lesson for her presumption."

"Pigs?" Anathae said as she brushed past him toward the adjoining room. "Oh, I quite agree with you—some people *should* be taught a lesson."

He followed in her wake, thought of something that might get her attention again, and spoke to her back.

Since she was slightly ahead of him, he could not see the change in her expression as her eyes narrowed and her hands made a few quick gestures. He thought she was saying something in response to his little joke, but her words were too low for him to make out.

In the parlor, Willis Baxter was too deep in his own brooding thoughts to listen to what the governor had to say to Rockhurst.

His own quick appraisal of the clothing and expressions worn by a good number if not all the ladies present, however, left Willis in little doubt as to just what kind of party this was likely to be. His worst fears were about to be realized.

The professor stopped at the self-serve bar, a short distance from the doorway, and turned back. Despite the distance between them, he thought he heard the governor's tenor voice saying something to Anathae, although the only words he could make out were "magic acts" and "cunning stunts."

He saw Rockhurst return to the room to summon a servant and say something into his ear. The servant crossed the room to a dark-skinned raven-haired beauty and said something to the young woman which apparently surprised her. Willis was not altogether sure if her expression was one of anger, so quickly was it replaced by a look of icy hardness. She took an envelope from the servant and, after setting her drink aside, got to her feet and walked from the room, looking neither left or right.

Wondering what it was all about, he turned to survey the rest of the room and collided with the bar, causing several bottles to ring together. He caught his balance and barely managed to grab the one which was in most danger of falling. The jangling had caused a few heads to turn in his direction, so, although he had planned to drink little or not at all at this particular party, he picked up a large glass, poured some of the contents of the bottle he had caught into it, and drank it.

Straight bourbon.

Willis replaced the bottle, grabbed a napkin, and tried to wipe his tongue. "Ach," he said to himself, spitting bits of paper napkin into the air, "this'll never do."

"Baxter." It was Rockhurst. "I have your equipment set up at the front of my little theater. We'll be ready to start as soon as the governor returns."

"Of course," Willis grated, feeling as though an army of Janissaries had ridden through his mouth, throat, and esophagus, hacking with their scimitars all the way down. "Let me get another drink."

Rockhurst nodded.

Willis grabbed a bottle, poured, and gulped. Unfortunately, the bottle was not the one he had had before—this one containing Scotch.

Thus, Willis was quite blissfully unaware of the passage of any time.

Presently, however, he saw Rockhurst walk into the center of the room, raise his hands for attention, and say in a commanding voice, "Gentlemen! Gentlemen and ladies, the live entertainment is about to begin. For that, we must move into my private theater, since we'll want to start our movies after that. I regret to say that my theater's rather small, so we'll be a bit crowded—a few of you may even have to sit on each other's laps. But I trust there'll be no objection to that?"

The men roared their approval while the women smiled their acquiescence.

Willis hurried into the small theater as the others were getting out of their seats to follow.

9

As noted, in the week during which Willis had been uncertain as to whether or not he and Anathae would attend Rockhurst's party, he had checked out books on parlor magic from the library and practiced, before his mirror, the tricks he had purchased, since Anathae had convinced him that if they did attend, he might reasonably be expected to perform more than one trick, however impressive that trick might be.

He had not, however, been very good at it. But Anathae had reassured him on that score by helping him spice up his "patter"—the line of humourous talk which goes along with the performance of feats of legerdemain—and had even promised to help by covering any mistakes he might make with real magic.

And at first, everything went as planned.

The stage, such as it was, was only a small riser at the front of the little indoor theater; a magician's table had been set up there for Willis's use. The lights dimmed as the governor was taking his seat beside Rockhurst, and Willis was suddenly in the center of a spotlight. The faces which looked at him from the audience were eager, but the spotlight kept him from seeing them or feeling stagefright.

He launched into his patter and relaxed as soon as his first joke brought a gratifying response of laughter. He handled the rings and balls and boxes and chains quite well, he thought. The audience was with him.

But then, as the dim shadow of another late-comer was taking one of the two remaining seats down front, Willis unwittingly exposed a mirror which should not have been exposed.

Although the audience laughed both with and at him, he felt annoyed and wondered if this was how Anathae kept her promises. Then Willis gave away a punch line too early in his patter. He was so disconcerted by this that he realized, too late, that fully three-quarters of the audience could see he was removing the bouquet of flowers from his sleeve.

Wondering what could be occupying Anathae and deciding he wanted to be out of this place as quickly as possible, he deftly improvised a quick cut in his patter to bring himself to the trick before conjuring her—and then groaned when the cards slipped out of his hands, losing their all-important crimp in the pile they made at his feet.

Silence.

He smiled and said, "Conjuring up a demon is serious business—not something which should be tried by a bumbling magician—but for your sakes I will attempt it." He swallowed; the audience seemed to be with him again to the extent of being willing to accept his mistakes as having been planned.

"The first thing I have to do is make a pentagram within a circle. It is, when conjuring *any* demon, very important that the lines be solid—otherwise the demon we summon would be able to work through and control *us*, rather than the other way around. I'm sure we all have our own demons, as it is, without needing any more."

The audience provided a few tolerant chuckles for this totally improvised line.

Willis looked on his magician's table but failed to see the chalk he had requested be placed there. To his surprise, the late arrival quickly stood and handed him a piece.

"Here you are, Professor."

If the man's features were still indistinguishable beyond the spotlight, his voice was not.

It was Larry Hawthorne!

"What are *you* doing here?" Willis whispered, taking a step backward. For an instant, forgetting what Anathae had said to him, he pictured police surrounding the mansion to make arrests that could well result in the scandal of the century.

Hawthorne merely said, with a smile which was malicious even through the dimness, "I couldn't miss this chance to see you perform."

Willis wanted desperately to announce that he was ill and could not go on, but it was already too late—his mistakes had made the audience restless.

So he drew his pentagram and circle, accurately enough, but then rose, pocketing the chalk, and began the wrong chant: "*Eiris sazun idisi, sazun hera duoder.*"

This was of no consequence, however, since this was not, of course, to be a real conjuring; Anathae would simply appear when Willis reached the end of this old pagan charm, and Willis now felt that this was just as well, since he didn't want Hawthorne to hear the authentic version again anyway.

"*Suma hapt heptidun, suma heri lezidun.*"

"That's not right!" Hawthorne's voice cut through the silence.

"Shut up!" came Asque's tenor. "He knows what he's doing!"

"*Suma clubodun umbi cuoniouuidi.*

"*Insprinc haptbandun, inuar uigandun.*"

Willis waited.

The audience waited.

Hawthorne waited with bated breath.

Nothing happened. Nothing. No blinding flash, no cloud of smoke, no nude Anathae sweeping out in horns and tail.

Hawthorne stepped onto the stage and shouldered past Willis to take the spotlight, eyes gleaming. "Since Professor Baxter cannot summon up his demon, it is now time to consign that demon's spirit to Hell forever. I have the incantation written down here—and if *he* won't read it properly, *I will!*"

But as Hawthorne finished speaking, there was a blinding flash of light and a billowing of smoke that encompassed a good part of the audience.

Better late than never, Willis thought.

Yet, as the smoke cleared a bit, there was still no nude Anathae to be seen in the pentagram. Instead, there was a two-hundred-pound pig—wearing, or at least lumped up inside of, a man's pearl-gray suit.

"What the hell?" someone exclaimed. "Where's the girl?"

"You're supposed to give us Sweet Anny!"

Another voice: "Is this some kind of joke?"

Hawthorne cursed.

The lights came back on to reveal that most of the audience were trying to get out of their crowded seats and leave in disgust.

Willis could hear Rockhurst's voice saying, "Izzy? Izzy? Where are you?"

"Look out!" someone yelled, adding, "The pig!"—as if that explained anything.

The pig in the pearl-gray suit was not to be seen—at least, not in the flesh.

Because the pig, after a bewildered look to its left and right, had quickly scampered off the riser and, in the first moments of confusion, where many people in the audience were crowding into the narrow aisle, tried to make its escape. The progress of the pig was easy to follow as guest after guest, and lady after lady, began to scramble out of its way. But, like the majestic redwoods, sabotaged from below by a trusty woodsman's ax, or at least a scurrying pig in a pearl-gray suit, many of these persons now toppled forward and back, falling over each other and the seats with accompanying crashes.

Rockhurst shouldered his way through them all and grasped Willis by the wrist.

"The governor," he said. "Where's Governor Asque? If you've offended him with this stupid prank—putting that pig in a suit like his—I'll have your head!"

"Don't push!" came a woman's voice from the crowd. "Don't push. Goddammit, I said don't *push!*" This was followed by a sound which is unlike any other—that of a balled fist connecting.

Then for some reason the crowd—flailing arms, rushing feet, crushing torsos—surged in a new direction, and both Willis and Rockhurst were pushed aside. Rockhurst lost his grip on Willis's arm, and the crush of the men and women pushed by others wanting to get out, wanting to get back in, wanting to avoid the pig and wanting to be anywhere but where they were, easily parted the professor and the millionaire.

Willis was slammed to the wall, lost his footing, and sank beneath the waves of moving people like a ruptured duck.

It was not so bad, really, down below. His head was swimming more from the blows he had received than the drinks he had consumed. In fact, he felt almost sobered. Instinctively, he rolled himself into a ball, for fear that the herd of people would trample him, and closed his eyes.

He opened one of them again when this did not occur to see what was protecting him. The first thing he saw was a big brown loafer—which seemed to be on the back hoof of the pig. Most of the mob were trying to get out the door, which was at the back of the theater, with considerable pushing and shoving—and whenever a clump of people were pushed in their direction, the pig braced itself, put its weight behind its hooves, and pushed back. Being between the wall and the pig provided Willis with something of a shield.

Then the pig turned its snout in Willis's direction. "Hey," it said, "are you responsible for this?"

Funny. Willis shook his head. Only a moment before, he would have been prepared to accept a bet for any amount of money that the evening's series of unexpected events had left him stone cold sober. But apparently not.

"Did you do this to me?" the pig asked, trying to raise an unpickled pig's knuckle threateningly. The pig seemed almost to be crying.

Willis opened his eyes to study the pig as an idea occurred to him. "No, Governor," he answered, in part testing his thesis. "It's not my fault. Believe me!"

"*Fault?*" the pig replied. "I don't give a good goddam whose *fault* it is! You turn me back to my old self immediately or I'll initiate proceedings to restore the death penalty in this state, and let you guess who will be the first to pay it! I'll have your returns audited and your taxes reassessed, I'll have you investigated, harassed, and hounded until—"

Willis put his hand over the pig's mouth.

"Just keep quiet and I'll do what I can. The first thing is to find Anathae—she could undo this in an instant."

The governor freed his snout from Willis's grip. "That girl of yours? She's gone off with your assistant, Hoffbug."

"Hawthorne?"

"Yeah, Hawthorne. I saw him leading her out the front door when I almost made it out of here."

Willis didn't know what to think. While it seemed unlikely that Anathae would follow Hawthorne anywhere, for any reason, why should the governor—the pig—lie to him?

Several members of the crowd, seeing the egress totally jammed, now surged back toward the front of the little theater, and the pig—the governor—had to put his back into keeping them away. "How does Hawthorne fit into this?"

As quickly as he could, Willis told the governor about Hawthorne, about Anathae, and offered a tentative theory—that Hawthorne, for some reason yet to be fathomed, had turned the governor into a pig. The Higher Forms of magic, Willis realized, needed a magical being such as Anathae to perform them—but there were feats even a human could perform, and, with the evidence of the governor before him, he could only conclude that Hawthorne had found such a spell in one of the books he had been reading.

"That's the best guess I can make," Willis said, "although he was probably aiming it at me. I'm puzzled, though, as to why Ana went along with Hawthorne. He's not a friend of ours."

"Then why'd he give her the necklace back?"

"Necklace?"

"When I was taking her to the other room," the hog explained. "He came up, put it on her, and said, 'Here, you forgot this.' At first I thought she wasn't going to accept it, but when he put it on her she kind of settled down. Then he said he was your assistant and told her to go into the room, which she did."

Willis tried to puzzle this out but couldn't. "Well, whatever happened, we have to find her. She's the only one I know who might be able to help you."

"She went with him, so I guess we look for him first. Know where he lives?"

Willis said he did.

The governor eyed the not-much-diminished crowd. "You hit 'em high, I'll hit 'em low," he said and, giving forth a high-pitched squeal, plunged into them. Several women joined in with high-pitched squeals of their own.

Willis, rising both to his feet and the occasion, staggered after the hog, stepping over the men and women it had knocked aside in its rush. He lurched through the door into the next room, collided again with the portable bar, and then scrambled past the people who had made it out ahead of him and headed for the front door.

"The pig! The pig!" someone yelled. "The pig's getting away!"

"So's the guy responsible for this," someone else bellowed. "That magician—look!"

Willis pulled open the front door. Before he and the pig ran out into the darkness, he saw a number of the company (how many make a posse? how many a lynch mob? never mind—a *number* of the company) were following, with the obvious intent of seeking restitution for the wrongs done them.

Willis slammed the door and fumbled in his pockets for the keys to his car before he recalled that he had not come to the party in his little green Volks—Anathae, with her demoncraft, had transported them both to Rockhurst's doorstep.

"Glug," he said.

"What?" the hog asked.

"Nothing."

"Sounded like you said 'glug,' " the governor said.

"Never mind. We're going to have to run for it."

And with that, Willis started off at a lope toward the front gate of the Rockhurst estate, far off in the distance. The pig followed right behind.

Scant seconds later, the front door of the mansion slammed open and a small but angry bunch of men and even a few women poured out. "There they go! Get 'em!"

Willis continued running toward the gate. The hog also continued running but turned his head over his shoulder—not an easy thing for a pig to do—to look back.

"They're after us," Asque said, redoubling his speed and passing Willis. "I think that's Norman swinging a bottle over his head."

"Good grief," Willis replied as he passed the governor.

"Where's your car, Baxter?" the pig inquired as he was coming by.

"That's what I was glugging about—I didn't bring one," Willis answered as a new burst of speed put him out ahead.

The gate was in front of them. The hog was waiting, none too patiently, as Willis came up and pushed it open. "Here they come," Asque said. "Run for it. Along Seneca. Traffic's *got* to thin out in a minute—then we can cross and hide in the woods."

Willis and the hog, both badly winded, ran between the hedge and the street, looking for a break in the cars and trucks whizzing by. Willis glanced back toward the gate just as the vigilantes came through it.

"There they are!" came a shout.

"Into the street!" Willis yelled, jumping out into the glaring headlights of an oncoming car. Horns sounded, brakes squealed, and a taxi came to an abrupt halt just inches short of the unlikely pair. The driver—a dark shadow behind the lights—leaned out his window and shouted, "You trying to kill yourself, or what?"

Willis didn't answer. He ran to the side of the cab, opened the door, and gave Asque a boost in. Willis turned to see the mob running in his direction, then hopped in himself. "Drive!" he yelled, locking his door.

The driver, in no particular hurry now that he'd been forced to stop, turned in his seat. He was a twentyish man with long hair, a Fu Manchu mustache, and a beard. "Sorry," he said, "can't do it. I'm on call. You'll have to get out."

Willis, his heart sinking, looked out the window and could distinguish features on the faces of the angry mob closing on them. Rockhurst, he saw, was still brandishing a mean and heavy-looking bottle.

"Glug," Willis said again.

10

"Hey," the cab driver said suddenly, "is that a pig?"

"Yes," Willis said.

"Far out," the driver replied. "Never mind, then." He turned around and pulled his cab out into traffic, forcing his way into the left lane. "The guys aren't going to believe this one. Uh, where you want to go?"

Willis let out a sigh of relief. Most of the pursuing crowd had stopped; a few of the heartier—or perhaps only angrier—members continued the chase for a bit, but even they gave up as the cab cruised blithely through a red light.

"Or do you just want to ride around?" the driver asked when Willis did not reply. "Just you and your pig?"

"Oh, no," Willis said. "Take us to the Idylwood Apartments, just off the P.U. campus. The best way to go—"

"I know the way," the driver said. "A pig. This is the first time I ever carried a pig in my cab. I bet there are guys hack twenty, thirty years and never carry a pig." He seemed to be making the last statement to himself.

But then, to Willis, he said, "It'd be somewhere between twelve dollars and thirteen on the meter—but I'll high-flag you nine."

"Fine," Willis said.

The driver picked up his hand mike and spoke into the receiver noise. "Twelve, twelve," he said.

"Twelve, c'mon," the radio sputtered.

"Turn me around on that Arrowhead Avenue—I picked up a flag."

"Sure thing, dirty dozen," the receiver said.

They rode in comparative silence for a while, the only sounds being the squawk of the radio, the rush of musty heat from the vents under the dash, and the occasional murmurings of the driver: "A pig! If *I* can't believe it, how can I expect *them* to?"

Fewer and fewer cars passed by until, at last, the cab pulled into Idylwood Avenue.

"Which building?" the driver asked, slowing.

"Here will be fine," Willis said, peering through the mist on the window. "In fact, this is just perfect."

The driver stopped the cab, switched on his flashers, and turned around to face Willis. Willis dug around in his pocket and at last pulled out a clip of bills. "You said nine dollars?"

"Right," the driver replied. Then, in surprise: "Hey, he's got a suit on—pretty ragged and dirty, but your pig's got a suit on. He a trained pig?"

Willis handed the driver a ten-dollar bill and said dryly, "Highly trained. This pig could be governor."

The cabby laughed. "*Any* pig could be governor of *this* state," he said loudly as he turned back to get a single in change. He laid the bill on Willis's hand expectantly.

"We'll just keep the change," Asque said. "Open the door, Baxter—the company in here's not fit for pigs."

The cabby did a double take, but Willis didn't wait for the exchange of any further repartee.

He jerked open the door and nearly fell onto the pavement as Asque pushed by him to get out of the cab. There was a thud as the governor jumped to the sidewalk, and Willis turned quickly to shut the door.

The driver stuck his head out the window. "A ventriloquist. I shoulda guessed by your tux, right?"

"Right," Willis said, putting the dollar bill in the cabby's hand.

"Even pigs should get a little respect," Asque shouted. "Especially *this* pig!"

"You don't even move your lips," the driver marveled.

"Years of practice," Willis replied.

The cab pulled away with, perhaps, unnatural speed—although, with a cab, who's to say?

Asque, sputtering and mumbling, turned in time to see Willis going down the long walk toward one of the high-rises. The hog scampered after him, yelling at the top of his lungs, "You're not going to lose me, Baxter!"

Willis rounded on him so quickly that the governor's hooves skidded on the pavement as he came to a stop.

"Be quiet!" Willis said. "We *don't* want to draw attention. This is where Hawthorne lives, and from what you said I guess he has Ana with him. She's the only one I know who can possibly do you any good—and if you get us caught before we get to her, well . . ." His unspoken words were ominous.

Asque shut his mouth with a snap and looked mournfully up at Willis.

The governor didn't have just any pig's face, Willis realized. There were recognizable features about it—a certain sculpturing about the cheekbones, a kind of fullness under the eyes. To anyone looking for the resemblance, it was blatantly obvious that this hog—this mountain of pink flesh in the tattered shreds of a pearl-gray suit—was Governor Isador Asque.

Willis walked to the outside door of the apartment building and opened it; he held it for the governor.

"Not a sound," he said, his fingers to his lips. Asque nodded so contritely that Willis was tempted to pat him on the head, but he resisted the temptation.

Although Willis was still as confused as ever about what was going on, he was beginning to worry about Anathae, recalling what Hawthorne had said when he had mounted the stage back at the mansion: "Since Professor Baxter cannot summon up his demon, it is now time to consign that demon's spirit to Hell forever. I have the incantation written down here—and if *he* can't or won't read it properly, *I will!*"

Willis was very well aware that Hawthorne might be doing precisely that at this very moment.

"It's three steps up the foyer," Willis whispered to the governor. "Can you make it?"

Asque snorted. "Just because I'm a pig doesn't mean I'm an invalid."

Willis started up the stairs, the pig behind him, and thanked his lucky stars that no one was around to ask what a man and a pig were doing tiptoeing through the foyer.

"Did you say something, sir?" an unfamiliar voice asked.

Willis started.

There was a room, off to the side, with a large archway cut out over a long countertop. This would be, he realized, where the high-rise dwellers collected their mail. Behind the counter was a switchboard, and behind the switchboard was a man, obviously the source of the unfamiliar voice.

Fortunately, Willis realized, the man, provided he did not get up from where he was sitting, could only see Willis from the waist up. Which meant he could not see the governor at all.

"Uh," Willis said, "just mumbling to myself. Which way are the elevators?"

"Are you a resident, sir?" the man asked, putting aside a magazine he had been reading.

"No," Willis answered, "I'm an associate of Professor Hawthorne's."

"Ah," the man said. "He just came in with one of his students, I believe. Shall I ring him and tell him you're coming?"

"No," Willis answered, "he's expecting us."

" 'Us'?"

"Me. He's expecting me. Which way did you say to the elevators?"

"Down the hall to your left." The man seemed about to say something else, but Willis turned and walked down the hall indicated and out of view.

Asque, who'd frozen at the sound of the man's voice, took a few cautious steps. Nothing happened, so he took a few more. As he rounded the corner, the governor almost collided with Willis, who was tiptoeing back.

Willis peered around the corner. The man was once again absorbed in his magazine.

"That was close," the hog whispered.

Willis said nothing but turned back down the hallway, and the pig fell in behind him. The hall was carpeted in worn yellow Herculon which muted their foot- and hoofsteps.

There were two elevators. Willis pushed a button, and the one on the left opened immediately. Seeing no one inside, he gave a sigh of relief and stepped in.

When Asque was safely inside with him, Willis pushed the button marked 11, and the door closed. The light over the inside of the door went from L to 2 with a few accompanying squeaks and shudders, but then the elevator picked up speed and the light went from 2 to 3 and from 3 to 4 quickly, slowed on the way past 5, and stopped—"Oh, no," Willis muttered—on 6.

Three people, two men and a thin woman, were standing in front of the elevator on the other side of the door when it opened.

"Down?" the woman asked Willis.

"No," said one of the men, with a lopsided grin. "See— the arrow's up. We'll have to wait for the next one going down."

The second man, whose untrimmed beard and mustache made his grin also appear lopsided, although in fact it was straight, pointed an accusing finger at Asque and said, "Now what the hell's *that*?"

Willis tried to assume the air of an uninterested, if not precisely bored, elevator passenger; a common, ordinary, unremarkable passenger in a tuxedo sharing an elevator with a pig. When the man pointed, Willis looked down at the governor but then turned back to looking forward as though pigs in elevators were so commonplace as to be unworthy of mention.

"Goodness," said the thin woman, "I do believe it's a *pig*!"

The first man blocked the closing of the elevator with his hand. He eyed Willis keenly. "That your pig?"

Willis looked down at the pig again, as if to ascertain whether or not it might in fact be his pig, before he said, "Heavens, no. He got on at the second floor."

Asque, taking his cue from Willis, sat on his haunches in

the middle of the elevator, staring at nothing in particular while trying to radiate nonchalance.

"Oh," said the man, taking his hand from the door.

"What did he say?" the woman asked.

"He said the pig got on at the second floor."

Mercifully, the door closed and the elevator ascended.

11

A few moments later, Willis and the governor stood outside apartment 1102. Without ado, Willis put his ear to the door and quietly tried the knob.

"I can hear crying in there," Willis said, his face darkening. "It's probably Anathae. And the door's locked."

"If she can do what you say she can, you have the governor's permission to break down this door." Asque's tiny gray eyes glittered.

Willis thanked him for his permission but pointed out that the door was solid and he was not exactly built for breaking it down. Then he searched through his pockets and came up with a pen, a clip of bills, a piece of chalk, a package of gum (with two sticks still in it), a handkerchief, a matchbook with five matches (people frequently asked him for lights), half of a theater ticket, and finally, his wallet.

"You got a key?" Asque snorted.

"Something almost as good," Willis said, flipping through the plastic pages of his billfold. "I read about this in a mystery novel," he added. He drew out a card. "BankAmericard comes in handy, even if you're not paid up." He pushed the plastic through the crack between the door and the latch in the molding and smiled with satisfaction as it eased open with a click.

Larry Hawthorne sat in a fetal position on the floor in the corner of his living room sobbing hysterically, his face pasty-white, his whole body trembling, his white shirt and black pants soaked with the sweat of fright and his long black hair drooping in disarray. The room itself was bathed in abnormally bright light, and even through the small crack in the door, Willis could feel intense heat.

The door wasn't even half opened before Asque slipped past Willis and into the room—but then he jumped back squealing with fright. "Don't go in!" he yelled to Willis and promptly wet what was left of his pants.

Willis looked at the sharp shadows cast on the peeling paint of the wall—and then realized the paint was *in the process of peeling* before his very eyes. Heedless of the governor's warning, he flung open the door and saw, in the middle of the room, the source of that light and heat.

It was a flowing, congealing giant glob of Hellfire, a demon figure made of living flame, standing in the middle of the pentagram which had been chalked onto the bare parquet floor. The fiery demon's eyes were wide—the staring eyes of a madman. In them was an irrational hatred of all living things, a hint of gleeful amusement at the prospect of torturing and maiming for its own sake. Those eyes, ebon voids in a face of red flame, bespoke a promise of pain and death; they seemed to see the certainty of the triumph of malevolence and evil over kindness and good.

The apparition swayed and fluttered like a candle, reaching out for Willis with its long sinuous fingers.

Hawthorne, seeing Willis, slithered across the floor and grabbed him by the ankles. "I can't *do* it," Hawthorne babbled. "I tried to send him back before, but he was here when I came back! He says he 'worked through' and I can't do anything about it! Send him back, Baxter, and I promise, I swear, I'll *never* try to conjure again! Never! I swear!" He let go of Willis's leg and cringed, as if he were afraid Willis might kick him.

Willis looked wildly around the room and caught sight of Anathae lying, turned away from him, on a couch beyond the pentagram. She still wore the sparkling red dress, but around her neck was a silver chain bearing an inscribed silver disk. At first, he thought she was sleeping.

"Anathae!" Willis yelled.

Very slowly, she turned her head. Her red curls spilled

over the edge of the couch, and Willis saw that her eyes were and had been open all along.

"Will." She smiled weakly, and her voice was strained, as though she spoke with difficulty. "I can hardly . . . move with this . . . medallion on. Can't do anything. And look at . . . the pentagram—*look at the pentagram!*"

Willis looked. A line in the pentagram was broken—smudged.

"Oh, no," he muttered. Willis surmised that Hawthorne's unwary foot must have stepped or even slipped on the line, causing the break.

"Oh, no," he said again as a tentacle of fire grew from the flaming apparition and edged toward the place where the line of the pentagram was incomplete. But then he realized he was still holding his BankAmericard, his wallet, half a theater ticket, a matchbook, a handkerchief, a package of gum, a clip of bills, a pen—and a piece of chalk!

Willis dropped to his knees in supplication. "Spare me, Evil One! I'll make a deal with you—I don't care about these people. Just spare me!"

A stench filled the room that made Willis gag as the demon spoke. *"I will take your soul Down with me as I go—of what other use could you be to me, petty mortal?"*

"Humans have served you before, O Prince of Darkness," Willis said, bowing in what he hoped might be considered a worshipful manner before the fiery apparition, trying not even to think of what he planned. "I only ask that you spare me—spare me and let me serve you as they have."

The black abysses in the flickering fire glared at Willis. *"I have no use for you."*

However, Willis, the sweat from his body wilting his collar, continued to make bowing motions, inching closer to the pentagram. It was not hard to focus his thoughts on the fear he felt. Then he reached out to the smudged line and quickly made it clear and distinct again with his piece of chalk.

"Gotcha!" he yelled.

The fiery form howled so that even a banshee's cry might seem like a baby's coo; every square inch within the pentagram burst into a flame so intense that it knocked Willis over backward. He saw, even as he toppled, that the pentagram was smudged in yet another place—one closer to the couch where Anathae lay helpless.

Willis, without any plan of action beyond the hope that he might attract the demon's attention, hopped to his feet and sprinted like a quarterback toward Anathae. At the last minute, he dodged the fiery fingers which had slipped through the smudge and were reaching for him. But then he slipped on a throw rug, almost caught his balance as he stumbled forward, but fell full over Anathae and the couch to catapult headlong into a pile of dirty laundry on the floor; he turned a somersault and landed on his back.

"I didn't know I could do that," he said to no one in particular.

"The medallion." Anathae's voice was strained almost beyond recognition. "Get . . . the . . . medallion."

Willis pulled himself to his feet in time to see flame reaching toward Anathae.

"No!" he yelled. He grabbed the medallion and yanked; the chain broke. With a pitching motion, he tossed it directly into the fiery form.

There was a puff of smoke.

And then, all at once, it was quiet. Very quiet indeed. The apparition had vanished.

But evidence that it had been more than illusion remained—peeling paint, burned spots on the floor and ceiling, and the strong smell of brimstone.

Anathae sat up slowly. Then she got to her feet and stood statuelike for a moment before pointing at Hawthorne, who still lay sobbing. "He did this," she said imperiously, "and he'll pay. He had it all set up, thinking you'd have to consign me to Hell forever—"

"I know," Willis interrupted.

Anathae's fingers and hands moved like a karate fighter's in Hawthorne's direction, save that they remained widespread, as she whispered a few words.

With a flash, Hawthorne vanished—and, in his place, a large slug appeared. The light, dimmer by far than the light which had so recently illuminated the room, nonetheless glanced off the slug's shiny body as it oozed along the floor, which it touched occasionally with its feelers.

Willis stumbled around the couch. "Larry!" he yelled. "My God!"

"And now," she said, turning toward the doorway, where the hog still stood shivering with fright, "it's time to take care of this pig of a governor."

Not liking the tone of her voice but unable to move, Asque said, "No! Please! Don't hurt me!"

Anathae went on: "This uncouth, vulgar, ungentlemanly, racist, insulting, bigoted, degrading pig of a governor."

She muttered again and pointed a long slender finger at the pig, and then he, too, was gone, vanished, but with nothing in his place.

As if in answer to Willis's unasked question, she said, "He's home. And we should be, too."

12

Immediately thereafter, Willis found himself holding Anathae close to him in their bed. In his old familiar bedroom. With the cluttered mahogany chest of drawers and the lace panties on the night table.

"Ana," he said, his heart pounding, "the governor—"

"—is back to his old self, with a stomach full of whiskey. Right now Rockhurst is trying to slap him awake to get him home before the governor's wife calls and makes a big stink. They just found him in one of the upstairs bedrooms. In a bit they'll find some embarrassing photos of Asque and the woman he had sent away from the party. But he's coming around and Rockhurst's telling him he shouldn't have made such a pig of himself."

Willis propped himself up on his elbows.

"There's something I don't understand, Ana. Why did Hawthorne want to turn Governor Asque into a pig?"

"*He* didn't turn Asque into a pig," Anathae said. "*I* did."

"*You?* But why?"

"I thought maybe a pig's-eye view of the world might improve certain aspects of his personality." She sighed. "It probably won't, though. He won't recall much of this in detail, and what he does remember he probably won't believe— one tends to think of one's drunken experiences as well, one's drunken experiences. But it'll be there, like a hard-to-forget nightmare. So it might do some good. Anyway, I'm pretty sure he'll be uneasy enough about it that he'll keep Rockhurst from making any complaints about our performance."

"Well, that would be a relief, anyway," Willis said, touching her shoulder softly. "But, really Ana—a pig! You should be ashamed of yourself!"

"I'm not, though," she said, as her fingers began to tickle the hair on his chest. "You forget, if it hadn't been for that, Hawthorne would have had what he wanted—that medallion made me quite powerless, you know, and he wanted our trick to fail because he thought you'd then be forced to read the rest of the incantation. You weren't doing the right one, of course, but it just didn't occur to him that there was no reason for you to use it again. If you refused to say it, he would have done it."

"Even so," Willis said, "I'd still have to send you back before that could happen—and I've no intention of doing so."

"But no, Willis, *he* could have brought me in and put me on your pentagram and sent me back himself, right in front of you—and with that medallion around my neck, I would have done it. That medallion made *him* the one in control of me, not you. Luckily, I'd already tied my spell on the governor so he'd appear as a pig in the middle of your pentagram when you finished your chant. Which caused the havoc which made Hawthorne decide to come back to his apartment—he had the pentagram there which he'd used to call up the Boss in the first place."

"Why didn't he do it, then? I mean, why did he stop to conjure up the Boss again?"

"But he didn't, Will. He must have made that smudge *before* he conjured the Boss. In a way, Hawthorne's extremely lucky—since he brought the Boss up into an incomplete pentagram, he could have been destroyed right then. But I suppose the Boss knew—well, really, there's no way the Boss *couldn't* have known—what Hawthorne intended. So he gave Hawthorne what he asked for and when Hawthorne 'dismissed' him, he just disappeared and stayed there in the pentagram. Because that way, when Hawthorne came back, the Boss would have us *both*." Anathae shuddered.

Willis allowed himself to lie back in bed without removing his hand from her shoulder—which, he realized, she needed for comfort at the moment. But eventually Willis said, "Ana, there's just one more thing."

"What?"

"Larry," he said. When the girl-demon did not reply, he added, "You just can't *leave* him like that."

"A slug? Why not? Don't you think it suits him?" She snuggled closer to Willis and put her arms around him.

"Ana," the professor said, his hands savoring the soft, smooth warmth of her back, "Ana . . . you . . . we . . . just . . . *can't*."

Anathae sighed.

"All right, Will. I'll turn him back—but only because you want me to." She paused before continuing, "But at the same time, if it doesn't seem too extreme for you, I'm going to make it so that the *next* time he tries to mess with magic, in any way, shape, or form, he'll have to put his index finger on top of his head and start singing an aria from *Madame Butterfly*. Okay?"

Willis laughed.

"Sure," he said, drawing her closer still.

Anathae sighed again. "Anything for you, Will." She snapped her fingers, mumbled a few words, then slipped a hand behind his neck. "Anything."

With her free hand, the girl-demon made a gesture at the bedroom light, which went out just as her lips found his.

PART THREE

13

Consider, dear reader: Life and Death. Good and Evil. Law and Chaos. Black and White. Sex and Oblivion. All the veriest stuff of Life whose churlish churnings and infinite interweavings, confusing comings and linear leanings constitute the essence of the universe's febrile fecund fabric.

All of which, alas, really have very little to do with this section of our saga.

No. Rather, dear reader, consider ice cream and bitter strawberries, Ping-Pong balls and chalky halls, yin and yang, a cozy college and the frazzled civilization in which it is entombed, magic and boredom, lust and dust and how the best-laid plans of mice and men, both in and out of academia, gang aft agley.

Anathae and Professor Willis Baxter, dear reader—consider them, for they, after all, are our protagonists.

First, Anathae.

Where does one begin a suitable description of this cuddly vixen, this seeming Lolita of Powhattan University who has made Willis Baxter appear her Humble Humbert and made him love it? How shall we outline her to you as she stands, at the beginning of this our (unlucky?) thirteenth chapter, in the good professor's office? Shall we call attention to the flame of tawny red hair which covers her head, framing the storybook beauty of her apparently teenage face, and licks down her classically formed shoulders to end just even with her eighteen-inch waist? Shall we point out other aspects of her lithesome figure, poking out and in and curving provocatively and cathartically under the dreamy creamy silk of her dress—surely a prototype of pubescent perfection? Shall we alliterate until we are illiterate, pulse and pound with our prose, purple with our passion over her full lips, full hips, sparkling eyes, and sparkling teeth, her short dress and that which lies beneath?

No again.

Rather, let us catch our breath, contain our emotion, and explain that this little half-demon, half-human is older than she looks. (Of course, if you've been reading this Very Closely, dear reader, this will come as no surprise to you at this point. But, what the hell.) Rip off that short silky dress she wears there in Willis Baxter's office on the P.U. campus and you will find a cute, very expressive tail curling out from the base of her spine; take off her gleaming calf-high boots and you'll see curly hair a slightly lighter red than her tresses leading down to genuine Satan-patented cloven hooves; push back the bangs of her fire-engine hair and you'll note two pert horns.

Yet take warning, dear reader, if you are at all literal-minded—for rip off her dress, take off her boots, push back her hair without her expressed permission and chances are quite likely that, unless your name is Willis Baxter, you'll end up bare-bottomed at the South Pole before you can twist the curls of your handlebar mustache and say, "Ah, me proud beauty!"

Enough of Anathae—and on to Willis Baxter.

You may think you've sized him up ere now, and, indeed, you may think you've seen his type before. The Rumpled Young University Professor with Chalk Dust on His Hands. The Absentminded Bumbling Bookish Boob a Bit Too Frequent in His Use of the Sauce.

Or, in a word, a klutz.

But scratch the stereotype and find, beneath, the man.

As he sits before us now in his new position as Chairman of the Arts and Sciences Division of old Powhattan University, let us remember that it was this seemingly meek-mannered man who precipitated these adventures by performing a drunken invocation at a party which brought the nubile Anathae to our attention. Let us also not forget to recall, dear reader, that just a few short chapters back the supposedly meek and mild Willis Baxter, for the sake of his beloved, unflinchingly faced the Dark One Himself.

So, although he may yet be a bit of a bumbler, something of a bookish boob, a man given to a bit too much drinking, and still a klutz much too humanly prone to err, let us keep sight of the fact that he is learning something of the verities of Life—for he is, above all, a man of good intentions.

Thus, we reach a quick end of this "unlucky" chapter.

Had anyone but asked your humble author, he would have opined that this work could have just as readily done without a thirteenth chapter—after all, practically every damned book you read has one.

But there are Conventions and Forms and Standards to which All Must Conform, and your author has too many troubles, more than you, dear reader, can ever know, to bother wasting his valuable time trying to argue this point with an editor.

Pausing only to reflect soulfully on this sobering thought, your author proposes to make the best of a sad business, keeping this as brief as his style will allow and then pushing on.

Shall we push on together?

14

"I won't do it," Anathae said flatly, her delicate hands on her hips.

"What do you mean, you won't do it? A few weeks ago it was 'anything for you, Will.' What's different now?"

Willis clamped down his teeth so that his jaw muscles twitched to show his exasperation—a trick which had served him well in the classroom—and rose from his seat, dislodging a sheaf of papers which fluttered to the worn carpet of his office and were ignored.

"Nothing's changed, Will. It's just, of all the hare-brained schemes—"

"You're a demon brought into this world by my magic," Willis interrupted, "so you're supposed to do whatever I ask, aren't you?"

"Yes," she admitted. "Let's just say, then, that I don't *want* to do it, that the demon part of me must do as you say but the human part is asking you not to ask *this*."

Willis's features softened visibly. He was much aware by now that Anathae had a human side.

"Oh," he said. "Well, I think I can understand that." He crossed the office to take her in his arms. "But Ana, dearest, don't you realize that regardless of how beautiful your magic may make Gertrude look, it couldn't *possibly* dim my affection for you?"

"That's *not* what I meant!"

"Then," he said, "I guess I *don't* understand." He let his arms drop to his sides. "Or maybe I do. Maybe it's really the demon in you that doesn't want to do this—because it would be the charitable thing to do."

Anathae's green eyes—eyes with which Willis Baxter had not yet come to terms—narrowed. Her eyes were ageless, like the land of Egypt in which she had been spawned and from which she had been taken into Hell thousands of years before by her demon parent.

She said, "Is that what you think? Is that *really* what you think?"

"I . . . don't know," he said hesitantly, backing away. While he realized she was growing angry, he did not as yet know her well enough to recognize the signs for when he should seek a graceful retreat. "It certainly seems . . . well, suppose you tell me."

"Because it *isn't* charity, Willis Baxter! And who the hell are you to give Gertrude charity, even if it were that? But it isn't—it's guilt, pure and simple guilt. You let her keep you under her thumb for eight years, then dumped her when I came into your life. So now you want to 'make it up'—as if *you* had *anything* to make up to *her*—by having me make her beautiful."

"Just a damned minute," Willis said. "Maybe you're right. Maybe it *is* guilt. I've been a dumping spot for it all my life. My parents wanted my brothers and sisters to grow up healthy and guilt-free, so they dumped it all on me. The very words 'judge' and 'jury' used to make me cringe with paranoia, and whenever I heard about horrible crimes in my neighborhood I used to wonder if maybe I'd committed them in my sleep.

"But so what? Ana, dearest, *I'm on top of the world*! I assume, with the aid of your powers, I could have fabled wealth or tremendous power, if I wanted—but I've asked for neither. I have *you* and"—he turned to gesture toward his desk—"a position which exercises my best qualities and requires my talents. So why *shouldn't* I do something for Gertrude?"

If the demon-girl appeared to have softened somewhat from the professor's description of his new life, she tensed again at his final sentence.

"Because—" she started.

"No, no, dearest, let me finish. The fact is, Gertrude was the closest thing I'd ever had to a girlfriend—until you came along. I 'dumped' her after eight years—and I feel bad about that. So maybe I've decided that the least I can do, the *very least*, is to have you use your magic so she can have a better life and get another man. What's so terrible about that?"

Anathae let out a pent-up sigh of exasperation. "You really don't know, do you? No, I guess you don't. Will, you know where I come from, don't you?"

"Certainly," he said. "Egypt."

"No," she said. "I mean the other place."

"Oh. You mean the Other Place. Hell."

"That's right. And do you know what they say the road to Hell is paved with?"

Willis smiled. "Good intentions, I've heard. But, you know, I suppose I really must meet your father *some*time. And on the way down, I can tell my fellow travelers I helped provide some of the road's building materials."

Anathae stamped her delicate hoof. "Very funny, Willis. Don't you see that while your intentions are good, your motives are base? You just want to salve your conscience. But if you'd stop to ask yourself why your conscience is bothering you and whether there's any good reason to feel that way, and consider the consequences of—"

"I've done that already," Willis interrupted. "I don't care to do any more. As for "consequences'—aside from the fact that you'll have a little competition for the whistles and stares of the underclassmen—I fail to see how making Gertrude look beautiful could harm anyone. And I'm sure it would do her a world of good. So I'm beginning to wonder, Ana, if you dislike the idea so much only because you're jealous—"

"Huh! Jealous? Me, jealous? Of Gertrude? Now *that's* the last straw!"

"What else am I to think? You certainly have no competition—as long as Gertrude looks like Gertrude. But what if she looked better, eh? What if she looked like, say, a combination of Marilyn Monroe and Raquel Welch, eh? Yes, Anathae, I really think I *am* beginning to understand things a little better now."

Anathae stood for a moment in sulky silence. While she

knew Willis was goading her deliberately, she seemed unable to resist responding. She took a deep breath and tried to speak calmly. "It's not right," she said, "to mess with Mother Nature."

"Hah!" Willis retorted. "You're a fine one to talk about messing with nature, after turning Governor Asque into a pig and Larry Hawthorne into a slug!"

"I changed them back," the girl-demon said defensively.

"Only because I insisted. And poor Larry still can't say so much as 'Goddammit' without putting his finger on his head and singing something from *Madame Butterfly*." (For what indeed, dear reader, is even the most simple curse—from "Go to Hell" to "Goddammit"—but an imploring of Higher Forces to act as we would wish? And what is that, dear reader, if *not* an attempt to "practice" magic?)

Although he was trying to use this as a point against Anathae in his argument, Willis could not help but smile and add, "It wouldn't be so bad if only he didn't try to sing the soprano parts."

"Now, Willis, you know that little spell I put on Professor Hawthorne was for everyone's protection. But all right, have it your way. I've tried to warn you. If you won't listen to it, you're quite right—I'll do what you want because I must."

Willis took her in his arms again. "You'll change Gertrude?"

Anathae nodded. "I'll do it carefully and slowly, over a period of a week or so, so it won't look like magic. A little here, a little there, looking better every day, until it all falls into place. That what you want?"

"Yes. I knew I could count on you."

"Just one thing," Anathae nodded ominously.

"Oh?"

"No matter what happens, no matter what the consequences, I want your solemn oath that you won't ask me to use my magic to help her—or you, in this circumstance—again. Do you understand? Once I've changed Gertrude, that's it."

"All right," he replied. "I think I can understand that. You have my promise."

"Very well."

Anathae made a few circling gestures in the direction of the front office. She also said something which sounded to Willis a little like "Whoop-dee-doo," although he wasn't sure, despite the fact that she was still in his arms. But to him she said, "It's begun—nothing can stop it now."

Willis kissed her warmly; she returned his kiss with a peck on the cheek. And before she vanished, she said, "Remember Epimethius? He couldn't return a gift once he took it. This kind of deal works the same way. For your sake, I hope the time will not come when you'll regret this—but if it should, I trust you'll recall that I gave you plenty of warning."

Now, dear reader, as painful as it might be, before we exit this chapter let us consider Gertrude Twill, department secretary, "jilted girlfriend" of Professor Willis Baxter.

Much time would be saved by going back to read the description of Anathae in Chapter 13 and pondering its opposite number. Suffice it to say that Gertrude Twill, from the tip of her mud-colored hair to her often tennis-shoe-clad feet, demonstrated to most who bothered to look that it simply wasn't worth bothering to look at Gertrude Twill.

It was true that the braces on her teeth made her kisses something only a masochist could enjoy. It was true that she had often been voted by students and faculty alike as Most Likely to Be Traded to the Los Angeles Rams. It was true that while she had been Willis's girlfriend, the combination of his shyness and her repressive attitudes had forced intimate caressing to stop upon reaching the elbows. It was true that she had maintained her hold on Willis through most of their relationship by harassment and intimidation. It was even true that while no one had ever used the words "cute" and "cuddly" to describe her, it was equally true that—in her present form—no one with any respect for the meanings of words would ever want to.

And yet, what of that?

Which of us, dear reader, are such Adonises or Venuses that we can laugh at physical ugliness?

Which of us has such a perfect personality that we cannot overlook another's faults?

What sheltered individual amongst us has never known beautiful women or handsome men so twisted by their own beauty that we would gladly trade their company for that of a Quasimodo with nary a qualm?

And who of any sensitivity whatsoever has never seen true beauty in a form which nonetheless offers no physical competition to the *Playboy* and *Playgirl* pinups?

Eh? Eh?

Think about that, dear reader. And at the same time, ponder one other question, while keeping in mind that it is one which has been taken up without resolution by the Great Thinkers ever since there have been Great Thinkers: *What is beauty?*

15

It was Day Three.

If Gertrude Twill had noticed a certain firming of her legs, stomach, and breasts, an added luster to her hair, a softening of her facial features—and attendant attention from the males around her—they were nothing she could not herself explain.

Years of mental discipline—always getting to sleep and rising at an early hour, attuning herself to office routine—combined with plenty of exercise and liberal doses of broccoli soup were doing what she had long known they would; they were beginning to pay off.

It was Day Three, a little before her usual rising hour, and her phone was ringing.

She pulled the covers off herself, noting as she did that her nails were beginning to curve and taper, although she'd never had a manicure in her life. She got up and, walking with a grace which had been denied her ere now, reached the phone and picked it up.

"Hello?"

"Uh, hello, Miss Twill?" The voice was feminine and unfamiliar to Gertrude.

"Yes."

"I'm really terribly sorry to disturb you so early, Miss Twill. I'm Miss Townley, Dr. Henderson's assistant."

Gertrude was still not awake, but she recognized the name of her dentist. "Yes?"

"I really don't quite know how to tell you this," Miss Townley said, "but we've recently discovered a mistake. Do you recall, Miss Twill, several years ago, you came to us when your orthodontist, Dr. Isakmof, died?''

Gertrude said she did.

''Well''—and from this point on Miss Townley went on in such a rush that Gertrude could not interrupt her—''it seems Dr. Isakmof kept his records—which, of course, we sent for when you came to us—in a rather peculiar fashion. He indicated your braces were to be removed—in fact, he indicated they *had been* removed. And yesterday we had some temporary help and one of the girls we brought in had worked for Dr. Isakmof and she noticed, going over your file, that he'd removed the braces two days after he died, which she remembered because he died the day after her birthday.''

''But that's impossible,'' Gertrude said. ''I mean, he never did. Remove my braces, that is.''

''That's my point, Miss Twill,'' Miss Townley said. ''We know that now. She—Mrs. Rolfe, the one who used to work for Dr. Isakmof—Mrs. Rolfe told us that often the doctor couldn't get office help and sometimes he made his notations in advance. As, apparently, he did in your case.

''But anyway, when I asked Dr. Henderson about this, he said he was certain he'd told me or one of his other assistants to make an appointment for you with his associate, Dr. White, so your braces could be removed.

''But the thing is, Miss Twill, as best as we can figure it out, whoever was supposed to do this would check your file—that's standard office procedure—and when they saw Dr. Isakmof's note about removing your braces, it didn't make sense to make an appointment to do something that had already been done.''

There was close to a full minute of silence before Miss Townley went on, ''If you have the time, I could squeeze you in at ten-thirty tomorrow. Dr. Henderson doesn't ordinarily have anything to do with removing braces, but he'll do it himself—he says this time he wants to be certain that it's done. Under the circumstances, considering that this is a terribly embarrassing mistake and it must have been quite inconvenient for you over all this time, there will be no charge.''

''What? Oh. All right. Tomorrow at ten-thirty.''

Gertrude put the phone back on the hook, eyed the alarm clock, which was within a few moments of going off, and shrugged.

She had a little difficulty getting dressed. Her pants suit was baggy in some places, too tight in others. She had been noticing that of late and telling herself she would have to dip into her savings to buy herself some new clothes if the trend continued.

The trend, evidently, was continuing.

Day Four.

"Startin' rather early, aren't ya, Doc?" asked Mike Schultz, the bartender at O'Leary's Bar & Restaurant.

Dr. Henderson nodded in acknowledgment. "But I really need it today, Mike," he said.

"Well," the bartender replied as he mixed the doctor's daiquiri, "I ain't here to knock the business. What's the problem?"

The dentist let out a sigh, as if by preparing to talk about it some great weight were dropping from him. "I think I'm flipping out. Losing my hold on reality. Flipping my cork. *And* going crazy."

"Oh?"

"Yeah. Mike, I see ten, sometimes twelve people a day— but I've still got . . . no, I *used* to have a pretty good memory for faces. I had this lady patient today, though. As I remember it, I used to have to constantly remind myself that she was a secretary down at the university and not, say, a truck driver."

Mike, knowing better than to comment, poured the doctor's drink.

The dentist picked it up and took a long draft before he continued. "Only, see, I was *wrong*—wrong as I could be. I mean, yeah, I had the face right, somehow, and even the person right, somehow—but Christ, at the same time I was wrong because she was beautiful! No, not beautiful—gorgeous! No, not gorgeous—fantastic! Skin like peaches and cream, a figure you wouldn't believe—like a goddam movie starlet!"

Mike just nodded.

"You've seen my wife, haven't you Mike? Sure—we've

eaten together here a few times. We've been married going on six years now—and if there's any doubt about it, I still think she's lovely. We have no problems to speak of—I've got a good practice, a nice home, I love my wife, our sex life is wonderful, and I couldn't be happier; I've never cheated, or even *wanted* to cheat, on her.

"Oh, yeah, sure, I can appreciate a good-looking woman as easily as the next man—but I'm quite happy with what I've got and don't want to mess it up. *Didn't* want to mess it up. But Mike, honestly, it was all I could do to keep my hands off this lady.

"Let me have another, will you?

"Well, fortunately, I couldn't talk to her—wasn't able to. I guess it was fortunate. I mean, I tried to make small talk but all I could say was 'Uhhh,' and 'Ahhh,' and other meaningless nonsense like that. I couldn't take my eyes off her, and I was so nervous I cut myself six times taking out her braces. Luckily I'm the only one who got hurt.

"And that's a funny thing, too. I mean, I took off her braces and her teeth were *perfect*! Well, hell, I know our office records were screwed up—*had* to be or she'd've had those braces off long ago—but there wasn't anything wrong with her teeth. Not anything! Now, as I said, I remember her, and even if my memory is shot all to hell and gone, I know I've worked on her before. But nothing's there—no fillings, no cavities, nothing. It's not often I can say it, but that lady needs a dentist about as much as Alexander the Great needed someone to plan his military campaigns. I dunno, Mike—I just don't know."

Mike wiped the bar as the doctor took a sip from his second drink. "Lucky for you," Mike said. "I mean, that way, you won't be seeing her again."

"I'm afraid that's not the case," Dr. Henderson said after downing the rest of his drink. "I've made appointments—one a month for the next year—to clean her teeth."

He looked up pitifully into the bartender's eyes and added, "Free of charge. I think I'm really flipping out."

Day Seven.

It was so short a walk from Willis Baxter's apartment to

the icy sidewalks of Powhattan U that, on these bracingly cool mornings, he disdained driving over in his trusty VW.

Willis had been working very hard with the Finance Office over at North Administration, in any event, and it was easier to walk the distance than it would have been to drive the meandering and often student-packed road which twisted lazily in and out between the buildings on campus.

In his zeal, he'd met with every official affecting monies to A&S, arranging appointments from early morning until late in the evening for every day of the week—except Wednesday, when he "kept his hand in" by teaching a class of grad students—since he had extracted the promise from Anathae.

Thus, he had not seen Gertrude in the interim; he *might* have stopped by on Wednesday had he not suddenly gotten a line on what seemed to be troubling some of his students and spent half the day wondering what he could do about it.

But today, he decided, he was going to see his handiwork.

Willis smiled at everyone he met—even long-haired boys, at whom habitually he had previously only thrown disapproving stares.

The world is changing, he thought as he admired the graceful snow-covered firs that lined the walk. He was going through his own spring, so the winter could have no effect on his feelings: Everything seemed new and beautiful, and life was worth living.

At last he attained the creaking doors of the snowy-pillared Administration Building and marched down the tiled hallway.

He paused momentarily before the reinforced oak doors of the Division of Arts & Sciences and tried to peer through the wired glass. But the view inside was obscured by peeling gold letters which boldly stated *Dean and Department Heads— A & S*, with his own name immediately below the dean's.

So he took a deep breath, pushed open the door, and walked in, and it hit him in the stomach—a seemingly invisible pile driver.

"Uhhh," he said, as the breath he had taken was forced out of him.

Gertrude Twill, beautiful—no, gorgeous; nay, fantastic— from the tip of her dainty toes to the top of her rich brown wavy hair, seemed to broadcast sensual sexuality with the slightest of her movements.

She looked up.

"Professor Baxter," she said, acknowledging his presence.

"Ahhh," he said nodding.

She smiled, her teeth a flash of even-sparkling whiteness.

"The dentist took them off this week," Gertrude said, tilting her head provocatively. "As I was sitting there getting my mouth in shape for the first time in years, it suddenly occurred to me that I should probably sue the bastard. I may still do that—but first I think I'll let him clean my teeth free for a while." She laughed. "I feel great."

"Uhhh," Willis said, again nodding dumbly, his retinas suffering severe overload as he noted the new strain at the front of her lacy white blouse and the smooth sweep of her legs as she turned in her swivel chair. Finally, finding the remnants of his voice, he whispered hoarsely, "You *look* great."

Gertrude's smile twisted, became almost a sneer. "Not as great, I'm sure, as a certain teeny-bopper I could mention. But thanks." And she turned back to her desk, ignoring Willis completely.

Now that she was turned away from him he was only mildly disturbed by her supple back and the rippling waves of her hair, and not by her wide liquid eyes with the heavy, sultry lashes, or her moist red lips.

"Ahhh," he said, "I guess I'll be going. I have, uhhh, lots of work to do."

"I'm sure you do," Gertrude said without turning back to him. She began sorting the morning's mail and slicing it open with a letter opener—and it occurred to Willis that she could have done just as well with only her long, red nails.

At last he tore his eyes away and lumbered past her down the hallway toward his office.

16

After his week of appointments with finance officials over at North Administration, it was a long and lonely morning for the professor. He shuffled through the routine reports which had accumulated, and he read and approved the new curricula for Physics and French Language, although he did not really feel qualified to make the decision on the former.

Then he found the following memo:

To: Willis Baxter, Chairman, A&S Div
From: Cromwell Smith, Dean
Re: Duties of A&S Chairman
Date: February 12

It has been brought to my attention that the spectrum of duties which have been ascribed to the Chairman of the Arts & Sciences Division requires a broad understanding of each department. Therefore please submit to me, no later than 2/20, a detailed analysis of each department and suggested changes, if any.

CS:gt

Willis let the memo fall from his fingers onto the desk and sat in his chair for a long time staring out the open door of his office. The hollow echo of distant footfalls brought him back to himself.

It was a simple enough matter, he decided. He could easily request reports from all department heads and compile the data. With all the ideas he'd had and never been able to implement in the ten years he'd been with the university, "suggestions" would also be no problem.

But why?

Why had this "understanding" been brought to the dean's attention—and why had Smith seen fit to add that little fact to the memo? Had it also been brought to the attention of President Mellon? Was there perhaps some implied threat here? Was his competence being questioned before he'd had a chance to demonstrate it? Had there been some complaint from some source considered unimpeachable? Or was he just being paranoid again?

Willis noted that Gertrude had typed the memo but knew there was nothing unusual about this. Gertrude did most of the dean's typing, as well as his own and that of a few others, when she was not overseeing the work of the other women in the office. Indeed, there was nothing of import to be noted here, other than the fact that Gertrude was—and always had been—a superlative secretary and office manager.

Willis took up a Bic and a yellow pad and started drafting a letter to all department heads. But it was hard to concentrate— someone was laughing out in the hall, and the echo multiplied the sound disproportionately.

He muttered a "Dammit," and threw down his pen, and walked across the worn yellow rug to the door, intent on admonishing whoever it was who was laughing.

But as he reached the doorway he saw Gertrude Twill in the hallway—standing, so that he could see that her dress not only clung but was much too short for February—with her arms wrapped tightly around Dean Cromwell Smith!

Willis drew his head back, his breath quick and shallow, and eased his door closed.

Could he believe what he'd just seen?

Had Dean Smith's hands really been where they had appeared to be?

Willis staggered back to his chair and dropped down. He spent a long time staring at his hands. He kept hearing laughter long after it had disappeared; the sound of it hung in the air like an obscenity uttered during Mass.

Then, with a sigh, pushing the incident out of his mind, he got back to work on his letter.

Noon trudged by on leaden feet. His letter finally finished, he shuffled more papers, skimmed more reports. There was the usual afternoon slump at three o'clock. He took a drink from the bottle he kept in his desk, and, after what seemed subjectively to be several hours, four o'clock finally arrived.

Willis packed his briefcase and was striding down the hall toward Gertrude's office by four-ten. He was hoping—despite what he'd seen in the hallway earlier—that she had not left for the day; he knew she often stayed until six or six-thirty to finish up.

He did not want to hurry, since he still was not certain what he would say to her if she was in—although, for some reason, he had to admit that "Ahhh" and "Uhhh" seemed to have been used overly much, and therefore felt he should try to think of something new.

But Willis found as he approached her office that while coherent thoughts about what he might say to her diminished, the pace of his steps nonetheless increased.

When he stepped out of the hallway onto the plush green rug which decorated her office, his heart leaped and his brains seemed to scramble as he looked in her direction. There she was, a vision of long-legged slinkiness, her skirt clinging to her like nylon pulled from an electric dryer and her blouse seeming to have become so small that the four top buttons had to be undone to allow room. And on her desk sat his old archrival, Professor Larry Hawthorne.

"Baxter!" Hawthorne jumped up somewhat guiltily. "So how's the job?"

Willis looked from Hawthorne to Gertrude, then with difficulty back to Hawthorne again. He pondered Hawthorne's furtive jump when he'd entered and wondered if the two of them had perhaps been talking about him.

Stop it, Willis, he told himself. *This way lies paranoia.*

"Uhhh," Willis said, "fine. What're you doing these days?"

Hawthorne drew back his long black hair with a flick of his head and pulled himself up to his full six feet, two inches. "I assumed you knew. I'm back on the staff. My curriculum reports are probably on your desk right now—Survey of Renaissance Lit.''

"Yes," Willis said, nodding, mentally checking the clutter on his desk and sifting the course outlines he'd reviewed that day. "Of course, Larry. I'm uh, glad to have you back on the staff—glad to hear your troubles have cleared up."

"I'm grateful," Hawthorne said, "that your lady friend never pressed charges." He glanced at Gertrude, realized she would not understand him as Willis would, and added, "And for other considerations, too."

"It was a complete misunderstanding, and an unfortunate one," Willis said. "Anyway, you have a lot to contribute."

"Indeed he does," Gertrude said, standing up. Her hand traced Hawthorne's sleeve and came to rest at the nape of his neck. "You'd be surprised at the innovations Larry could have implemented if he'd been—" She bit her ruby lips in concern, apparently having said more than she'd intended.

Although Willis felt a sense of foreboding, it was all he could do to keep from replying with another "Ahhh" or "Uhhh" and say instead, "If he'd been appointed chairman instead of me?"

"No hard feelings," Hawthorne said quickly. He put an arm around Gertrude, his hand nearly cupping her left breast, and smiled. "You win some—you lose some."

"That's true," Gertrude said sardonically. "Even *you* lose sometimes, Willis." She moved closer yet to Hawthorne.

"It's late," Hawthorne said, making a show of checking his watch. He gave Gertrude a kiss and said, "Pick you up at eight?"

"Of course," she answered.

He disengaged himself and walked off down the hall as Willis and Gertrude stood looking after him.

Gertrude put her purse over her shoulder, a delicate hand on her shapely hip, and turned back to Willis to say, almost conversationally, "He's afraid of you, for some reason. I know because I tried to get him to come in with me on my little . . . project. But *I'm* not afraid of you, Willis Baxter!"

"Why, Gert," Willis said, aghast, "whatever do you mean?"

She smiled sweetly. "Whatever do I mean? Why, only that

whether he wants it or not, whether he's afraid of you or not, I'm going to make *him* the next Chairman of the Arts and Sciences Division. And at the same time, of course," she fluttered her eyelashes at Willis, "utterly *ruin* you!"

"What?"

"I've already got the dean wrapped around my little finger," she said. "He's already looking—critically, I assure you—at each and every thing you do." She laughed. "But that's only 'harassment,' just something to amuse me until I can *really* go into action. You see, Norman Rockhurst's delivering his check to the university in the next few days—and you know what sort of man *he* is. Frankly, I don't think there's a damned thing you can do to prevent the kind of influence I can wield on a man like him. What have you got to say to *that?*"

"Uhhh," Willis said.

"I thought so."

And as she walked away from him, her hips undulating in a motion that Willis still found disconcerting, he began to understand, too late, Anathae's warning. Like Epimethius, who had wed Pandora and accepted a nonreturnable gift, there seemed little he could do but await whatever hand Fate dealt him, having given Fate a free wild card.

Willis Baxter knew he had delivered a powerful weapon into the hands of an enemy and realized, reluctantly, that only Anathae—promise or no promise—could help him.

17

"I told you!" Anathae said, flinging herself down onto the couch. "You gave her the ability to do something she'd wanted to do all along—she's been through a lot of humiliation. The thing is, Will, despite her faults, despite what I said about her before and despite how she manipulated the relationship she had with you, she has some beauty *inside*—but it's been so bruised by this sudden physical manifestation of beauty that she's just not prepared to handle it. But enough I-told-you-so's."

Anathae rolled over onto her stomach and peered over the arm of the couch at him. Willis sat slumped in his old purple easy chair; his face was creased into a frown, and he stared at some unresolved point beyond her.

"I didn't know she could be so vindictive," he said.

"Come now," Anathae said. "You wouldn't be saying that if she'd fallen into your arms after I'd completely fulfilled your wish."

Willis bristled and then slumped back down again. "Yeah, I guess you're right. I mean, I did sort of go off today with the idea running around in my head that she'd be grateful for what I'd done."

"Even without having been told you were responsible," Anathae said.

"Right. Crazy, wasn't it? And you did make her, uh, quite beautiful."

Anathae rose from the couch and put her soft hand on

Willis's cheek. "I don't mind if you desire other women, Willis. It's completely normal."

Willis waved a distracted hand at her. "I know. I'm glad you're not seriously annoyed—although, if anything, I'd have to say I'm more annoyed at myself on that score than you could ever be. But where you can help me . . ." Here Willis paused, took a deep breath, let it out, then continued, "Where you can help me is by changing her back the way she was. If she loses her beauty she'll be no threat. Maybe you could fix it so she lost her job."

"Now I *am* disappointed in you."

He had expected this reaction and had tried to steel himself against letting it affect him—but the steel melted and he felt dismal. Yet, by virtue of feeling so low, he was able to force himself to go on. "If there were any other way, Ana, I wouldn't have to demand this of you. If there were some way I could do it on my own—but there isn't. She's got the dean on her side. She's working on Larry Hawthorne, who's afraid of what you might do to him right now. But if I don't use you against her, that won't last for long. And I have no doubt she'll find Rockhurst an easy conquest. I need a weapon to use against her, and that weapon, unfortunately, is you."

"Demand? Did I hear you say *demand*?"

"Yes, Ana, I . . . I guess I did. I know that's breaking my solemn promise to you, but frankly I don't see any other way out of this."

"No. I won't do it. I refuse to help you. N-O. No. No help."

"I . . . was hoping you wouldn't refuse," Willis said, "because, if you won't help, I'll have to send you back to you-know-where."

The moment he said it, he wished he could take it back. But she had, he reminded himself, told him early in their relationship that one of the things he lacked, one of the things she had hoped to instill in him, was forcefulness.

She didn't say anything for a while. She stood in front of him, searching his eyes—and her eyes, for once, almost looked her age. "If you could do that," she said, "then I don't think I could miss you."

"You realize, of course, if anyone's come across your

name in Wilheim's book and tried to summon you, you'll most likely never be able to come back here again.''

"That, Professor Baxter, could be a blessing in disguise."

"Is that your answer?" he asked. "I guess it is. Well, all right—I'll show you I mean what I say."

Willis went to the closet, pulled some chalk from a coat which hung there, turned, threw back the rug, and expertly drew a pentagram on the floor.

"Your place," he said, pointing, "is over there."

She took her place in the pentagram. "I'm ready," she said.

Willis swallowed hard. She wanted forceful—he'd give her forceful. A woman who loved you should do what you wanted—wasn't that what she herself believed, what she'd implied when she'd admired his forcefulness? But then, damn it, why did he feel like such a louse?

"*Ubele* . . ." he began the incantation.

She closed her eyes.

He went on, ". . . *Canet minen* . . ."

Willis could not help but recall the last time he'd done this and how fortunate he had considered himself at having been able to summon her up again. But this time she'd really forced his hand, blast it—how could he stop now?

". . . *Teryae* . . ." he continued.

She'd practically been in tears the time before, protesting that she really cared for him. Where were tears and protests now? And why did everything he do feel so damnably wrong?

"*Exconae chanet!*"

If she didn't believe he'd really do it—well, he was coming to the end of the chant now. Let her speak or forever . . .

". . . *Isnel* . . ."

Damn, double-damn and blast it! *She* knew the words as well as *he* did—but she wouldn't even open her eyes to look at him. One more word from him, just *one more*, and she'd be back in Hell—probably permanently. Well, why didn't she speak? Say *some*thing? If that's what she wanted, then . . . if eternity in Hell was what she really preferred, why then by God he'd . . . he'd . . . he'd . . .

The wave of guilt and self-disgust which washed over him

sent a cold frosting over his back and chest, and his shirt clung clammy against his skin.

Very gently, Willis pushed Anathae out of the center of the pentagram. Once again he swallowed hard, then erased the features of the pentagram with his foot. "You knew I couldn't do it," he said. "You knew it all along."

"No, Willis," she said, opening her eyes to reveal two tears, "I didn't. I'm glad you find you can't, just as I couldn't willfully do anything to hurt you. But I didn't know it in advance, until you proved it just now. I hoped you wouldn't, but if you didn't feel that way I'd've been better off in Hell."

Willis walked slowly back to his chair, nodding to himself. "I understand now why you didn't want to make the change in Gert in the first place. But maybe you'll tell me, since I can't figure it out, why you extracted that promise from me, why you're so insistent on holding me to it."

"Because it's always wrong to force a change on any human being, Will. An internal change is the worst, but even an external change is bad. And because the real answer to your problem, Willis, is in you, and in Gertrude, and, yes, in Larry Hawthorne too—in your power and in theirs. In your beauty, if you will, and in theirs. Do you understand?"

"No. The first part, maybe, but not the second. Not really—but I'll think about it," Willis said.

Anathae sat down opposite him on the couch. "Will, look at me."

Willis looked at her seemingly youthful freckled face and into her eyes, those deep green eyes into which he had tried too often not to look directly; the disturbing quality about that icy green which usually made him shiver was not in them now.

"I'm four thousand years old," she said, her voice seeming to echo inside his head. "I've known many people in this world and the other, and few of them possess the power. But Gertrude has it—she's an excellent secretary, a credit to the university. She may be shallow, petty; she's not grown up with the physical beauty we've given her, and she's trying to use it in a despicable way against you because of the hurt you caused to her pride. These are not good things, but don't confuse not being good with being evil. I have known evil, Will."

"And Hawthorne?" Willis asked. "I suppose he's a credit, too, and maybe should have gotten that appointment instead of me? Is that what you're thinking?"

"He's not much of a person, Will, as a person," she answered. "He's vain, ignoble, loud, and a bore. He's frightened of us—of me, really—but can you blame him? And his fear bothers Gertrude, whatever she might say, because however much he wants your job and despite the lures she's thrown out to him in an effort to get him to do it, he's much too scared to join her.

"But, in answer to your question, yes, he has his own beauty. Besides being a good Professor of Renaissance Literature, he spends every free moment studying the psychology of the motivation of learning. Teaching is his life, just as it's yours, and for all his personal defects he can't help but want to inspire others. He may bore the socks off elephants when he tries to be the life of the party, but he *doesn't* bore his students. He's the best student counselor in your whole division, and you know it.

"And what about you, Will? Despite your temptation to send me back a few minutes ago, you had the courage to realize you were wrong and to act accordingly. You've got more character and integrity in your little finger than both of them put together. You'd step aside if you thought Hawthorne—or anyone else, for that matter—could handle this job better than you. And for all that you've asked my opinion, you know you're the only one really capable of handling the whole picture, and it's your opinion of yourself that really matters. Your ideas about education have scope—the kind that's needed if Powhattan isn't going to turn into a diploma mill, the kind that no one else at the university has, not Joel Mellon, not Cromwell Smith, not Larry Hawthorne, not Gertrude Twill. You're also a scholar, top-notch in medieval literature—and though no one knows it, you're the foremost authority on demonology; your books are the last word on the subject, and you've proved yourself best by conjuring up the last available demon in Hell—me.

"You think you need a weapon to use against Larry and

Gertrude? Well, I can conjure up one, if that's what you really want.''

So saying, she said a few words Willis did not understand, gestured, then reached into the air and pulled from it a tape cassette, which she handed to Willis. ''But before you use it, know that it also will place you on the horns of a dilemma—for if you do use it, it will implicate Hawthorne, even though he's really not a part of this. Take some advice from me, Will, and look inside yourself. *You* are the answer. You're the needle; they're the thread. It's not a magic spell but a whole cloth you want to weave.''

''But what about my job?'' Willis asked in dismay. ''I can't do it if I have to be constantly on guard against the next stick they may try to thrust in my wheelspokes. Especially since Gert's so strong with Dean Smith that—''

Anathae drifted close enough to lay her fingers against his lips. ''The power must be preserved wherever it is found,'' she said. ''When I perceive it, I cannot destroy it. We've wreaked a sort of havoc in Gertrude's life by making her beautiful—it would be a double cruelty to take it away from her, no matter how she misuses it, now that we've given it to her.

''Besides,'' she said as she landed in his lap and slid her arms around his neck, ''inside, you know the real solution. You don't need any help from me.''

Anathae's dress vanished. And for a while Willis did not think about his problem at all.

18

It rained when it did not snow for all the next week, and twice the temperature fell below zero.

Willis sat staring out his office window at the gray sky that seemed to clamp onto the horizon like a helmet. He was alone, but by the way he sat tapping his pencil on the desk, it was obvious he did not expect to be alone for long.

Indeed, there was a knock at his door.

"Come in," he said firmly.

The door swung open, and Gertrude Twill, the latest epitome of female beauty, and Larry Hawthorne, erstwhile slug, entered together. Neither smiled; Gertrude looked grim, Larry wary.

"I've been expecting you," Willis said.

Hawthorne's hand floated across Gertrude's back as she sat down, as if he were seeking some kind of reassurance from the contact. Then he slid into the chair next to hers. "What's this about, Baxter?"

"I'd like to think of this as a continuation of a discussion Gertrude and I had last week."

Gertrude started to rise. "I have nothing to discuss—and Larry isn't involved."

Willis waved her back into the seat. "Sit, Gertrude." And miraculously she did. "I rather think we do—all three of us."

"If you're looking for a bargain," Gertrude said, "I suppose I'm willing to offer you one. All you have to do is admit your own incompetence in that report you're writing for the dean, which you're being so secretive about, and recommend that Larry be named in your place. If you do that, then as far as I'm concerned you can continue on here as a Professor of Medieval Literature."

Hawthorne looked horrified at the suggestion, but before he could protest that this idea was not his own, Willis said to Gertrude, "No. I won't do that, Gert."

Gertrude unpursed her pouting, Clara Bow lips. "Then I'll break you the hard way. I already have a memo from Norman Rockhurst stating that he would be just as pleased to see Larry in your position. You really shouldn't have offended Rockhurst, Willis."

"I suppose I must agree," Willis said. "However, I didn't call you here to discuss what you have planned for me. Hah! Although, you know, maybe I did, at that. But the thing is, I don't need you to tell me what you've done, Gert, because I have it all here." He held up a tape cassette. "Would you care to hear it?"

Although for different reasons, the two shared the same expression—one of bewilderment.

Not waiting for their answer, Willis put the tape on a cassette player and turned it on. Then he sat watching their expressions as, slowly, it began to dawn on them precisely what they were hearing. The fidelity was not very good, but it was clearly Hawthorne's voice that first came from the machine:

". . . can put the screws to you if you don't do as we say. Gert's got Dean Smith wrapped around her little finger, and she's working on Rockhurst. You can say what you want about us, but the Dean won't hear a word . . ."

"But I never said that!" Hawthorne protested.

"I know you didn't, Larry. I realize you know how I came by it, though, even if Gertrude doesn't."

The two exchanged glances, and Willis felt a little sorry for Hawthorne, who knew the truth of the matter but could scarcely tell it to Gertrude, since if he did she'd believe him to be crazy.

The voice coming from the tape player was now Gertrude's:

". . . I'll do whatever I have to to make Professor Hawthorne the next Chairman of the Arts and Sciences Division, so you might as well give in. I suppose I'm willing to
offer you a bargain. All you have to do is admit your own
incompetence in that report you're writing for the dean,
which you're being so secretive about, and recommend
that Larry be named in your place. If you do that, then as
far as I'm concerned you can continue on here as Professor of Medieval Literature."

Gertrude looked from the machine to Willis and back at the
machine. She knew the tape had been in his hand, and
therefore that he could not have used it to tape her remarks of
just a few minutes before, so the look she turned back to
Willis was almost as horrified as Hawthorne's had been
pleading.

With a swift movement, Willis clicked the tape player off.
"See? I admit the fidelity's not the greatest, so if it were all
up to the dean, I suppose he could believe it wasn't you—or
at least *say* he believed it wasn't you."

Gertrude slowly smiled. "There's always that possibility,
Professor Baxter."

"Unfortunately, Gert," Willis went on, "the matter *isn't*
up to Dean Smith. You seem to have forgotten that I'm a
tenured professor here—and if I chose to protest it, he'd have
to take it before President Mellon and the Board of Gover-
nors." Willis paused to let this sink in before he continued.
"I would be a fool to deny that you could, in all probability,
tempt some of them as well—you've really turned into quite a
beautiful woman, Gert. But there are some fifty of them,
altogether, and some are old, others remarkably straightlaced,
a few of them are women, and surely not all of them can be
as weak-willed as the dean or as crude as Norman Rockhurst.
And you'd only have two weeks to do it."

Willis removed the tape from the machine. "Of course, it's
possible enough of them wouldn't believe this tape. They
might think I trumped up the whole thing—not too likely, but
a small hope that you might save something of your careers
here. What do you think?"

Hawthorne protested, "But I didn't have anything to do with this! You *know* I didn't. And you know *why* I wouldn't!"

Gertrude glowered at both of them.

Willis held the small tape between his thumb and index finger. "Yes, Larry, I *am* aware of that. My question was rhetorical, in any event—we'll *never* know what the board might make of this, because I have absolutely no intention of ever using it. I just wanted you both to know that I *could* have played your game if I wanted to." He tossed the tape to Hawthorne.

Hawthorne, although startled, caught it, then held it up and looked at it in disbelief. "I don't understand."

"You will," Willis said, "after you've read my report. It's already been approved by Dean Smith, by the way. I suppose he'll be wanting to talk to you fairly soon."

"Wha—what about?"

"I shouldn't tell you, but I will. Dean Smith concurs with me that you're the best man to head up our new Department of Student Impetus."

Hawthorne's mouth dropped open in surprise. "Well, uh, thanks. I suppose I'll be reporting to you—"

"Oh, no," Willis said with a smile. "The department will be university-wide—not just A&S. I'll be glad to cooperate with *you* in any way I can. Will have to, in fact—the position will carry the title of assistant dean. This could be the beginning of elevated academic achievement for our students—*all* our students."

Hawthorne looked bewildered. "I—but—that is—why?"

"Why? Well, actually, Larry, there are a couple of reasons.

"First, if you were under me, you'd keep bucking for my position—or, if not bucking for it, at least keep on believing that it should be yours. And quite frankly, I don't think you can handle it. You'd get swamped in the paperwork; you'd focus on your narrow if useful band of interest and everything else would fall by the wayside.

"Second, I think it's high time we called an end to this useless rivalry. There might have been some point to it back when we were both just professors competing to give our students a better education. It might even be to the same purpose if we were still in competition for this job—the best man would win and the students would be the beneficiaries. But that's just not the case here.

"So what it boils down to is that I want you out of my hair so I can do my job but in a place where you'll be of most benefit to the students. I don't find it all that unfortunate that the 'place' puts you in a position higher than mine. Understand?"

Hawthorne seemed almost on the point of tears. "Yes, I . . . I think I do. And I agree. Willis, I don't know how to thank you. But may lightning strike me if I ever . . ."

A strange expression crossed his face. "On, no, not again! I—"

He rose and placed his right index finger on top of his head, then began to sing a soprano aria from *Madame Butterfly*. He went out the door, his hand on his head, still singing.

Willis turned to face Gertrude. "And then there's you."

Gertrude was distracted. "He keeps *doing* that." But when she focused on Willis, her expression returned to a glower. "What about me? You can't buy me off with a fancy position. Nor could you blackmail me with that tape even if you still had it. I'm still out to get you, Willis, and if Larry Hawthorne won't take your job I'll just find someone else who will. And you can put that on one of your tapes and send it to Dean Smith for all I care!"

"Did I really hurt you that much?" Willis asked.

Gertrude sneered. "You? Hurt me? Why, that's the most ridiculous—"

"Not so ridiculous, Gert. Why else would you be working so hard to hurt me?"

She did not deign to reply.

Willis sighed. "I almost wish you were one of my students— because then I'd have a right to lecture you. I can't even claim that right out of friendship—because while I think you thought I might marry you and I think I thought you might be right, we really weren't very good friends, Gert, even when we were going out together. I suppose I disliked letting you bully me almost as much as you must have despised me for letting you. I was grateful to you for paying any attention to me at all—and I probably *would* have married you if I hadn't met and fallen in love with someone else."

Willis sat up a bit in his chair, considered what he had said, but then went on, "And I suppose it must have seemed that I rejected you. But I'd just like to suggest, Gertrude, perhaps that wasn't the worst thing that could have happened. Maybe someday you'll look in a mirror and see the lovely woman looking back at you and you'll wonder why it ever mattered to you that I went to someone else. I think you have an inner beauty that will someday far outshine the other one, and when you find it you'll discover you can have any man you want. *If* you want.

"In the meantime, I hate to see what you're doing to yourself. I'm not worth it. Getting your vengeance on me isn't worth it, if you have to degrade yourself to do it. Larry Hawthorne. Dean Smith. *Norman Rockhurst*, for God's sake.

"Oh, hell, I wasn't going to lecture."

Gertrude let her now tear-brimmed eyes slip from Willis to the stained yellow carpet at her feet. "No, Professor Baxter—Willis, I mean. I think you may be right. I'll need time to think."

"I hope you do think about it, Gert," Willis said gently. "I hope you do. We have a university to run here, however, and let's hope some of the young men and women who come through here will learn something and make all our lives better for having been here. We really need you, Gert—Dean Smith, myself, Larry. You know as well as I do that this place would run down completely without you. But if we can't work together, you and I, if we're going to be at each other's throats . . . Gert, if we can't work together as friends, I'll have to—"

"—have me fired?" Anger flashed across Gertrude's face again. "You just try it!"

Willis shook his head. "I'll have to give you this." He handed a paper to Gertrude across his desk, and she crackled it smooth before her and began to read.

She looked up suddenly. "Your resignation?"

"Not because of your threats—I played that tape just to let you know I could answer your threats with threats of my own, if that were what I wanted. And not because you can get the dean or Rockhurst or any number of influential individuals to arrange it. I'm giving it to you because you seem to want it and because a house divided cannot long stand."

Gertrude's eyes softened. "Willis, I—"

"You've got it—keep it until you've thought this matter through. As you can see, I've signed it, addressed it to the dean, and given other reasons—I didn't mention any of this. I owe you at least that much."

Gertrude had grown very solemn. She crumpled the resignation paper and tossed it in Willis's wastepaper basket. Rising, she said, "If you don't mind, Professor Baxter, I have more important things to do."

She turned and left his office before he could say anything more. Willis turned back toward the window behind his desk, contemplating the leaden sky and the wind, which had begun to send the powdery snow into deep drifts. It would be a cold walk home.

It was only for an instant that he saw the reflection of his own face in the glass and Anathae's impish smile superimposed over it. She seemed to be gesturing and mouthing words.

There was a snapping of fingers.

Then Willis Baxter disappeared.

PART FOUR

PART FOUR

19

"That's it," the skinny young male passenger in the backseat of the VW said, pointing, a nervous tremor in his voice. "The one with all the bushes. That's Rudy Narmer's place. The party's already started."

The '75 VW had stopped in front of an old house shrouded by ancient leafy oaks. The driver, a thirtyish fellow, switched off the engine and put out its lights with a brisk slam of the heel of his hand on the outthrust knob.

Night sat softly on the woodsy suburban neighborhood in which the house, a modern gothic memory of slower dreamier times, was situated. The bushes came close to constituting a hedge, but the house was all muffed up in ivy against the snow, and through it mere patches of brick and wood could be discerned. Behind this air of antiquity, lights were shimmering dimly through partially curtained windows, and muffled but wild music was throbbing from one section of the house and hanging in the cool night air.

"You're certain," the driver said, "this Narmer guy's the reason?"

The young man nodded his head up and down emphatically, his smile hidden in the darkness. "Yes, Professor Baxter. It's the stuff he passes around at his parties that does it."

"Speaking of which," said the apparent teenager sitting beside the driver, "how about a couple of tokes of Colombian before we check all this out?"

She picked a perfectly rolled joint out of the air—but so

that the backseat passenger would not see her, since only a select group of people at Powhattan University knew she was a demon who had been conjured up from Hell by Professor Willis Baxter during a faculty party. (Well, a select group from Old P.U. and, of course, *you*, dear reader!)

"No, uh, I'm doing all right," said the youth.

"Ana," said Willis in a kind but firm voice, "this is not exactly the best time to be getting high."

Not that Willis smoked marijuana anyway, despite Anathae's infrequent urgings. While from his ivory tower he had noted that use of this drug seemed to cause little or no harm to his students, he nonetheless shied away from its use himself. He had even made something of a joke of it: He wouldn't want other teachers using it during classes, and he had to provide something in the way of moral leadership. "That way," he had punned, "I retain control of all of my faculties."

Anathae tossed back her tawny red mane, careful not to reveal her two little horns. "Okay, okay," she said, shrugging her shapely shoulders. "Just trying to cheer up this dreadfully dull atmosphere, Willis. Gee, you'd think we were going to a wake or something instead of a party!"

"It's not a fun party, Ana," Willis said.

The grad student in the backseat said, "You don't know what it's doing to some of my friends—coming to this place, freaking out on Rudy's stuff. That's why I volunteered to cooperate with Professor Baxter on this, even though it might be dangerous for me." On this last note, his voice dropped to a whine. "I want my friends back the way they were—they've really gone through some heavy changes lately."

"I didn't give Ana the entire story, Neal," Willis explained to the younger man. Staring ahead at the cars parked along the street in the driveway, Willis added, "It's like this, Ana. I told you I wanted you to help me check out this character, Rudy Narmer—"

"He's from Turkey," Neal interrupted. "That's where he gets his drugs."

"Right," Willis said. "And these drugs seem to be messing up a lot of students at Powhattan, including a couple who, like Neal here, are in a graduate seminar of mine. They seem totally out of things now—no interest in their studies. You really should have seen the results of the last exam I gave!''

Willis could not help but recall the incredulity with which he had read the papers they had turned in: "Define courtly love" answered with "Making love in court;" "Discuss Siegfried" alternatively with "A German salute" and "A breakfast made with matzoh"; and "Give two interpretations of the love potion in *Tristan*" answered by "Powdered rhino horn; Spanish fly." Until Neal Barski had shown up with a better explanation, Professor Baxter had wondered if perhaps it had suddenly become fashionable not to pass his course.

And even when Neal had come forward, Willis had been so caught up with his own problems that he had considered simply turning the whole matter over to the police. But he also felt he owed these once-promising students his best efforts—he could not just wash his hands of them. At some earlier time in his life he might have been forced to do so with the realization that it was the only thing he could do to help them—but with Anathae's aid, he knew he could find out if this was the cause or only a symptom of what had been happening.

Anathae said, "And you're pinning the blame on the drugs this guy's been dealing? Never heard of any drugs like *that*.''

Neal laughed without humor. "Sure, you think you've heard of drugs, but Rudy's stuff is different. It does things you wouldn't believe.''

"Like?" Anathae asked.

"I did some once," Neal admitted, shifting uncomfortably. "But the others've been doing it every night since Rudy came. That's why they haven't studied—why they don't *want* to study, even if it affects their grades and the rest of their lives. Anyway, it's not just the drugs—it's Rudy, too. He has a strange effect on a lot of people, and the drug just seems to intensify it. You can *feel* his presence in a room—charismatic, you know, but sort of sinister too.''

This was followed by such a dark moment of silence that Anathae, looking back and forth at the two men, suddenly stuck her thumbs in both ears, wriggled her fingers, made a face, and yelled, "Boo!''

Both men jumped in their seats, and Anathae giggled.

"You see," she said, "the two of you are too keyed up. Maybe you're right about this Narmer guy and maybe you're wrong. But relax! You're not going to get anything out of anyone if you're all nervous. People will tune you out."

"Yeah," said Barski, sucking in some fresh air. "She's right."

"We have to be cool," Willis acknowledged. "Observant."

Willis sought to adopt the proper mien—something, he thought, between that of Humphrey Bogart in *The Big Sleep* and Basil Rathbone in *Hound of the Baskervilles*. He refrained, however, from either checking to see if he had his gun or pulling down the brim of his peaked cap, both of which were entirely imaginary in any event, and clicked open the door on his side of the car. He put a foot on the pavement, stepped out calmly, coolly, observantly, and clunked his head smartly on the top of the door opening.

"Ouch, damn, ouch!"

He heard Neal snickering in the backseat.

Anathae, out on the other side of the VW, asked, "What happened?"

"Nothing," Willis said, grasping his head, "nothing." He asked himself what Philip Marlowe or Sherlock Holmes might have done in such a situation but could think of no answer.

Neal clambered out of the backseat, and they made their way to the front door of the Narmer residence without further incident.

Willis paused outside the entrance and glanced at Anathae. "Do I look all right?" he asked. "I just don't feel natural in this old T-shirt. And these jeans are all faded and—"

"It'll do, won't it, Neal?"

Neal nodded, gesturing toward his own casual outfit. "If you wore anything formal, Professor Baxter, you'd look like an elephant in church."

Willis sighed and rubbed his aching head. He had to admit that Anathae looked rather good in the loosely tied halter and hip-hugging jeans. Yes, he rather envied those jeans at the moment—there was just enough about her figure left to the imagination that one imagined everything about her. And her magic, to Willis, at least, had made her all the more alluring, mysterious. He was even tempted, for a moment, to call the whole thing off, forget about this business, let his students do what the hell they wanted to do, while he went back to his apartment with Anathae to lose the day's tensions and headaches in her arms.

But no, he had responsibilities. He had a duty to his students as a teacher and as the head of the Arts and Sciences Division, and he braced himself to perform it. After all, he told himself, what more could be involved than meeting this Narmer guy, getting a look at his drugs and what they did to people, and having Anathae look at what was going on inside the guy's head? Depending on what was motivating him and how successful he was with it, they could then decide whether it was worthwhile to talk sense to him and get him to lay off Powhattan U and its students, or have Anathae use her magic powers to discourage him.

So Willis rang the doorbell, the sound of which was all but drowned in the steady throb of music coming from inside. A throb, Willis noted, which was more than echoed in his head.

20

After a moment, the screen door opened slightly and a tall dark young man slipped through and stood on the step before them. He was perhaps twenty-four or -five, with olive skin and blue-black hair, and his steely blue eyes held a kind of intense gaze, as if they were constantly analyzing everything they viewed. Perhaps because he had been thinking of movie stars earlier, Willis could not help but think of Omar Sharif.

The voice, which was deep and slightly accented, however, made him think of Topol.

"Hello, Neal. We haven't seen you for quite a while. Who are your friends?"

The young man's smile was warm, friendly, even disarming, but he looked at Willis suspiciously before turning to Anathae. Then his eyes seemed to soften and his voice began even more suave. "I'd remember *you* if I'd seen you before."

Willis could almost feel Anathae step up her sexual presence, either to match this guy's or to impress him. Willis hoped it was the latter, since he felt there was not much which he—or, for that matter, almost any other male—could do to match this fellow's obvious sexual attractiveness.

"Hi, Rudy," said Neal calmly. "This is Willis Baxter, a pretty hip professor at the Pow How. And his ward, Anathae—"

"Ana," the girl said breathily, her eyes wide, pupils large even in the light. "Please—just Ana."

"Oh," said Rudy, obviously very taken, "but Anathae is such a, well, such a *charming* name really, redolent of sensual perfumes and mysterious musics. Can't I be allowed to call you Anathae? It feels so good in my mouth.''

That mouth in which it felt so good to say her name curled up in an even broader smile that would steam the pants off most women and that had no little effect on Anathae, obviously.

Good in your mouth, huh? thought Willis, fisting a hand behind his back. *I have something right here I'd like to put in your mouth.*

But he held himself in check: Anathae had her little games, there was no doubt of that, and she was playing one right now. Had this Rudy Narmer right where she wanted him. That must be the case, Willis told himself. She couldn't really have the hots for this . . . this *dope dealer*. This handsome, sophisticated, Omar Sharif–looking, Topol-talking, friendly, smiling dope dealer.

Could she?

"Entrez," invited Rudy, eyes half lidded and focused on Anathae's loosely wrapped figure. "Tonight's party is holding forth quite nicely in the den, mostly. Everyone's very much into music at the moment. It would be a notable pleasure to enjoy it with two new people."

The interior of the house was an interior decorator's delight, fitted with only the most modern of furniture, paintings, lamps, and rugs—clean, neat, perfectly arranged.

"I'm very much a man of the moment, a creature of now," explained Rudy, alluding to the entirety of the house with a single graceful gesture. "Tell me, Anathae, does it suit your taste?"

"Oh, yes," said Anathae. "Definitely."

"Good. I take pleasure principally in the pleasure of others. But the entire house is not done up in the style you see here. The den, as you'll soon observe, is modern in different ways."

So saying, he effortlessly swung open a door in front of them. Loud music pulsed through—churning electric guitars stitched tightly with a smooth melotron backing, grounded with thick base and delicate drumming.

"Italian group," Narmer commented. He nodded his head to the complex rhythms. "Lovely stuff."

The large room which was the den had a twilight effect,

brought about by the absence of electric lighting and the presence of candles. On the obviously comfortable antique furniture lounged various students of Powhattan, some twenty strong. Some Willis recognized, some he did not.

Here and there on the baroque wallpaper were weird and fantastic works of art, and an almost palpable cloud of smoke hovered over everything—clear enough to see through yet dense enough to be plainly discerned as smoke. Conversations buzzed mildly below the music and through the smoke, barely audible.

Willis had to admit the atmosphere was most intriguing.

"Drinks?" asked Narmer, obviously well practiced as the gracious host. "I've got the full run, so don't balk at anything."

"Pepsi," said Neal.

"Yoo-Hoo?" asked Anathae. Narmer smiled and nodded.

"Rum and Coke," said Willis absently, looking about for his students.

"Certainly. Make yourselves comfortable. I'll be but a brief moment." Narmer turned and strode gracefully from the room.

"Goodness," said Anathae, hugging Willis's arm, "he *seems* nice enough, doesn't he, Will?"

Willis made a grumbling sound in his throat, then bent over to whisper in her ear, "Have you tried looking inside his head yet?"

Anathae appeared nonplussed for a second, then smiled with a touch of a blush on her cheek which all but made her freckles disappear. "Sorry," she said. "He was so nice I just, uh, forgot."

"What?" asked Neal.

"Nothing," Willis said.

Neal plopped down into an empty chair, and Willis eyed the group of people playing cards in one corner of the room. Two were in his Chaucer seminar: Linda Weinstein and Rich Schwartz.

Willis asked Neal who the other two were.

"Oh—the guy in the funny shirt's Dan Stuffing; the other's Dave Cardinal. All four of 'em are heavy into Narmer's stuff— 'powder blue,' they call it. They mix it with their drinks—

tasteless but heavy stuff. And they've been into doing strange things lately.''

''Playing cards is strange?'' Anathae asked.

''That game is. They're playing Broken Hearts—a variation of Hearts in which the winners get to whip the others. Literally.''

''Bleech!'' said Willis.

''Well, they don't actually draw blood or anything. It's all very ritualistic. But it's pretty strange anyway.''

''I'll say,'' Willis said.

He watched in amazement as a young girl in the middle of the room opened a large bag of potato chips and set to work eating them, casting furtive glances over her shoulder at others nearby lest they might try to take them from her, until in record time the bag was empty. With hardly a pause for breath and without wasted motion, she ripped open a package of Oreos and began eating them in like fashion, stopping only to pick them up and clutch them to her if anyone came near.

''Don't get too freaked by Laura,'' Neal said, indicating the girl. ''She's on powder blue too. It affects everyone differently. She'll go on like this for four or five hours, but don't worry—I mean, when she comes down, she'll eat hardly anything at all.''

Willis nodded but noted the tone of disgust in Neal's voice. *He doesn't believe what he's saying*, Willis thought. *He knows this girl's turning into a glutton but not only won't come out and say so but defends the practice. Why?*

Suddenly, above the sound of the music, someone screamed, ''Duck!''

Willis ducked, and the others laughed.

''Don't worry, Professor Baxter,'' Neal said with a grin, ''that's just Dan. Dan's into a duck trip. I just hope he doesn't get too freaked—''

Cards flew up above the corner table, then fluttered down over the head of one of the players. ''Ducks on the wall!'' Dan said loudly, holding a hand to the side of his face and pointing with the other toward a bare wall. ''Ducks on the ceiling! Ducks everywhere! I gotta get out of here!''

''Uh, oh,'' said Neal. ''Dan's done too much blue. I hope he doesn't create a scene. Rudy doesn't like it when someone does that—particularly when we have new guests in the house.''

Dan Stuffing was a large, rotund, friendly-looking fellow—a giant teddy bear. He turned around and walked—no, waddled, like a duck—toward the center of the room, quacking to himself.

But then he espied Willis, and his eyes lit up. ''Donald!'' he cried happily. ''There you are, Donald! I've been looking all over for you.''

Dan waddled excitedly toward the professor, coming to a stop just before crashing into him. ''Oh, wow, Donald, really glad to *see* you. Walt died ten years ago, and, if I do say so, the studio's really been messing up your image.''

Willis started to say something, stopped, and before he could get a word out Dan was gushing hurriedly onward. ''I was just speaking to Mickey at the Seven Dwarves' cottage the other day and he was saying that he hasn't seen you for years and years, and for all he knew you'd been shanghaied by the Chinese to make Peking Duck. And oh, wow, it's just great to *see* you again. Huey, Dewey, and Louie are going to be *very* pleased. . . .''

''Say, Donald, you recognize your old Uncle Scrooge, don't you? Sure you do. Yeah, me. Hey, Donald, where's your sailor suit? And how come you're wearing pants, eh? And—''

Abruptly Dan halted, looked over Willis's shoulder, and froze.

Willis turned to follow his gaze.

Rudy Narmer stood in the doorway, eyes aflame; Willis had never seen such an intense, sinister stare from the eyes of a human before. Shivers marched down his spine. Very cold shivers.

''Dan,'' said Narmer in a cool, steady, commanding voice, ''Dan, this is not Donald Duck. This is my very special guest, Willis Baxter. There is no need—no need whatever—to trouble him, my good friend Dan.''

''Uh, sure, Rudy,'' said Dan in a soft voice. His gaze returned to Willis's face and he asked pitifully, ''Spare change?''

Startled by this non sequitur, Willis absently reached down

and pulled a quarter from his pocket and dropped it into Dan's pudgy outstretched hand.

"Hey, duck—man, I mean—thanks!" Dan turned and waddled slowly off to rejoin the game of Broken Hearts.

"I apologize for Daniel," said Narmer, his eyes cooling down considerably. "He gets a bit enthusiastic, and therefore rather annoying, about his illusions at times. If you'll excuse me, I've got your drinks on a tray, which I'll bring along in just one second." And again he was gone.

While Anathae, it seemed, was staring wistfully after him.

Willis wondered idly what had brought Narmer back to the room without the drinks just when Dan Stuffing was going into his act. Willis put a hand on Anathae's arm and again whispered in her ear. "Have you taken a peek at what's going on in Narmer's mind yet?"

Anathae looked perplexed again and then a little annoyed. "I'll get to it," she said.

Turning to Neal, she asked, "How come Dan asked for spare change? He doesn't look like he's exactly starving."

"He's not," said Neal with an inappropriate grin, as if he were really talking about someone or something else. "Dan's the son of one of the richest men in the state. He's got a huge allowance. But he's also on this great miser trip. Getting very bad. That's why he fancies himself Scrooge McDuck. You should only see him when he's Ebenezer Scrooge, not to mention his King Midas thing. With that, he just goes around touching things and giggling to himself."

"I'm really not sure if I'm going to be able to handle this evening," Willis said, looking to Anathae for support.

But Anathae's eyes had gone back to staring at the door through which Rudy Narmer had left the room. What the devil was *wrong* with her?

"You're not thinking of leaving?" Neal asked, seeming truly upset. "It would spoil—I mean, you know, what we've planned and all. . . ."

"No," Willis said, waving an assuring hand distractedly at Neal, "no." Thinking half about Anathae and half about what Neal had said about Dan, Willis asked, "And do all the people who do this powder blue stuff act like tightwad ducks?"

"Uh-uh. No more than it makes 'em all scoff down cookies and potato chips. Like I said before, it affects each individual differently—you know; you've seen what it's done to Rich and Linda.''

Yes, Willis acknowledged to himself, quite true.

Linda Weinstein had been one of his most serious, studious pupils. Once quite reserved and given to wearing sedate modest clothing, shy and soft-spoken, she had become a brazen temptress, flirting outrageously even with Willis when she showed up for his class. And when he had called her in to discuss her recent performance in the class, for no reason at all she had started to unbutton his shirt and tell him she would "do anything—anything at all!" to get a good grade.

And Rich Schwartz! Rich, at the beginning of the semester, had been clean-shaven, sharply dressed, alert, and nimble-witted; now he wore his hair long, shaggy, and unruly, had an unkempt beard and a straggly mustache. He slept during class all the time. His clothing not only looked slept in; Willis knew it *was* slept in.

Two promising students turned into extreme parodies of faults previously hidden to the point of inversion deep within themselves. A completely puzzling mystery—until Neal Barski had come to explain how these changes could be attributed to a strange drug called powder blue and an even stranger man named Rudy Narmer.

21

As the name entered Willis's thoughts, the man himself popped into the room bearing a tray of drinks.

"Sorry about the delay, my new friends," Narmer said as they helped themselves to their respective glasses, "but I think you will enjoy the drinks. Please do make yourselves comfortable if you have not already done so. We are not very formal at these affairs. We just get together to enjoy each other's company, listen to some good music, and do some drugs. Speaking of which"—he slipped a hand into the large right pocket of his bright yellow lounging robe, which he must have donned, plucked out a marijuana cigarette, fitted it into his mouth, produced a Cricket lighter from the other pocket, lit the joint, and puffed—"how about a hit?"

Narmer offered the cigarette to Willis, who took it, drew as little smoke from it as possible, then passed it on to Neal. Willis inhaled through his nose and then let the smoke he'd sucked into his mouth go a few seconds later, hoping he'd convinced Narmer he had taken the smoke into his lungs. Finding the taste of the smoke mildly unpleasant, he took a large gulp of his rum and Coke—which seemed to be mostly rum. All the better; he much preferred booze to other sorts of intoxicants.

Then, looking around, he found an empty chair and sat down on it. Across from the chair was a couch; Narmer seated himself on this, and Anathae sat down beside him.

"I take it you do not entirely approve of drugs, Mr.— Professor?—Professor Baxter," said Rudy mildly, not really looking at Willis. Rather, he regarded Anathae with a gaze which, if one were of a mind to describe it with understatement, one might dub "desirous." "I am heartened to see, however, that your lovely ward seems to take the delight in cannabis which it affords to those who savor it properly."

"I indulge only when it seems socially expected of me," Willis admitted.

Blast the man! If Rudy Narmer's eyes were hands, Anathae's clothes would be peeled off by now!

"Drugs, Professor Baxter," Narmer continued in his offhand manner, "properly used, are merely utensils to a greater, more far-reaching consciousness. They are not ends in themselves. It is the mind—indeed more—the *essence* of the individual using the drugs which is important, not the mere effect of the drug."

Narmer took a long drag off the joint, inhaled deeply, casually gazed about at his ongoing party, then blew a stream of smoke that rose slowly into the greater cloud of smoke hovering over everything. He said, "Just as that cloud of smoke connects the physical bodies of my friends and myself intangibly, so does the *effect* of the smoke connect our minds and essences. With greater drugs, it is even more so. There is a oneness developed between individuals which is invaluable in this lonely, solitary existence. Don't you find that so, dear girl?"

He gazed fondly at Anathae, a smooth smile saying so much more. He delicately brushed her forearm with his finger. "Contact, whatever its form, is both very basic and very important, is it not?"

Anathae seemed entranced.

What's going on here? Willis wondered, feeling troubled. What was this clown doing with *his* demon? And why didn't she protest?

The fury slipped upon him slowly; things seemed to take on a green shade. And although jealousy seized Willis, so did a sudden strange overwhelming numbness. He felt as though all his consciousness had been gathered in a tight furious little ball somewhere behind his eyes—and the arms, legs, and body that surrounded it were somehow not his own. He could call upon them to perform some service and they would turn to him as a stranger and ask, "Now, really, sir, I must protest—just who are you to tell *me* what to do?"

Come to think of it, *who was he?*

He watched, feeling incredibly detached, as Narmer slowly began to caress Anathae's bare shoulder. The handsome young man seemed utterly alien, unearthly, yet encompassing the whole atmosphere with his presence. His hand flowed naturally down to cup Anathae's breast.

Abruptly, Willis realized why his students had turned to Rudy Narmer, and with the realization came the sensation of relaxation.

It was all so simple, so obvious. Rudy Narmer was not merely handsome and charming and well-off, he was as fascinating and marvelous an individual as any human could ever hope to be—the most dynamic, magical, charismatic, interesting . . . yes, Rudy Narmer was almost godlike. Except, of course, that even this comparison would have to be judged a disservice to Rudy.

Narmer leaned over, whispered something in Anathae's ear. The demon-girl nodded slowly, her eyes far away. Narmer rose, extended a strong hand to her, helped her gently to her feet. And together, arm in arm, they drifted out of the room.

The little ball of Willis's consciousness was at war with itself.

On the one hand, everything seemed perfectly normal and as it should be. Rudy and Anathae obviously liked each other, and Willis felt complimented and happy to please both of them by letting them both please each other.

But, on the other hand, he was in a murderous jealous rage.

His left hand said, "How wonderful that the two of them should find each other through me." His right hand responded, "Bunk! Let me but grasp his throat and tear his head off!"

His right foot said, "Savor the beauty of this moment! Consider, with humility, bliss, and grace, how two people whom you love also love each other." But his left foot replied, "Let me strap on a steel spike to gouge in his groin, his kidneys, his eyes, drawing rich red blood, slashing veins and ripping out entrails."

His eyes, his ears, his blood vessels and internal organs vied with each other, sending contradictory messages to his brain as he sat on the couch stupefied. The jealousy and acceptance battled each other—changing positions, attacking, then defending against attack. Sinews rippling, they gripped each other in sure fingers and strong hands. They dueled. They hurled grenades. They dropped atomic bombs—all in his brain.

Eventually, his own augmented rage rather than what Narmer had intended proved to be the victor. Willis suddenly jumped to his feet and cried out, "Narmer, you lay off my girl!"

He would have bolted after them had he not been jumped from behind and pulled down to the floor. His head hit hard, and consciousness swirled away, only to drift slowly back again.

When it did he felt quite normal, except that his head hurt and his arms and legs were numb because four of the students who had been attending the party were now sitting on them, effectively pinning him to the floor.

Though his vision was blurred, Willis recognized them: Rich Schwartz, Linda Weinstein, Dave Cardinal, and Dan Stuffing. The Broken Hearts players.

"Neal," Willis cried out. "Neal! Help!" He tried to struggle, but the four students had no problem keeping him fast to the floor.

Then, looking up at the drugged expressions on their faces, he recalled that gluttonous girl and suddenly realized he could name similar basic sins for at least three of the four who were holding him: avarice (Dan), lust (Linda), and sloth (Rich). And even as he was thinking this, he heard Dave complaining, "Why do I have to hold a foot instead of an arm? Why do other people always get the *easy* part?" Envy! And Willis himself had been furious with jealousy.

Narmer had put powder blue in their drinks!

But at least, Willis thought, it had partially backfired in his own case, working on his natural reaction to Narmer's attentions to Anathae. The direction Narmer had wanted the drug to take him and the direction Willis had been inclined to take had been at cross purposes—and the two had canceled each other out.

Because now Willis was all right. Normal, even, if having four strong (and in some cases, heavy) college students sitting on his arms and legs was normal.

"Neal!" he cried again. And then he saw that Neal Barski's skinny frame was leaning over him, hands on hips, and Neal was smiling.

"Sorry, Professor Baxter," he said, not sounding a bit sorry as his smile turned into a lopsided leer, "but I seem to get quite a kick out of this sort of thing since I met Rudy."

Barski's eyes glazed over, and his hands reached out to gesture in the empty air, as if they could grasp and help form his meanings there. "It's really just so great, you know. Taking truths and shading them and shifting them, balancing them all in such a way so that they hide truths from the seekers of truth. Bending reality to unreality and making unreality the master. Ha ha! I mean, it's *really* great!"

Deceit! Another mortal sin.

"Why, Neal? Why?"

Neal shrugged as his eyes lost their glaze and focused on Willis. "Rudy told me to do it, so I did it. I, we, don't ask questions of Rudy—after all, he's given us the means to focus on what we really are. Anyway, when we do our thing on our own, it's never as much fun as when we do it because Rudy wants us to. Like now. What ecstasy!"

"Ecstasy!" Dave Cardinal snorted. "Everyone *else* gets ecstasy, while *I* get left holding someone's legs. It isn't fair!"

Dan Stuffing tightened his grip on Willis's arm. "Sorry, Donald," he said. And, for what little comfort it might be to Willis, the big fellow did sound as if he were sorry. "But we gotta take care of you," he added in explanation.

"Let's get him up," Linda said.

"Fine," Dave said. "Then my help's not needed—not that it's likely to be appreciated anyway. With everyone else, it's 'Thank you, Dan,' and 'Thank you, Neal.' But not for me, no." Cardinal got off Willis's legs and walked over to sit in an easy chair as Dan, Linda, Rich, and Neal stood Willis on his feet.

They continued to hold him tight. A medallion Rich had been wearing under his stained T-shirt slipped out in the process, and he let go with one hand to put it back inside. But not before Willis had caught a glimpse of it—a goat's head, one of the symbols of demon worship.

But this only confirmed what Willis had already started to suspect. The indications were certainly clear—for if the sins he had identified were not enough, there was the simple fact that no mere drug could have had such an effect on Anathae. If the understanding taking form inside Willis's head was correct, it would explain why she had never been able to look inside Narmer's thoughts, why she had been so helpless under his gaze.

"Linda, Neal, Rich, Dan! Don't you realize? Narmer's an agent of *evil!* He's a *demon!*"

22

"Evil?" said Linda, the perplexity coming to her eyes in sharp contrast to the sophomoric smile she had worn all evening. "No! Rudy is *love*."

"Besides," Rich said lazily, "we're not going to do anything evil to you, Professor Baxter. We're just going to give you some more powder blue—you're so full of hate, you *need* some of the love drug."

Willis could see no point in trying to argue with them. What he needed, he realized, was some sort of a weapon.

But, wait! He *had* a weapon—each of them represented a sin, and every sin is, in fact, a weakness. He would only have to find a way to use what he knew about them to their disadvantage.

"I appreciate that, Rich," Willis said, his mind racing, "but I really do think you're holding me a bit too tightly. Not because it hurts, mind you, but I have to wonder why you're expending so much effort when others here, like Dan, are much stronger and capable of holding me much better. It's not as if I'm not bright enough to see how fruitless it would be to try to escape. Really, why exert yourself so much?"

Rich, all at once cross-eyed and slack-mouthed as he considered Willis's statement, could only nod; while he did not release his grip, it eased noticeably.

Linda was also holding that hand, but farther down, yet she did not resist as Willis turned it so that he cupped her breast. Her eyes almost closed as she began to breathe slowly and deeply.

Turning to Stuffing, Willis said loudly, "Quick, Dan! Look out! The ducks are at your feet and they're after the money in your boots!"

Dan let go of Willis's other arm and jumped back across the floor, fright welling up in his eyes.

Now only Neal Barski held Willis in a firm grip. It was but the work of a second to withdraw his other hand, his right, from Linda's breast and jerk free of Rich's halfhearted grasp.

"Hey, Neal," Willis said, "your shoelace is *not* untied."

Neal looked down at his sandals, perplexed. Willis, who was not very strong but was nonetheless stronger than the slim student, hit him hard on his nose with a balled-up fist, and Barski let go of Willis's hand to clasp his wounded proboscis, which began to bleed profusely.

Had he been quicker on the think, Willis knew, he might have maneuvered himself into a better position. Even though he was now free of the four who had been holding him, he realized several others were between himself and the exit which Narmer and Anathae had taken. While the four who had held him were shaken and confused, Willis knew the others could stop him should he attempt to rush in that direction.

His only hope—and Anathae's—lay in escape.

A hallway, a kitchen, then another hallway seemed to fly past him. Excited shouts behind him told him that the pursuit had begun, and he cast about desperately for an escape route.

When he saw the open window he didn't think, just jumped straight through it; he ripped his T-shirt on a bush and landed heavily on the slushy ground.

He scrambled up instantly and charged straight into the bole of an oak tree. Dazed, he picked himself up again and staggered forward to where his car should be. Tripping, stumbling, puffing, and panting, he finally reached the edge of the lawn and pushed through the bushes to where he could see his Volkswagen.

Only then did Willis look back at the house to see his pursuers boiling out of the doorway and scattering in his general direction.

He fumbled his keys out of his pocket and made the final

dash to his car, opened the door, and was just getting in when the first pursuer pushed through a couple of bushes.

"He went thataway!" Willis yelled, pointing down the street.

The boy nodded, said "Thank you," and turned in the direction Willis had pointed. He halted suddenly, angrily, and whirled with a snarl of rage on his lips. But Willis was in the car, had the engine revved, and was in first gear.

Eight more pursuers spilled out onto the street; no exit there. They began to run toward him. Willis popped the clutch, spun the wheel hard, gunned the engine, and in a split second was over the curb. He whisked between two bushes, and his tires spun up muddy divots from the grass. He came alongside the driveway, turned out onto the open street, and left the students screaming behind him.

He knew this would be a night which would feed his paranoid feelings about students for years to come.

He had to think. He had to figure out some way to rescue Anathae.

Willis glanced into his rearview mirror to see if anyone was following. He didn't see any cars behind him; he saw the shadow of Rudy Narmer sitting in his backseat!

But when he turned to look over his shoulder the backseat was empty. When his eyes returned to the road, he saw he was going through a red light—and a large diesel truck was blaring its horn and coming down right on top of him from the left. Panicked but galvanized into action, Willis tromped down hard on the accelerator and felt as much as he saw the big truck, its brakes screeching, whiz by inches behind him.

He kept on going. He had to think and act in such a way as to secure Anathae's release as soon as possible—and staying to explain to the truck driver, and possibly the police, didn't fit in with such plans. Besides, what could he say? "Sorry, officer—you see, I thought I had this demon in my car."

No, that would never do. It would only complicate an already complex situation.

Willis checked his rearview mirror again and gulped. This time it was not a mere shadow which he saw. It was the distinct features of Narmer's face.

"What is it you want?" Willis snapped.

"What I'll eventually get, Professor Baxter," Narmer said smoothly, "what I'll eventually get. But for now a bit of rational discussion will suffice." Narmer's voice had an odd hollow quality to it, as if he were talking from inside a tin drum.

"I'm listening," Willis said. *Not that I have any choice*, he thought.

"You have escaped me for the moment, Professor, but for the moment only. You know something of Anathae's powers, and it should be obvious from what has happened that mine are even greater. Were my presence not required here at the moment, I could as easily transport my physical self into the backseat of your vehicle as this apparition you see in your mirror."

So. Something unnamed "required" Narmer's presence at the house. Anathae, perhaps? It could be that Narmer feared to leave his residence until he had her completely under his sway. That seemed to jibe with what little Willis understood about one demon's power over another.

Willis said, "So?"

"Unimpressed? So be it. Underrate me, I don't care. It'll just make it that much easier for me when I can turn my full attention to you. You are but a minor thorn. After all, it was Anathae I was after, and in that I was successful."

"I wondered about that," Willis said, noting that his own voice remained remarkably firm and steady. "Why you did all this, I mean."

The face in the mirror smiled. "Trying to pump me for information, Professor? Well, all right. I don't mind telling you. At first it was just because I was aware that another demon was nearby. Quite simply, she could have been quite a bit more than a mere thorn in my side, so I stayed hidden until I found out what she was and what she could do—"

Willis had abruptly turned a corner, and the face in the mirror had disappeared; the voice stopped as if Willis had turned off his radio.

He continued on for a few blocks before the face reappeared, still smiling. "Ah, there you are," Narmer said. "Don't do that, Professor. You've no idea how difficult it is to accomplish this projection."

"Far be it from me to do anything to make your life more difficult, Narmer," Willis said sarcastically.

"I said there were two reasons," Narmer went on, ignoring Willis's comment. "Actually Anathae is quite lovely, as you yourself know. I've grown tired of human women—I need one of my own kind."

"Anathae's half human, too, Narmer."

"Yes, it's unfortunate—but being the only choice I have, I'll make the best of it. It's also unfortunate that Anathae should want to resist me, but, being the stronger, I will bend her to my will and it will be as if she wanted me. And really, there's nothing you can do about it, although it would amuse me no end to see you try."

"That's me," Willis said, "nothing but a clown, a buffoon, somebody for you to toy with. Only you know what, Narmer? It seems to me that *you're* the one who's going to all this trouble to talk to me with this 'projection'—which makes me wonder, if I'm such a 'minor thorn,' why you bother."

"Like all mortals, you're a fool, Baxter. I'd thought to offer you your life. Quite frankly, if you put your foot to the floor and kept going till sunrise, you'd be beyond easy reach and I'd let you live. Why not? Ana would be mine and you would be far enough away that it would be more bothersome than not to go after you. Surely you understand. Would you stop making love to chase a gnat, no matter how it may have bothered you, after it had left your house?"

"I'm not a fool, Narmer," Willis said, "and I wouldn't buy my life at that price. And even if I did, I *would* be a fool to trust you."

"Then I'll hear from you again. Very well, let me get on to my real reason for visiting you in this way. It's to deliver a simple warning. If you should try—"

Willis swung his VW sharply into a driveway, slammed on his brakes, threw his car into reverse, and burned rubber backing across the street (narrowly missing a car that had been half a block behind him, Narmer's "projection" having obscured Willis's view). He almost lost control on a patch of ice but veered slightly again to back into the mouth of an alley he had seen.

Narmer's face was no longer in the mirror.

Willis kept backing through the alley, knocking over occasional unseen but noisy trashcans, until he reached a street which ran parallel to the one he had first been traveling. He turned his VW back in the direction from which he had come, turned sharply left again at the second corner, floored it for ten blocks, turned right, then left into another alley, and finally left again.

The face still had not reappeared in the mirror.

Willis stuck out his tongue and gave his rearview mirror a resounding Bronx cheer. "Stick that in your hookah and smoke it!"

Then he felt truly juvenile. He'd given in to the impulse to try to shake Narmer because he was tired of Narmer's having both the upper hand and the last word. He'd played the hero but now realized that if he'd only held himself in check, Narmer might have said or done something which Willis could use.

For right now, Willis Baxter knew precisely what kind of hero he felt like: Theseus without Ariadne.

23

It was the first time Willis had ever yearned for the sight of Larry Hawthorne's corpulent face.

Willis had spent some time driving around aimlessly, telling himself he was doing a fine job of "losing" any students who might have tried to follow him ("If I'm lost, they must be").

He discovered he was on Idylwood Avenue, and a familiar-looking high-rise apartment loomed ahead. Familiar-looking in part because it looked like all the other high-rises on Idylwood Avenue but also because it was the one in which Larry Hawthorne lived. Willis had known he would need help; his subconscious had answered the question "Who?"

He had already discarded the idea of going to the police. He knew he didn't have to say a word about demons—he could simply complain about a wild drug party or claim a young girl had been dragged kicking and screaming into Narmer's residence. But Narmer, with his charm and smooth talk, could probably convince the police that black was white or green or brown or maroon or any combination of the above. And if he couldn't, his magic could.

Willis pounded on the door of Larry Hawthorne's eleventh-floor apartment.

Had the students tried to follow him in their cars?

He pounded again, harder.

Were they even now searching the streets of the city, looking for him or his car?

Or had they already sighted him?

If so, when would they spring their trap?

At least, he thought, *I didn't go back to my own apartment. They could be counted on to look for me there.*

Was that the elevator door opening?

Willis turned to look, at the same time bringing his fist up once more in front of the door.

Larry Hawthorne opened the door and got the knock square in the mouth.

"Ummph!" said Hawthorne, stumbling backward away from the door. "Arrgh!" he said as he backed into a chair, the arm of which caught him neatly behind the knees, causing him to topple into the seat. "Blurgh!" he exclaimed as the chair, in reaction to the momentum he had imparted to it, rose up on two legs under him and carried him down with a resounding *whump* to the floor, knocking the wind out of him.

"Oh, damn, Larry," said Willis, horrified, but not so upset as to forget to dash in and slam and bolt the door behind him. "I'm sorry, I didn't mean—"

Hawthorne worked his mouth, but only wheezes issued forth.

"Listen, Larry, I'm in big trouble." Willis gestured so wildly with his arms that Hawthorne cringed back. "What's the matter with you?" Willis asked before stopping to consider his own actions. Then: "Oh, no. No, I've not come to 'get' you or resume our—misunderstanding. That was just a klutzy mistake. No"—he pointed to the outside—"it's just that there are students after me."

"It must have been that exam you gave, Baxter," gasped Hawthorne, recovering his composure somewhat. "If I were them, I'd be after you too."

"You don't understand," said Willis. "These students are under the influence of a demon!"

Hawthorne had shifted his bulky frame into a more comfortable position so that he could pay better attention to what was being said. At the mention of the word "demon," his eyebrows shot up. "You got Anathae mad at you?"

"No, not Ana. Another demon—a very *evil* demon. Are you okay?"

Hawthorne felt his jaw as if assuring himself that it was

still there. "Yeah, I guess so. You ever think of becoming a prizefighter? You may have missed your calling." Then what Willis had said finally registered with him. "Is that possible—another demon? Except for the Boss, I thought Anathae was supposed to be the last one who could still be summoned."

"So did I," Willis said. "But evidently I was wrong."

As Willis helped Hawthorne to his feet the latter asked, "When did you take up dressing like that?"

Willis looked down at his jeans and now somewhat muddied and ripped old T-shirt. "I'll tell you about it," he said and then picked up the chair.

When they had both seated themselves, Willis launched into his story, telling all that had happened up to his escape, hardly pausing for breath. When he finished, Hawthorne said nothing. The big man sat with his chin on his fist, thinking.

Then he started to ponder aloud. "The thing that bothers me is that if anyone should know what conditions prevail in Hell, it should be Anathae. And she assured you she was the only demon who could still be summoned?"

"That's right," Willis said. "She told me the de la Farte theory was correct."

Hawthorne said, "So doesn't that mean this Narmer character can't be a demon?"

Willis thought for a long time before answering. "No, Narmer's a demon, all right—he acknowledged as much when he said he wanted Ana because she was 'one of his own kind.' So, even though Anathae said—"

He stopped as if hit by a sudden thought.

"What?" Hawthorne asked.

"Of course! Narmer's a demon who never went back! Somehow Narmer was summoned by a sorcerer or magician who was careless, and Narmer's never been back. The consignment of a demon's soul to Hell forever takes effect only if the demon is in Hell or returns to it."

Hawthorne yawned. "Sorry," he said, looking at his watch. "You're not boring me, but it's one a.m. You might be right—it's a good enough theory to work from. Almost puts you in de la Farte's class yourself."

The big man got up from his chair and stretched. "You know I can't help you with the performance of any ritual, but

I'll tell you what. First I'll make some coffee, then we'll both hit the books. If we can find Narmer's True Name, maybe you can do something.''

Hawthorne's library of demonological lore was not as big as Willis's, but it was quite large. And although they confined themselves to Mediterranean countries—"He said he was Turkish, and while his accent and features fit, who knows?"—by five in the morning the pile of discarded volumes stood quite high: *Solomon in Egypt, the Hittite Conspiracy, Daemons of Greece, Gods of Asia Minor, Demons and Spirits on the Continent, The Road to Antioch*, etc., etc. The words were blurring on the pages, while between them the two men felt as though they had consumed enough coffee to fill a waterbed.

Willis continued to read, scowl, and turn pages as if it had become something of a ritual. From time to time he sipped the whiskey-laced coffee Hawthorne had provided, but it did nothing to keep his eyes from feeling like marbles resting in their sockets. Seeing had become an obligation instead of a natural function; he hardly noticed that day had dawned.

Hawthorne sat in a comfortable chair, a volume in his hand, resting his eyes. "Hey, wait a minute, Baxter," he said.

Willis turned his bloodshot eyes away from the book at which he had been scowling and gave Hawthorne his attention. "Huh?"

"You said something about drugs?"

"Right," Willis acknowledged. "Narmer uses this stuff called powder blue. Makes the kids subservient to his huge, powerful ego and emphasizes a mortal sin in each of them."

"Drugs. I'm so stupid I could shoot myself. You ever hear of the Shastis?"

"Of course. That is, I've seen references to them."

"The Shastis were a clan of demons. They augmented the spells they cast on the minds of humans with drugs. Operated in Turkey around the eighth century. And very, very clever."

"Yes," Willis said, "that might be it."

Hawthorne chewed on his lower lip. "For your sake, I hope he's only a minor one; the major ones were some kind of hairy. I could tell you a story about what a Shasti did to a sultan through his harem that would make your short hairs fall out."

"I wouldn't even want to have Ana mad at me—and she's a minor demon," Willis said. "But I don't suppose I have any choice."

"Well," Hawthorne said, "if he's a Shasti, I think I can get a peg on him."

The big man rose and placed the book he'd been reading face down, pages open, on a nearby table. He pulled a huge volume from his bookshelf. "I've got a rather complete history on 'em. Characteristics, names, everything."

Hawthorne placed the ornate, musty volume on a desk and began paging slowly through it. "Hmmm," he said every once in a while as he paused at a page, punctuated alternatively with "Nope" and further pagings.

About three-quarters of the way through he became absorbed in his reading. He looked up at Willis. "I think I've got it."

"Are you sure? If you're wrong, you'll never see me or Ana again."

His ex-enemy smiled. "A month ago, Baxter, and I'd've been tempted. But no, I'm sure. First, he's the only one who uses this particular drug—the translation from the Turkish is 'blue powder.' Eh? Second, says here he's got a very powerful ego, very vain, likes the attentions of *young* people. Feeds off them, likes them around. Right? Other stuff too—dashing appearance; his mother was a succubus."

Willis nodded. "Yeah, that would have to be either Narmer or his twin brother. Let's assume he doesn't have one."

"He's also one of the major ones," Hawthorne said. "There's an account here—well, a magician claimed he had complete mastery over this demon. Rose from rags to riches; lived in a castle, all that. And then he went quite mad—fits in with your theory, doesn't it?"

"Major or minor, I've got to deal with him," Willis said with a sigh. "Give me his True Name, Larry."

"Right," said Hawthorne. And he told him.

*   *   *

Willis borrowed Larry Hawthorne's Volvo for the drive home; it was critically important to his plan that he get as far as his apartment, and he knew his own VW could be recognized by almost every student on the Powhattan campus.

As he eased Hawthorne's car to a stop less than half a block from the entrance to his garden apartment, Willis saw two students lounging around out front—one of whom he recognized from Narmer's party.

But they had apparently been watching for him for most of the night, and the combination of the long hours of waiting and the bitter cold of early morning in winter had taken their toll on the vigilance of the pair. One sat on Willis's neighbors' step, his head between his knees and his hand over his head to ward off the cold, and was either sleeping or on the verge of drifting off to sleep. The other, the one Willis recognized, paced back and forth, more to give his blood reason to continue circulating than to keep an eye on things, since he was avoiding facing into the biting wind and had his hands thrust deep in the pockets of his overcoat.

Got to make it, Willis thought, fixing his latch key firmly in his hand. He did not believe he would make it; his stomach revolted at the thought of a fifty-yard dash, possibly slipping on the icy sidewalk, and then perhaps a scuffle with two heavy-set young men who would consider no holds barred. But this was no time for indecision.

He slipped out of the car and, using others parked on the street for cover, got within twenty yards of his front door without being seen. Then he bolted for it, running with his shoulder forward, reminiscent of basic training at Fort Dix.

"Gaaah!" he yelled as he threw himself past the young men, one of whom turned, the other jumping to his feet, both only half awake. Their eyes bulged in astonishment as Willis lumbered up the walk and slid the last five feet to slam into his door.

"Hey," the one who'd been on the steps yelled, pulling his long blond hair from his eyes. "Hey, it's Baxter! Get him, Bo!"

Willis had grabbed the doorknob to keep from falling back from the impact when he hit his door, and now he pushed his key into the lock and twisted. The door shuddered for a few seconds, as if it knew time was of the essence and it must, therefore, stop to consider the matter before conceding to open. But the door gave up its struggle and Willis rushed in, slamming it shut and locking it behind him.

There were shouts from outside, and a heavy fist pounded on the door.

"Come out, Baxter! You have to come out sometime!"

They couldn't keep making that kind of racket for long, Willis knew; someone—mostly likely Miss Bradmorton—would complain to the police if they did. The two must have realized this, for the pounding stopped.

Willis yelled back at them, facing his door: "Get Narmer! Get that stinking crumb bum and tell him if he's not afraid of me I'll be right here, waiting for him!"

There was the muffled sound of discussion outside his door, and then even that died away. Willis went to change into more normal attire and fix himself a stiff drink.

24

Narmer would come. Of that there was no doubt in Willis Baxter's mind—Narmer was too proud a being to let any human challenge go unheeded for very long.

So Willis, despite the warmth he felt pouring over him from the Scotch he had had and despite his fatigue from the long night, pulled all the furniture off the rug onto the parquet at the edges of the living room; the TV was the toughest because of its heavy hardwood cabinet. He rolled up the rug, then the soft brown pad loaded with about two years' worth of dirt and paperclips, and on the underside he very carefully drew an X with a piece of chalk, then around it, with precision, the mirror image of the proper pentagram. He replaced the pad and the rug, and rearranged his furniture so that both of the chairs in the living room were inside the pentagram.

Then he made some coffee, hoping that neither his fatigue nor his present lack of sobriety had caused him to overlook anything.

Because if I have, he thought gloomily, *not only will I die and Anathae remain his slave, but a terrible evil will remain loose in the world.*

He drew the shades, lit candles for the atmosphere he wanted for incantation, and sank into his easy chair. The old grandfather clock ticked away seconds, chimed off the half hours.

It was chiming off twelve strokes as he sat up with a start. He realized he must have dozed off and found this confirmed by the half-consumed candles, which had been fresh when he lit them. But he felt somewhat better for his rest and then almost chipper when he realized that noon would be the nadir of any demon's power—and that he himself would need every edge he could get.

Willis tensed. Something was happening.

Although it was broad daylight, the shades kept the apartment dim; the candles cast shadows on the wall. As Willis peered into the shadows, he could see glimpses of whirling smoke holding glitters of bright light.

There was a gush of strong wind, the smell of sulphur and brimstone, and a brief, almost blinding flash. And out of the shadows and smoke into the fullness of the gutter and flicker of candlelight stepped Rudy Narmer.

He wore a floor-length black gown marked with strange and arcane symbols. The robe was open in front, and Narmer was naked beneath. Willis could plainly see his hooves, larger than Anathae's and rougher, with thick black hair rising up to his calves. There was the vague hint of a large tail through the finely muscled thighs. Also quite apparent now were Narmer's horns—big, thick, dark things curling out from his forehead which, Willis realized, must require constant illusion to hide in Narmer's human guise. Below the horns were flashing eyes and a distinct smile.

"Ah, Professor Baxter," boomed the night-throated voice, reverberating with authority and power. "So happy to see you awaiting your finish. So happy, so very gratified."

Hands on hips, widening the opening of his robe to reveal more details of his superb physique, the demon chuckled. "But *really*, Professor, your choice of words to describe me—'that stinking crumb bum,' indeed. *Most* distressing. You've hurt me to the very quick, as it were." And he threw back his head and laughed—a laugh which came from the depths of his diaphragm, from the depths of evil itself.

"You seem quite sure of yourself, Narmer," Willis said, fighting hard to keep the quaver out of his voice. "Perhaps you don't realize that many humans, such as myself, have just as much knowledge of magic as do the likes of you."

A bluff, of course. Discounting sleight-of-hand, at which he was none too good anyway, Willis's only act of magic had been to summon Anathae. And while she might have taught him some minor magic, Willis had never bothered to learn, because he realized it took a magical being to perform real magic with true power—a being like Ana, or Narmer.

Narmer's rumbling laughter rose to a high-pitched cackle totally devoid of human feeling or hope.

"You propose a match of skills, mortal? A battle of wits, power, knowledge?" Narmer tossed back his thick curls, placed a finger to his chin, and considered. "Yes. Yes, that would amuse me highly. Ana has been telling me how you raised her up, not once but twice, from Down Below. Basic parlor magic, of course, and most hilarious. Most hilarious indeed. You may not think so, Professor, but you lead a very funny life. A shame it must end with so little humor."

"I can see it all now," Willis said. "You're going to bore me to death with empty words—quite humorless, I agree."

A twist of the lips, a flash of the eyes, a scowl. "You have no idea, I assure you, Professor, what I intend for you. You, who had the nerve to resist my beautiful powder, you, who had the gall to resist the ecstasies of serving me."

"Oh, I have ideas, Rudy. I certainly don't expect anything original from you—poke out my eyes with red-hot knives, skin me with a dull penknife, hang me with my own entrails. Nothing with any imagination."

The scowl became a frown. Narmer pointed a long, sharp nail toward the floor. "There are those Below who like to keep souls, but I—" he swept over to one of the candles, thrust his thumb downward onto the wick, and plunged the room into deeper shadow—"I like to snuff them out!"

"Which is what you're doing to those poor kids—slowly snuffing out their minds with that drug of yours. Why do you fool around with drugs when you obviously have more powerful, forthright magic?"

"Curious, are you, mortal?" Narmer's smile returned. "That's ever been what is so admirable about humans—their questing intellects, their brief flashes of inspiration which raise their minds to achievements which even a demon might envy. But there you have it, the answer to your question. This facet of the human mind and the scope of human imagination make me envious—and at the same time give me the greatest of satisfaction when I snuff one out.

"Quenching your light will give me no such pleasure. You shrugged off my drug; you did not want me as your leader; you did not grant your mind and soul willingly, as did your students. But I will destroy you nonetheless. You know too much, and although you alone have no hope of dealing with me it is conceivable that you could band together with others who might."

"Like Anathae?"

"Anathae?" He snickered—a soulless laugh through bared fangs. Narmer's eyes lit with glee as he began twirling around, once, twice, his robe billowing out behind him. He abruptly halted his pivotings and thrust his right arm out perpendicular to the line of his body, his robe draping curtainlike down to the floor.

"You place too much respect and confidence in the meager powers of your she-imp, Baxter. You obviously don't realize the pecking order of the demonic power structure. Females of the same order are invariably less powerful than their male counterparts, and Anathae is of a lower order than mine. No, Ana was simplicity itself to deal with—easier than you, I regret to say. Observe."

He lowered his robed arm to reveal Anathae, standing where there had been but emptiness before.

She was as naked as she had been when Willis had first midwifed her from Hell's womb—a perfect collection of human female curves and impish sultriness that added to a total far beyond the sum of its parts.

Willis's pulse throbbed faster, but he shivered to look into her eyes now, because they mirrored a soul no longer familiar to him and a heart which had a new master.

The new master chuckled. "Shall I have her perform a few tricks for you, Professor?"

"That—" Willis's tongue stuck to the roof of his mouth. "That won't be necessary."

"What would you have of me, Rudy?" asked Anathae, unheeding, in a monotone so bereft of inflection that it did not sound like Anathae at all.

"A little dance, I think," Narmer said.

He gestured with his hands and suddenly held a violin and bow; he began to play a sprightly Irish air, to which Anathae began to move, prancing about the room quite mindlessly.

"You see, Professor Baxter—a puppet on the strings of my spells." Narmer stopped the music, and Anathae halted in midstride.

"Now, Professor," Narmer continued, "you mentioned something of a battle of skills, wits, power. Are you still quite so certain? Would you perhaps care to beg for something a little less painful for yourself in the way of a demise?"

"No, I'm still willing to have it out with you in a gentlemanly fight."

"But good sir," Narmer said with a grin. "I am neither gentle nor a man. Still, the notion of battle intrigues me. Very well, a battle it shall be."

"Good. I'll sit here—and," Willis said, indicating the chair opposite him, "if you'll be seated we'll just *see* which of us is the more powerful."

Rudy Narmer again shook back his dark locks proudly and advanced to the chair Willis had indicated. "I do think you are making a—"

He halted.

Damn it, thought Willis. *Why's he stopping? He's got to sit in that chair or—*

Narmer regarded the old chair before him, cocked his head toward Willis, and grinned. "Very clever, Professor. I commend you. Very clever indeed. You almost had me, but this is a most ingenious first—a pentagram chalked under the rug, your chair in the proper place and this one over the sign that would bind me and give you the power to use the *only* spell you know to send me plummeting back to Hell. Most ingenious."

How did he know? Willis wondered, rising from his chair. *It's almost as if he could—*

—*read your mind?* enjoined Narmer's voice in Willis's head. "But of course I can, Professor. Anathae could, and I've already told you that my powers are the equal of hers and more. Really, I'm most disappointed that you overlooked that."

Willis sank slowly and tiredly back into the chair he had chosen for himself.

All was lost now, and all because of his own fatigue, and his alcohol-induced stupidity! He wanted to hit himself for being so dumb. He had the feeling that Narmer would do much more than that.

Yes, all was indeed lost.

25

Narmer's smile of mock pity slowly altered into a frown of deep concern.

"A second, a second," he said, apparently struck by something in his own thoughts. "It occurs to me, Professor, if you truly expected this to work, then that must mean you know my True Name."

His bottomless-pit eyes sparkled with anger. "And I do not like the idea of humans knowing my True Name. *I do not care for that at all!*"

A quick gesture from Narmer, and Willis suddenly found himself floating upside down in the air.

Even had he known one, Willis would not have tried to mutter a defensive spell; Narmer's magic was too strong. But he struggled, squirming in midair, battling valiantly to right himself, and shouted, "I don't blame you, Narmer! I wouldn't like anyone else to know it if *I* had a Turkish name that translated 'Dung heap of a camel,' either!"

The demon flushed with fury. "I shall rip that fact out of your skull along with your brains, human filth!"

"Better than camel filth, Narmer!" Willis retorted, grabbing onto the top of the chair below him in an attempt to pull himself down out of the air. But his hands were ripped from their hold and he was hurtled against the wall. He slipped down heavily to the floor, groaning in his pain.

Narmer remained motionless beside the chair. Only his face moved, writhing with rage.

If only I could push him into the chair, thought Willis.

With all his remaining strength and despite the protest of every one of the considerable number of bruises on his battered body, he scrambled to his feet and launched himself toward Narmer, who simply raised a hand, causing Willis to smash into an invisible wall. Willis staggered back, crumpled, then sprawled, dazed, on the floor.

"Be still," said Narmer, "while I manufacture the instrument of your grisly death!"

The gestures were augmented by brief spurts of strange-language spells.

Willis managed to get to his hands and knees and, grappling weakly with the chair, to his feet. He was then halted by the wonder and horror of what was beginning to appear in the air behind Narmer.

Gobs of translucent muck began to form, suspended in mid-room. They spun slowly and sickeningly, moved together with a motion that inspired seasickness, and collected into one large scab-encrusted piece which suddenly began to take on a nauseating combination of colors; mauve, slime green, blood red. Glitters began to twinkle at the center as this glob, this amoebalike thing, began to pseudopod itself, streaming parts of its mottled form outward. These pseudopods glimmered, glowed, then hardened into suckered tentacles tipped with razor-sharp claws which gleamed in the flickering candlelight. The center of the thing transformed into a body which was mostly mouth. This dreadful maw was crammed to overflowing with spikelike teeth, the tips of which were stained with moist blood, and yet found room for a horrible purple tongue which dripped gooey phlegm. Above the mouth were huge bulging eyes which gleamed evilly in the dimness, eyes which had not only seen but delighted in seeing things of unspeakable torment and pain. And incredibly, the obscene lips of the thing widened and then widened farther yet; the tongue lolled out of the way, like that of an idiot, allowing a view of the Hell-beast's lower throat. No, not a throat—a void. A starless black *void* of despair, in which—*my god!*—human skulls and human bones floated.

And . . . were those wails of pain Willis heard? Screams of tormented, damned human souls without hope of reprieve?

Fear twisted Willis's viscera, bent his mind almost out of

shape. The slithering tongue slipped noisily back into the maw just before the mouth of the misshapen monster snapped shut, cutting off the incredible sight, but pushing out a rotting stench which was so foul that Willis thought he would certainly faint.

Narmer folded his arms and looked back over his shoulder at the thing he had conjured up. "Gracious," he said mildly. "I've been reading too much Lovecraft. Ah well, 'twill suffice!"

He raised a hand, drawing the thing closer. He indicated with gestures—for the hideous thing had no ears—that Willis was to be its prey, and slowly, ponderously, the monster began to move through the air.

"Really, Rudy, don't you think your friend needs some Scope?" asked a girlish voice.

Startled, Narmer turned slightly to find, standing beside him without a trace of stupor, Anathae—who promptly bopped him in the mouth with her petite fist.

Narmer grunted with surprise. "Anathae?"

"And what's this male chauvinist demon garbage about you being 'better' than me?" she demanded, her eyes flashing. "You may have more power than I do, meatball, but you're not as smart. Because now you've got more than poor Willis to contend with—you've got me." And with that, she kneed him sharply in the groin.

At first Narmer reacted as a man might if dealt a similar blow, doubling over with pain.

But then he jumped back a few steps and threw off his robe, standing in his full splendid nakedness, and he shook his curly head as if to shake off the blow. Offhandedly, he batted aside a fireball which Anathae had seemingly pulled from nowhere to throw at him.

Then Narmer stood tall and seemed almost to grow. His barbed tail was very long and stood straight up over his head with anger.

"Admittedly you fooled me," he said, "and for that you will pay with much pain. I thought your subjugation was perhaps a mite too easy.

"But now, Anathae," Narmer continued, growing even taller and more menacing yet, as he stepped back to hurl a potent spell, "we shall see if your dubious intelligence is any match for my power. *Thanos*—aieeeee!"

The first of his last two words was but part of the spell Narmer intended to cast, but the last was a definite and piercing cry of horrified pain.

It would be difficult to say whether the demon's tail, when he had stepped back the second time, had been thrust into the toothy maw of the advancing Hell-horror, or whether the gruesome beast had advanced upon Narmer's tail. But it scarcely matters, dear reader, inasmuch as the result was precisely the same.

The monster chomped down and its evil eyes lit up with a glee which could only be called devilish. It let out a sound like a thousand starving cats feasting on a just-discovered whale or a hundred cold chisels being scraped with force and determination across an equal number of blackboards.

Narmer yelped with pain. "Not me, dumb shit! Not me—*him!*"

But the ecstatic beast, besides having no ears, had closed its eyes with its joy and continued to suck the tail in, pulling Narmer off his feet and into the air. It floated back and sucked in the demon's tail, dear reader, much as you or I might a strand of spaghetti (although not, of course, in a fine restaurant, where one might be expected to behave with a bit more dignity).

Narmer wriggled about much as Willis had a short time before. Finally, turning to look up, he saw that the loathsome thing was about to begin munching upon the base of his tail. The captive demon screamed a few words, and waved his hand desperately, and the monster vanished in a puff of green smoke.

Rudy Narmer plunged downward—directly into the waiting arms of the chair in which Willis had invited him to sit.

Willis had recovered his senses enough to shout out the demon's True Name and part of the binding spell. "*Deve Gubrelik! Ubele Canet Minen.*"

"My tail!" cried Narmer, feeling the bloody stump behind him; agony was plain on his features. "My beautiful tail!"

"Don't worry about your tail, Rudy," Anathae said, moving beside Willis and gloating. "We've got your *ass!*"

"What?" screamed the demon. Narmer shot up out of, then bounced back into, the chair into which he had fallen as though he had hit a brick wall. He let out a hideous bellow and tried again, with the same result.

"*Teryae . . .*" continued Willis, unperturbed.

"All right. All right. I give up. But don't send me back. I'll go away. I'll make it up to you. I'll go away *and* make it up to you! Just don't send—"

"*Exconae Chanet . . .*" Willis continued his slow, measured chant.

"Anathae," the demon whose True Name was Deve Gubrelik pleaded, "talk to him. He'll listen to you, and surely *you* understand. The, uh, Boss is mad at me—very mad. That's why I turned on that magician hundreds of years back. Please!"

"*. . . Isnel . . .*" continued Willis.

"Look, I just *can't* go back. I can't. You've no idea what the Boss will do to me. He could overlook it while I was Here, doing what I was doing, but if I go back There I'll be no use to him. What can I say? I'll do *anything* to keep from going back." His smooth handsome features were imploring, his voice plaintive and begging pitifully.

I don't know what the Boss will do to you, Willis thought, hoping the demon was reading his mind, *and I don't care. But for what you've done to those poor kids, and countless others, you can go to Hell, camel dungheap!*

And Willis, pointing his finger at the demon, his voice steady, said ". . . *Canet!*"

Deve Gubrelik turned to black lightning-shot smoke and billowed away.

Willis sat up from their bed slowly, so as not to awaken Anathae.

He reached for his shorts, found them, and put them on, then moved into a chair where he could sit up and do a little thinking without disturbing her.

After the battle, Anathae had insisted on using her magic to heal his bruises; he had made no complaint. And they had both been very tired—not *that* tired, but very tired.

In bed, Anathae had told him she had never really been

completely under Narmer's power, that she had suspected something was amiss the second time she'd inexplicably "forgotten" to read his mind and so had been somewhat prepared for what had followed. She had only waited for the right opportunity, which showed itself when Narmer's power was occupied with summoning the monster and his attention was fully on Willis.

And none of this had disturbed him, then. They had made each other even a little more tired. Then they had slept.

But now what? Willis asked himself.

For he knew that while she had waited for the opportunity she had had to submit to everything or the subterfuge would not have worked. And the picture in his mind of Anathae's lithe softness in bed with Narmer's sinewy muscular body, responding to desires Willis dared not imagine, was not a pleasant one. Certainly it was no help to Willis's peace of mind that Narmer not only was better physically endowed but, with his experience, was probably a more skilled lover to boot.

The easy way out of this dilemma, he knew, would be to adopt the method of the ostrich—stick his head in the sand and tell himself it had never happened. (It was possible, of course, that Narmer simply had not had the time to do anything with Anathae. See? It was *easy* to do.)

"But not very likely," Willis whispered to himself.

What were his feelings?

How did it affect him?

How did it affect her?

How did it affect them?

What were *her* feelings?

Should he go into the kitchen and fix himself a drink?

Willis noted that he had left the light on in the bathroom earlier, which explained why it was so easy to see Anathae across the room, sleeping peacefully, nude as always, her too-young face nestled in her pillow. He had a momentary argument with himself trying to decide whether she was more beautiful asleep or awake, then decided to call it a draw.

Had she enjoyed it?

Did it matter if she had?

Willis knew he had to be very certain about his feelings, for with Anathae there could be no pretenses.

Then Willis laughed silently to himself. True, he had a lot of questions and they would require honest thought and searching of his emotions before he could find the needed answers, but one of them was *not* "Do I still love her?"

He eased back into bed, pulled a strand of hair from her freckled childlike cheek. She stirred a little, but when he did not do anything more she continued to sleep.

I love her, he thought. *I suppose, if demons are capable of love, that she loves me too. And that's what matters. And that's really the only important thing.*

And with that reassuring thought, he had no trouble getting back to sleep.

PART FIVE

PART FIVE

26

Strange are the ways of coincidence.

Right now there are only five people in O'Leary's Bar & Restaurant, just off campus from Powhattan University—although this is roughly average for four in the afternoon (there will be more people along soon, to take advantage of Happy Hour, although none of them need concern us here.)

That's Mike Schultz, the bartender, over there behind the bar—he serves drinks rather than a significant purpose in this portion of our saga. He wipes the bar and the glasses after they've been washed—sometimes, absentmindedly, with the same rag—and frequently gives the appearance of listening when his customers tell him their problems. Still, someone has to do the manual work.

At the moment Mike is serving a third sweet Manhattan straight up to a dentist, one Dr. Henderson by name, in the darkest corner of the bar. The dentist usually prefers daiquiris and to start his drinking later in the day.

But today his favorite patient—a lovely secretary who works at old P.U.—did not show up for her appointment to have her teeth cleaned. The doctor is certain he is in lust with her, might well be in love with her, even more certain that he could never win her—and, in his drinking, is trying to lose the certainty of his otherwise happy marriage to someone else. Part of the problem is that this secretary has the most perfect teeth he has ever seen—and so, even though he provides his service free of charge to her, he cannot persuade her to come into the office every month. So he sits here and, with the aid of alcohol, fantasizes about filling her cavity.

He also has nothing to do with *this* section of our tale. Strange are the ways of coincidence.

But the other three . . .

Ah, the other three, indeed! Two of them are in the bar drinking together, and they are known to us from old acquaintance. They are Professor Willis Baxter, head of the university's Arts and Sciences Division, and Professor Larry Hawthorne, for close to a month now head of the Department of Student Impetus.

The third, one John Smith by name, sits two stools down from them, a slender shadow on the edge of their perceptions, noticed but unheeded, a faceless face.

Let us join them now to see if they, in any combination, have anything at all to do with this portion of our story. . . .

"I absolutely forbade her to crawl around in my brain!" Willis was saying. He up-ended his Dewar's, then slammed the glass down onto the bar with a *clack*. "She's a doer, Larry. She does what she pleases."

Hawthorne shook his head sympathetically. He glanced sidelong at the man sitting down the bar, who sipped his beer and seemed oblivious to Willis's mumblings. Most people don't listen to what other people are saying in bars, so Hawthorne did his best to shake off the feeling that the man was listening intently to their conversation.

Still, the big man put off replying for the moment, choosing instead to sip at his rum and Coke.

Two men entered the bar at this point and found themselves a place over near Dr. Henderson. Mike Schultz went over and took their drink order (a Heineken and a draft Michelob), at which point two girls—obviously, by their books, from Powhattan—came in and found themselves a table, and he took their order (a Pink Squirrel and a White Russian) before going back behind the bar again.

"So how," Hawthorne asked at length, "do you know she's been in your brain?" He leaned a large elbow on the counter and stared past Willis toward the girls.

When one them—Hawthorne was certain he knew her—

leaned over to adjust her shoe, the décoletage of the top she was wearing exposed the full and creamy curve of her breasts.

One of the two men walked over to their table and said something; one of the girls said something sharp back. Schultz looked up from mixing drinks and put his hand on the shillelagh behind the bar, but the man laughed and walked back to his own table. (It should be noted, for the benefit of those who might venture into the neighborhood around the campus and in fairness to O'Leary's, that it generally did not cater to a rough trade but that Schultz—as bartender and bouncer [someone had to do the manual work]—was prepared for trouble if it should arise.)

Willis, oblivious to everything but his own problem of the moment, flagged Schultz from behind the bar. " 'nother Scotch, Mike—an' don't thin it down with so much ice. It isn't right to mess with God's Water." And then, for the third time, he said to Hawthorne, "*In vino, veritas;* in Scotch, oblivion."

Schultz, a balding man of fifty-one with permanent smile lines at his mouth and eyes, halted in front of Willis, two mixed drinks and two beers on the tray he was carrying; he glanced briefly at Hawthorne, then asked, "How many have you had now, Professor Baxter? Six or seven since you came in, isn't it?"

"Thing is, Larry, I need my secrets," Willis said to Hawthorne, not really having heard the bartender's questions. "Anyway, sixteen will get you twenty, or so I've heard."

Schultz's eyes narrowed a little, but he went on, "As I count, you've had about six, Professor, maybe seven. I'm sorry, but I can't serve you anything but coffee now. Wait a couple of hours and—"

Willis's eyes seemed to focus on Schultz for the first time. "What d'ya mean by that? I'm a perfectly reshpectable citizen. I wanna talk to the manager—no, the *owner*—of this joint. I wanna talk to O'Leary himself!"

"Now Willis—" Hawthorne looked around nervously. The man he'd thought he'd spotted listening to them was staring at Professor Baxter but turned away when he caught Hawthorne's glance.

Schultz pulled himself up to his full five feet nine inches.

"I own O'Leary's, Professor. Have since 1954 when I bought it from Luigi Monticollo."

Willis's mood changed abruptly. "Really? And you still tend bar yourself?"

Schultz's smile matched Willis's abrupt change. "The way I figure it," he said, "someone has to do the manual work. Now, do you have something to say to me as the owner that you wouldn't say to me as just the bartender?"

Hawthorne laid his large hand on Willis's shoulder. "He's got nothing to say, Mike. Give him a little while to sober up, okay?"

"And a cup of coffee to help me do it," Willis added.

Mike Schultz winked, said, "You've got it," then moved down the bar and out to the two tables to serve the drinks he held.

Hawthorne took his hand off Willis's shoulder, picked up his own drink, downed it, then turned back to Willis. "Now tell me what's bothering you, Will. What kind of 'problems' could you have with Anathae? She's such a sweet and lovely young thing, and with her magic you could have anything you—"

"Dunno, Larry," Willis said, shaking his head sadly. "Maybe it's that I'm average—not good enough to hold the interest of a sexy demon. Not that she's ever said or done anything to indicate she's not interested, you understand. Larry, you and I both know the ideas about 'demonic possession' are bunk—but *some*thing must have possessed me of late, because I've . . ." He let himself trail off; he'd been about to say he'd been living the life of a eunuch, not because of any disinterest on Anathae's part but because of several recent "failures" he had experienced.

Willis realized he had been on the verge of talking about a subject which, had he not been so drunk, he would have found acutely embarrassing. (Strictly speaking, of course, "drunk" was too simple a description of Professor Baxter's condition; in truth, no single word could serve to describe it at this point—"four sheets to the wind" being about as close a short summation as one might assay.)

Virility—particularly a lack thereof—is a touchy subject. When one has problems of potency, one does not easily confide about it to another male. Yet it was true that Willis was suffering from such a problem, one which he did not fully recognize himself. Anathae's youthful appearance, that of a saucy sixteen-year-old, which had once seemed almost enticing to him, was now among the factors which helped turn him off. It seemed to him that after years of hopeful and ready abstinence, in the crush of plenty supplied by his beautiful and willing roommate, and despite the fact that she had engaged his affections, his key had suddenly grown too limp to fit the lock.

And, anyway, if Anathae, who could read his mind until he forbade it for the duration, could not understand him ("I *know* you could 'fix it' with magic, Ana, but I've got to rise to the occasion *myself*, don't you see?"), how could he expect Hawthorne to do so?

As Mike Schultz arrived with a cup of steaming black coffee, Willis's eyes narrowed to consider the fragrant vapor and also whether or not Anathae had obeyed his wishes.

Did she know the uneasiness he felt when he considered their relationship? Was she aware of his trembling fear that his impotence might drive him to undermine what had been the only loving and caring sexual liaison of his life? Did she know how unsure, inept, bungling and, therefore, unworthy he felt when he approached their bed? Was she cognizant of how her youthful appearance was affecting him now, making him feel like a dirty old man debauching an innocent child?

To these questions he had no answer.

Hawthorne, two drinks behind Willis, had lost the thread of their conversation; he had been trying to catch the eye of one of the Powhattan girls but had not been successful. He realized that Willis had been talking about Anathae, his demon—his personal demon. He glanced around, but no one else seemed to be taking any note of Willis's complaint—no one, that is, except the man two barstools down. And besides, even he did not appear overly curious.

27

Ah, dear reader, if only Larry Hawthorne and Willis Baxter had but known! And yet, if they could have known the identity of that man on the barstool, if they had known this dark-haired man was John Smith—or, as he was known by mail-order diploma, the Rev. John Smith—how could they have guessed what was in his mind? How could Willis, in particular, guess how this man would fit into his future to complicate his already complex problems?

How, indeed?

But you and I, dear reader, are in a special position—we know, herewith, that the Rev. John Smith was the founder of the Receivers of the Lord, the modest congregation of which was made up of students at Powhattan. We know that the group had funneled a certain amount of funds to Smith—not quite as much, perhaps, as he had "acquired" when he walked off with the organ fund of a similar if older group of people down in Dothan, Alabama, nor near again as much as he had once made selling the same piece of real estate to half a dozen people—but still enough to live on. Not in the style to which he and many of the rest of us would love to become accustomed, alas, but enough to get by—bread and beans, an occasional hamburger, and, even less frequently, a beer.

As always, the Rev. John Smith was looking for an edge. He would be the first to admit that his group, RotL, needed new impetus—that certainly no new members would be likely to join at its present low ebb. Smith was not dumb—he would have been in jail several times over if that had been the case—but he had a tendency not to follow through on his thinking, which limited even his most optimistic operations to the "small con" or one-shot and minor blackmail.

Smith, a little down in the mouth over the turn of his fortunes and certainly not willing to stay in the divinity business here if it should remain on the same keel, *had* been listening intently to the overweight man two stools up from him at O'Leary's and also to his companion. It was rather hard to overhear while pretending to be absorbed in drinking his beer, but he felt he had taken in a great deal. And the fact that the larger of the two had almost caught him listening and had then spoken more quietly, and tried to get his friend to do so as well, convinced Smith there was something here worthy of his efforts.

The larger man was Larry, the other Willis. And the bartender had addressed the latter as Professor Baxter. They were from the university, no doubt. Both men had used a word he'd seldom heard in a bar before, although it was still used often enough among the Faithful—"demon." And he'd heard Baxter say he felt as if he'd been "possessed." But that had been about all he'd been able to hear clearly, besides the fact that Baxter had apparently made some kind of bet with Larry—and although 16-to-20 odds were a bit unusual, there did not seem to be anything useful he might make of this.

Still, there were possibilities in what he had heard—and Smith was willing to grasp at almost any straw if he thought he could find some profit in it, since at present he was down to (count them) two dollars and a beloved collection of baseball cards. It was a little hard for him to understand why a professor might believe in such bunk—his own followers from the university, with the exception of Arnold Davies, were a pack of lonely hearts and misfits, and Smith realized better than any of them why his "appeal" did not extend to many of their fellow students, who had inquiring minds which left them with a tendency to doubt, or at least to question, bold assertions.

But Smith was not the sort of person to look a gift horse in the mouth. As a former deprogrammer of religious nuts (which he had given up as being too much like real work), he knew how to earn money from the credulous. Gods, devils, demons, spirits, ghosts—they were all the same. Some people believed in such stuff, and it was easy to take advantage of them. Smith himself did not believe such nonsense, but he could see how this might give him the "edge" he had been looking for.

On the other hand, it seemed much more likely that the professor had only been speaking figuratively. If it was only an exaggeration, some minor problem he had been referring to, that would be disappointing; but if not, it could have even more intriguing possibilities. Despite Willis's mild-mannered appearance, Smith realized it could be anything. Drugs? Homosexuality? Wife-beating? Sleeping around—with one of his students, perhaps? Something which Smith might use to blackmail the professor or, failing that, the university itself?

It would all depend, of course, on what the professor had been "possessed" by. And to find that out, Smith would have to follow him, find out where he lived, and nose around until he discovered what it was. Since Willis had been denied any further drinks save coffee, no doubt he would soon be leaving.

Smith glanced bleakly out the window of O'Leary's. March was supposed to be the harbinger of spring, and although some pleasant weather at the beginning of the month had been nice enough to thaw some of the winter's snow, Mother Nature had played a little trick by dumping one last heavy load over the New England states. March was supposed to enter like a lion and exit like a lamb—and if the cold snow outside did bear some resemblance to fleece, Reverend Smith could not help but feel that this was not what had been intended by the saying. But while he did not want to go out into the cold outside, Smith reflected, he had nursed his beer about as long as might be considered reasonable.

Surreptitiously, he watched Willis as he contemplated but did not touch his coffee.

Willis leaned his elbows on the bar and stared at himself in the mirror behind the bottles. His five-o'clock shadow had begun to sprout, and his unfashionably short hair hung in a diagonal fringe across his forehead. Then he felt around in his inside jacket pocket for his wallet; his hands came out, instead, with a neatly folded piece of lined yellow notebook paper.

He unfolded it, dimly recalling what it contained. On campus earlier that afternoon, with nothing else to do, he had attempted to enumerate his troubles, listing them in the order of importance they held for him. He opened the note and read it:

1. Impotence with Anathae.
2. Ennui with respect to job I'm doing. *After only three months?*
3. The opinion of others, notably Miss Bradmortion, that I'm "contributing to the delinquency of a minor." (Contributing to "1" above?)
4. Am I becoming an alcoholic? (Contributing to "1"?)

Willis scowled at the note, pulled a pen from his shirt pocket, and with no further ado scribbled out item 4. He had, of course, intended to outline possible solutions to these problems when he had written them down, but had not had time to think of any.

Abruptly he said, "I think I'd better go."

"I'll drive you," Hawthorne said, knowing Willis had again not brought his car. "It's just a couple of blocks out of my way from here."

"No, thanks," Willis said loudly. Then softly: "I need the walk to sober up. The cold air and ever'thing. I'd gag on this coffee—O'Leary's is worse even than the Automat's. Anyway, for all I know, Ana could be in my head right now an' *pop*, justlikethat, might decide to jus' whisk me home at any second."

"Now, Willis—"

"Nope, nope, won't listen to reason—'m goin' now." And with that, Professor Baxter walked a circuitous path around the tables between himself and the door and, throwing on his camel-hair coat and buttoning it up, disappeared through the exit. The fellow Hawthorne had thought might be listening to their conversation put a dollar bill on the counter and, not waiting for his fifteen cents change, walked out after him.

28

Forget your woolens, dear reader? Then let us skip, forth-with, to Willis Baxter's apartment, avoiding the chilly trudge from O'Leary's, thus:

Willis slammed the door so hard the entire apartment shook. He stomped the remaining snow off his feet, glared at the girl-demon sprawled on his couch, threw down his briefcase, and stalked into the kitchen.

During his short, cold—but still not sobering—walk from O'Leary's, he had stopped a few times to pull the piece of yellow notebook paper from his pocket, snort, shake his head, fold it up, and put it back again. He had been particu-larly bothered by the ridiculous thing he'd had sense enough to scribble out. Sure, he was perhaps drinking a little too much—but, at the same time, he had more problems now than he'd ever had before, so if he could find even a little respite from them by taking a couple of drinks, that was perfectly normal. He'd seen alcoholics before, and he sin-cerely pitied them—grubby unshaven men in greasy trousers who shouted obscenities after those who would not give them money when they were panhandling for drinks. Even though (he grudgingly admitted) he could use a shave now himself, he had sense enough to know he wasn't like them.

"You lie around naked like that all day?" Willis half snarled, half slurred over his shoulder at Anathae, reaching far into the refrigerator to retrieve a glass decanter of pre-mixed martinis. "Got nothin' t' do?"

Anathae, in the other room, sat up slowly and stretched,

her long tresses falling back to reveal her small horns. During the past three months she had shared Willis's bed and board, his trials and tribulations, triumphs and victories—and, most recently, his spate of impotence and ill-humor.

"What would you like me to do, Will?" She floated toward him on a cloud of sulphurous vapor, her dainty hooves barely brushing against the carpet as she stretched again. "Shall I whisk away all the snow outside? Shall I change the walls of Miss Bradmorton's apartment to glass? Shall I—"

"Anathae!" Willis snapped.

"Sorry," she said.

He took a gulp of martini straight from the decanter. What the hell, he'd had enough to drink at O'Leary's to make him drunk but not quite enough to provide the warmth he had needed for that trek through the snow. As long as he already *was* drunk, he might as well have a little more to help him thaw out. He turned, looked at Anathae, shrugged apologetically, then walked past her back into the living room.

"I'm sorry, too," he said. "It's just my problem. And . . . oh, hell, it's just that things are so, well, *humdrum*. Over at Powhattan. Ever since my plansh—my *plans* for a decent curriculum started to be realized and my problems at the division were straightened out—"

Willis broke off and took another deep drink; he turned in time to see Anathae come out of the kitchen—fully clothed. Her long green dress brushed against him as she sat down on the couch.

"Do you mean to tell me," she asked, "after you've realized one of your life's ambitions—to head the division—that you're bored?" She curled up against the arm of the couch so that her small firm breasts bulged appealingly from her low-cut gown.

Willis sank into his purple easy chair and considered his martini. "I'm top man there an' all I do is push paper. Somehow, I thought it would be—*different*. You know? Back when I was just a professor I thought the problem with the people who were running things was jusht that they lacked imagination. Now I unnerstan'. I see what it's like. Most the stuff I deal with's got nothin' to do with education. Water pipes bustin', Student Union activities, registration, makin' sure the student store's got enough erasers. *Nuthin'* to do with education.

"And the memos! Who was it said, 'Blast the memos, full speed ahead!'? Damned memos. People coverin' their ass in paper. Yes, really, that's all it is. Nobody can do anything by word of mouth, gotta put it down in writing in a goddam memo before you can get anything done. And *then* it's no guarantee. Instead, most times you get twenty memos back for every one you put out." Willis's shoulders drooped as he set his martini on the table beside him. He covered his eyes with one hand and loosened his tie with the other. "I don't have time to teach. Or to learn. Or make love."

"I know," Anathae said—and regretted it immediately.

Willis looked at her, then turned away, teeth clenched, to stare out the front window at the frozen lawn which stretched out to the street. His sullen and angry thoughts chased each other for a while but then lost themselves in the corridors of his mind, and in a short while he was simply staring at the street.

"My whole life's been at Powhattan," he said. "Ten, going on eleven years, but it seems like my whole life. Every day I've walked those campush paths, eaten in the Shtudent Union, worried about campush problems. And sometimes my own." He shook his head and sighed. "An' next week I got to go to another stuffed-shirt faculty party. I got the job and I gotta do it. I just wonder, sometimes, how long I can go on like this."

Willis looked down at the tie in his hand; he vaguely remembered having loosened it and pulled it off. With a small disjointed motion, he dropped it on the carpet and turned back to Anathae. "There's a whole world out there, Ana! Isn't it mine, too? Or is it like Thoreau or Pound or whoever it was said—that we all lead lives of quiet deshperation?"

Willis gestured toward the window, indicating all the world outside, and as he looked that way again he saw a rather portly woman coming up the walk. *Gonna hafta keep my voice down*, he thought, smirking, *if I'm gonna lead a life of quiet desperation*. He put a finger to his lips to shush himself, then started to search about on the floor for the decanter, which he had put aside along with his martini.

Anathae stood up abruptly. "She's going to knock at our door," she said in a whisper.

Willis's elbow knocked over the decanter as he turned to Anathae. "Who is? What?"

"I read her thoughts," Anathae said, tracing a demonic symbol in the air and muttering those words which Willis could never recall after she'd said them. All at once she was dressed in a modest yellow suit and comfortable patent-leather boots. Her hair was momentarily electrified, then reassembled itself into a neat bun at the back of her neck; only a few curls remained loose at the hairline to hide the small horns.

With a few more indistinguishable words and a gesture in Willis's direction, the decanter of martinis and the resultant spill disappeared entirely.

"She's coming here because of me," Anathae said, trying to pull Willis into a sitting position. "Because of that nosy Miss Bradmorton, really, but never mind that. Listen, you can't be drunk. She'll—"

The doorbell sounded its three descending notes.

"Coming!" Anathae called brightly, then turned back to Willis. "Please, Will. This could be important. She mustn't know you've been drinking. She's from some county agency and could cause grief I'm sure you'd just as soon avoid. Don't say anything. And don't breathe on her!"

"I won't say a word," Willis assured her. He smiled inanely and settled back in his chair, which (unfortunately) fell over.

"Beelzebub!" Anathae said. She muttered and made another sign in Willis's direction, righting both Willis and the chair, then turned to open the door.

At the threshold stood a slightly plump woman of about forty with curled graying hair, modest makeup, and a plumb-colored suit one size too small.

"Good afternoon," the woman said, holding out a gloved hand to Anathae. "I'm glad to find you at home—I'm Mrs. Hayward, Julia Hayward, of Social Services."

"Yes?"

Julia Hayward stretched her dark-painted lips into a smile and, inasmuch as Anathae was not really barring her way, stepped across the threshold into the apartment and glanced around.

"Well," she said quickly, "a concerned citizen called our department about your welfare—Ana?—yes, Ana. You seem older than I expected. Anyway, I'm sure you can understand one citizen's caring about the situation of another. This person felt you were perhaps not receiving proper care. I believe you are the ward of Willis Baxter?"

"I was," Anathae said, casting Willis a secretive and threatening look, "until I came of age. My parents passed away some time ago. He's my cousin, twice removed."

"Your cousin," Mrs. Hayward said with a nod. Turning to Willis, she said, "How do you do, Mr. Baxter?"

Willis looked up at her and smiled like a cat who had just raped a canary and was trying to conceal the fact.

"He's not feeling well," Anathae said, drawing Mrs. Hayward to a chair on the far side of the room. "He's been working very hard at the university all day and had to walk home in the cold—you can never find a cab when you need one. I think he's coming down with flu. Or perhaps pneumonia."

The woman stifled a gasp that came out as a choke, then hastily pulled a handkerchief from her purse.

Mrs. Hayward, a well-meaning woman, had a secret phobia that she might catch some dreadful disease from one of the people she had been assigned to help—a phobia which was never far from her thoughts.

But after only a slight pause, she continued bravely, "My! Well, let me get right to the point then. Ana, my department is responsible for minors who have problems. Some minors are in a position where they're too embarrassed to admit they have any problems, if you know what I mean." She glanced at Willis, then gave Anathae a meaningful stare.

Willis looked at Mrs. Hayward, then at Anathae.

He smiled.

He chuckled softly.

He laughed.

He tried to stop.

But, uncontrollably, despite dark glances from Anathae, he began to giggle—some necessary part of his inhibition had given way. The fact that his behavior could only lower Mrs. Hayward's all-important opinion of him only made the whole matter seem even funnier to him, and he melted into helpless mirth.

29

"Awk!" Willis said as he suddenly found himself standing and then, again involuntarily, in a stiff-legged shuffle, walking out of the room. Mrs. Hayward's frowning attention had been too much on Willis for her to notice Anathae's gesture in his direction or to hear the words she whispered.

Anathae smiled unevenly at Mrs. Hayward. "He gets nervous when he has diarrhea," Anathae said by way of explanation. "I think he *is* coming down with something. . . .

"Now, where were we? Oh, yes—my welfare. Willis, I'm afraid, is the victim of the gossip of some malicious busybody—I'm sure you know the type. He doesn't share the details of his life with his neighbors, and as a result I suppose they find them easy to misinterpret. I know I must look a bit young to you—I'm always getting carded in bars and suchlike—but, as I said, I haven't been his ward since I came of age. Still, he was kind enough to take me in when I needed it, and since we're related I see nothing wrong with my keeping house and cooking for him."

"Now, my dear, I never said, never *hinted*, that there was anything 'wrong' with your relationship with Mr. Baxter—"

"*Professor* Baxter, actually," Anathae corrected. "He's head of the Arts and Sciences Division of Powhattan—you can check that out, if you like. I assure you, if there's any question as to his respectability—"

"No, no," Mrs. Hayward said, "you misunderstand. I never said there was anything wrong. This was just a report we had, which I am supposed to check out. Provided you're of age—''

Anathae sneezed violently. "I have my birth—*achoo!* —excuse me—my birth certificate around here somewhere, if you don't mind waiting while I look for it." Anathae coughed and added, "Sorry, Mrs. Hayward, but neither Professor Baxter nor I took the inoculations when they were offered—I hope you're not going to catch some dreadful disease from us or anything."

Mrs. Hayward trembled, spreading her handkerchief over her mouth, as Anathae went to a nearby desk, opened a drawer, and pulled an official-looking photostat from it. Mrs. Hayward had been too concerned thinking about the germs she was certain were surrounding her to notice the movement of Anathae's lips and fingers before she opened the desk.

Anathae sneezed again, bringing the hand which held the paper to cover her face. Mrs. Hayward knew it wasn't particularly logical but she thought she could *feel* tiny flu (or pneumonia?) germs crawling all over her, so she waved the paper away.

"No, everything seems to be fine here. I'm certain this is a false report. Besides which, I am *ter*ribly susceptible to colds and things like that, and . . ." She paused, then raised her voice so that Willis could hear in the other room. *"So nice to have met you, Professor Baxter!"* She continued to Anathae, "And the symptoms for what you have sound absolutely *dreadful!*"

The girl-demon nodded sympathetically as Mrs. Hayward got up, walked to the door, and let herself out.

Anathae walked to the window and watched Mrs. Hayward start up a gold-and-black Opel and speed away at a velocity which exceeded the maximum prescribed by law in this neighborhood.

Willis returned, and Anathae turned to look at him.

"You saved my tail again," he said, the residue of embarrassed anger underlying his voice, "but what if I'd wanted to save it myself?"

Anathae sat wearily on the couch. "Willis," she said, "if you won't talk sensibly—don't talk."

He started to reply, stopped, then nodded and made an

effort to sober up. "Okay—what do you think caused all that?"

"I already know," she said. "Our nosy neighbor, Mrs. Bradmorton. She turned in that report. I know, Willis, because I've been inside her mind, too. She told Mrs. Hayward—anonymously, of course—that you were screwing a minor. But she didn't use such delicate terms."

Willis seemed to be considering this, and so sober were his considerations that he hardly slurred his words when he finally spoke. "If she succeeded in bringing charges or in having charges like that brought against me, the newspapersh would almost certainly get hold of it. Then the university would have to fire me. I've told them my 'ward' is staying with me, and whether they believe it or not they've so far been willing to look the other way. I don't shuppose you know if she's tried to report me to the university?"

"Just a minute, we'll find out," Anathae said. She traced a rhomboid sign in the air and whispered a few guttural words, and a holographic vision glowed at the center of the room.

It was Henrietta Bradmorton herself! She stood staring as if she could not see where she was, as though she were in a dark and unfamiliar place and therefore afraid to move lest she trip over some unseen object.

"No," Anathae said after a moment, "she hasn't done anything about reporting you to the university—not because she hasn't wanted to but because she knows she's the unknown quantity there. She thinks the people at the university would not believe her or, if they did, wouldn't do anything about it. If she could find the handle to the brush, she'd love to smear you there—but she doesn't even know how to go about it.

"Now look at her, Will—really look at her." Anathae obviously had to concentrate to maintain the apparition. "Can you see the lines that have deepened around her mouth? Even careful tweezing and makeup don't hide the sadness about her eyes. She's not quite old but no longer young—and coming to realize that older is the only thing she can get, the only way she can move through time.

"She's dyed her hair the same brunette it was when she used to deny men. The pity is, she'd love to have a man—

there are few she'd deny now, but none are asking. She'd love to go to parties all the time as she sees us doing, and she'd love to have a job like most everyone else's—out in the morning and home at night. But she's locked into a telephone selling job that keeps her in her apartment all day. So she takes what entertainment she can.''

"Like hanging out her window and tending to our business,'' Willis said as he sank back down into his chair and looked away from Henrietta.

He did not like what he saw as an accusing expression in her eyes. Her presence, even in this form, seemed to say to him, *Aha! Willis Baxter! You child molester and closet pervert! Look at that girl—just look at her! She's young enough to be your daughter! You think you're doing her any kind of service by—*

"Get her *out* of here!'' Willis croaked. He felt very tired and shut his mind's ear against Henrietta's whining voice. "It's bad 'nuff she sends anonymous complaints to the county, but every time I go out or come in, just about, she's peering at me like a bat out of a cave and likely as not screaching something 'bout immorality or dishgrace!''

Anathae waved a hand at the vision, which promptly disappeared. She got up off the couch, sat down on the arm of Willis's chair, and put a hand lightly on his shoulder. "It seems I cause you a lot of trouble, Will.''

"You're worth any amount of trouble, Ana,'' he said truthfully, but thinking of the third point on his list of problems, which he realized could be related to the first, he added, "but it wouldn't hurt any if you looked just a few years older.''

But Anathae, whose eyes sparkled to the humor of some inner joke, did not really hear him. "If you want, I could *really* take care of her so she'd never do anything like this again.''

"No,'' Willis said. "Not worth the bother.'' He realized his chance to broach the subject had come and gone. "I just wonder where it'll all end,'' he mumbled. He gave up on the attempt to overcome the effect of all the liquor he had consumed, leaned his head back on his easy chair, and fell into an uneasy slumber.

30

Take note: Love is alive in the world. And it is written—right here in front of your eyes, dear reader, if nowhere else—that There Is Someone for Everyone. And if that means Cupid can be, on occasion, capricious with his darts, so be it.

Reverend Smith had had no trouble following Willis Baxter to his apartment. Well, minor problems only: He had to stop in the cold each time Baxter stopped to consult a paper in his pocket. *A treasure map?* the reverend wondered the first time this happened, his brain being a bit addled by the freezing cold. Then Baxter staggered on and Smith trudged after him. *On his way to an assignation?* Smith theorized a little later, with a bit more logic, when the professor seemed to be looking at the paper again. Smith was beginning to wonder which of them might freeze to death first—Smith's coat was undoubtedly the warmer but Baxter had the advantage of several strong drinks to his single beer (for which, he reminded himself, he had been forced to leave a fifteen-cent tip for fear of losing the professor)—when Willis turned and trudged up the walk to his apartment.

Not lost on Smith was the sight of the drapes being pulled back at the apartment across the way and a woman glaring at the professor from the window thus unsheathed as Willis did a series of little forward-and-backward two-steps in an attempt to get his key into the lock. The drapes snapped shut as the professor finally succeeded in gaining entry.

Ah, Smith thought, *someone who might be in the know.*

After checking out the name on the mailbox, he went up to the door of the apartment across from Baxter's and knocked. In a short while it was answered by Henrietta Bradmorton.

"Mrs. Bradmorton?"

"Miss," she replied.

"Miss Bradmorton," he amended. "My name is Smith— the Rev. John Smith. May I come in? I'd like to talk to you about your neighbor, Professor Baxter. I won't take more than a few minutes of your time. Please?"

Henrietta looked at Smith skeptically at first, but then stepped aside. "Come in, Reverend. For a few minutes, anyway."

What was that you said? Not exactly lines from *Romeo and Juliet*, you think? Perhaps not. *Indeed* not, for after extensive research your author must report that the protagonists of the Immortal Bard's romantic play were yclept Montague and Capulet and, further, that no one named Bradmorton or Smith appeared in that Elizabethan entertainment, not even as Supporting Characters. So much for that.

And yet from little acorns great saplings grow—to coin a cliché. Before passing judgment on this inauspicious beginning, we must consider how these two view each other—how their psychologies and separate needs intertwine and even, if we might say it without offense, embrace.

Henrietta Bradmorton was not all that bad to look upon, really, although in truth the bloom of youth was no longer upon her. Yet it had not been all that long since men pursued her, were spurned and dropped her like a hot (strike that, make it cold) potato—proving, if that old Russian adage was to be believed, that they did not really love her. (The old Russian adage: "Love is not a potato. You can't throw it out the window.") While she had never shown her disappointment with respect to the way things had gone in her lack-of-love life, it did not necessarily follow that she had never felt it: She had felt, at times, as if she had been thrown out the window.

Moreover, her activities as a busybody had come upon her as a result of her relatively recent isolation—for where, indeed, was she to meet a man of her own age and inclinations or find entertainment while chained to a telephone sales job? And why should she watch *The Guiding Light* or *As the World Turns* when there was real-life drama in the apartment across from hers?

Now she saw before her a man, as young as she considered herself to be, who, because of his Calling, she might be able to trust.

And that man, a mail-order reverend and at most times a small-time con artist, saw two things in Henrietta. As a neighbor of Willis Baxter's who seemed to keep her eyes open to the activities of the professor, she was a potential source of information. But as a woman, now that he beheld her up close, she was something more personal. Smith might lack imagination in some quarters and fail to follow through on some of his thinking in some areas, but the bedroom was not one of these. He had long had a yearning for mature female companionship—there were more joys to life, after all, than collecting baseball cards—but his true calling, that of a con man, in which he constantly had to be prepared to move on beyond the reach of the long arm of the law, had ere now denied him the opportunity for a long-term meaningful relationship.

Yet John Smith knew, from the moment he first saw her, that somehow he was looking on her with more than just passing lust—just as surely as he knew, by the way her hand rested gently upon his as she led him into the front room, that she had more than a passing interest in him.

Speaking of which, let us return:

"Miss Bradmorton—"

"Henrietta, please."

"Yes. Henrietta. And you must call me John." Pause. "Well, about Professor Baxter. You see, I was wondering—"

"Immoral. That's what he is. That professor. She lives with him—that teenage girl. And I can tell, by his eyes, he's doing terrible things to her. Terrible."

"Yes, I'm sure. But I—"

"Terrible things," Henrietta said. "I've done all I can, even calling Social Services. Fornication—I've tried, as God is my witness, I've tried to tell them."

"That's why I'm here, Henrietta. I want to help."

"Yes," she said, nodding, "you look like someone who'd try to help."

"I am, Henrietta," he assured her, moving closer to the divan, daring to touch her arm with his other hand.

"You know," she said, "it's not as if she was old enough to handle a relationship like that. One can understand, as one gets older, how things like that are more acceptable with a little maturity. I mean, there are *some* standards of decency, after all."

"I agree, wholeheartedly," Smith said, still touching her arm. "You're a mature woman, Henrietta—you understand a lot about these things."

"Those terrible depraved things they do."

"Yes, I can well imagine. We can both well imagine."

"Nights they spend together—"

"Alone—touching, holding each other, like—"

"Yes."

Let us draw the curtain here, dear reader, although things are just starting to get interesting and even though it might be said (and, in fact, let us come right out and say it) that dormant passions in Henrietta Bradmorton and John Smith have been aroused and both are being swept along in their wake.

Very well.

Dormant passions in Henrietta Bradmorton and John Smith have been aroused and both are being swept along in their wake.

And that, really, is all that need concern us, inasmuch as we've all been through far too many lyrical descriptions of lovemaking in our reading matter to need any more.

What matter that, in a few moments, the ersatz reverend and nosy neighbor will begin an embrace that will end only when both are disrobed and lustily getting to know each other—in the Biblical sense, of course? Need each conjugal push and shove, each joyful shout of "John!" or "Henrietta!" or "Deeper!" or "Harder!" or "This is wondrous delight, my love!" be described in graphic titillating detail?

Must each tender caress of breast and thigh and face and buttock, each nibble of lip and ear and throat and areola be paraded?

Indeed, not.

31

President Joel T. Mellon leaned forward onto the polished surface of his mahogany desk from which his graying hair and the lines of his clean-shaven face reflected in almost mirror image. He eyed John Smith, who sported a worn blue suit.

"Am I to understand, Mr. Smith, that you intend to publicize this information?"

Smith, who now knew that "sixteen will get you twenty" was *not* a bet, pushed his fingertips through the lush velvet on the arms of his chair. He felt ill at ease amid all the opulence of this French-doored office. He could see snow falling outside.

"Not if you don't want me to, sir. Well, after all, the university—and you—have been aware of Baxter's illegal behavior toward this minor for quite some time now. It would look very bad in the news—very bad."

Mellon sat back in his leather recliner. He eyed a cigar which lay still wrapped on the desk next to some papers but made no move to pick it up.

Smith paused for effect. "What I really wanted to discuss with you was . . . grant money. As I see it, a 'grant' to me for my work in analyzing but *not* publishing this story should run somewhere in the neighborhood of five hundred dollars." Smith tended to think small as well as being unaware of the fact that regular research grants averaged between one thousand and ten thousand.

President Mellon's glance did not waver.

"Do let us speak openly, Mr. Smith. We are alone, so I

197

feel I may speak frankly." Mellon sat forward; his eyes glittered. "Mr. Smith, this university won't pay one red cent in extortion." He pointed a blunt finger at Smith, who reddened. "You do whatever you like with what you know, but don't ever come onto this campus again—or you'll leave wearing gray."

Smith rose slowly, then went to the coatrack to get his heavy overcoat. When he reached the door, he turned in time to see Mellon lighting his cigar.

Smith said, "Think on it, Mr. Mellon. You may change your mind."

Mellon puffed on the cigar, then pocketed his lighter. His face was as cold as carved stone.

"Get your ass out of here," he said.

Smith left, so he neither saw nor heard the university president push the button on his intercom and say, "Sally, I want to speak with my friend Chief of Police Daniels. Would you buzz me when you have him on the line?"

Although he had been discomfited by the immediate and dismissive response he had received from the university president, the Rev. John Smith was not dismayed. It was always possible that the president might change his mind, particularly when he found out Smith wasn't bluffing. In the meantime, what "Mr. Smith" had failed to do, "Reverend Smith" might be able to accomplish in some other way.

With a careful turn of the knob, so as not to disturb the badly cracked window pane, he opened the door to his basement flat, a.k.a. the Holy Tabernacle of the Receivers of the Lord.

Because it served a dual purpose, it was not the sort of apartment that appeared to be lived in—the living room was filled with three rows of hard-backed chairs, all facing a mottled green divan near the door to the kitchen. There was also a john that worked, often as not. The floor was basic gray cement, the walls were hung with pictures of large-eyed children staring up into hazy light and clasping their hands, and the rent was eighty-five a month.

And the people awaiting him in this dim sanctified chamber? They were none other than the cream of Powhattan's lost and lonely.

Consider, dear reader, Simon Balfour—a senior after five hard years of study and a notable failure with women. But the latter could soon become a thing of the past—since his association with the Receivers of the Lord, he had been talked into taking a bath *at least* once a month whether he felt like he needed one or not. He had also, on RotL advice, cached a half gallon of Listerine under his dormitory bed and was now so confident that he was considering asking Susan Gates for a date.

And what of Susan Gates? Had she not, before her association with RotL, been terribly downcast? Indeed she had—with no group to belong to or at least none that felt the obligation to make her feel at home, she had known the loneliness that only a young girl with thick glasses, pimples, and a size twenty-nine chest could know. Now she could walk right up to any stranger and start talking—and although perhaps it might be argued that it would be better if she could find some subject other than the Way of the RotL, at least it must be conceded that this was a step in the right direction.

Then there was Arnold Davies, who was perhaps the least fanatical in this Gang of Four, although he still had his reasons for liking Smith. A big, lumbering, muscled ox of a fellow, Arnold understood sports better than people, from whom he generally tended to shy away. His lack of a social life had disturbed him so greatly that his grades had started to suffer, yet outwardly there were no manifestations to explain why he was the way he was. In fact, Arnold was considered handsome in a rugged sort of way and was extremely well mannered. Of the group, he was the least inclined to agree with the reverend on strictly religious grounds, although he was tractable enough to suit Smith's purposes. But only Smith knew why. In the frenzy of his initial conversion to "the Way," before he had started to balk at the reverend's pronouncements, Arnold had told him something he had told no other person since he had come to the Powhattan campus—that he had been a battered child. The sharing of this secret made Arnold's feelings of friendship toward the reverend stronger than any doubts he might have about the "truth" Smith said he wanted to spread to the world.

And lastly, dear reader, consider the fourth and largest member of the RotL in-group, Alan Bosnan. As his fellow students at Powhattan got to know him, they began to say he wasn't bright enough to tie his shoelace and chew gum at the same time. Eventually, however, the truth came out; Alan wasn't bright enough to tie his shoelace *or* chew gum. Indeed, whenever he sat his massive form down to eat in the cafeteria, it was possible to get an even-money bet that he wouldn't remember to open his mouth. And yet, somehow, he had miraculously managed to survive his sophomore year—no one, least of all his fellow students, really understood how. It had been speculated that his overlargeness might have had something to do with it—even Arnold Davies looked like a dwarf beside him—but since Alan always attempted, more so than any of his companions, to remain friendly and cheerful at no one's expense, if any teachers had passed him out of fear that Alan might sit on them, the threat would have to have been considered no more than their own overactive imaginations. More likely, the teachers had just felt sorry for him.

These were the crème de la crème, as it were, of Reverend Smith's flock; they were the four to whom he had delegated the most authority.

And it might be noted in passing that while Smith regarded the flock as a means of his own support, he had not altogether short-changed these four—he had, however peripherally, helped them find themselves. At the same time, realize—as Smith did—that to find maturity, they only needed to break free of the Receivers of the Lord. And that would, of course, present something of a financial problem to Smith.

"Hey, Reverend, how're you doing?" Simon asked, looking up from the group which was huddled over a Parchesi board on the floor.

Smith gave them all his beatific—that is to say, slightly daffy—smile and told them, "I'm doing well enough, although I'm a little hungry and depressed. Is there anything here to eat?"

Bosnan, who'd brought along a dozen bologna sandwiches,

as he often did, now offered a couple of them to Smith. Smith took them.

"What's depressing you, Reverend?" Davies asked.

Sitting himself down on the divan to do justice to the sandwiches, he said, "Well, you know the situation here well enough—"

"We need more publicity," Susan broke in. "Hardly anyone came to our last rally."

"Mmmff," the reverend said around a sandwich, "I agree. But that's not all that's bothering me. I'm worried over the state of this weary world we live in, and, though I fear to confess it, I'm beginning to wonder if Good can ever triumph over Evil in it."

If this seemed to shock at least three of the four people sitting before him on the floor, he knew quite well what he was doing. He let the fire of practiced zeal come into his eyes and, in the measured cadences he knew to be so effective, unfolded his tale of woe. He had heard some people talking about a professor at the university who was "possessed," but fearing not for his own safety—"for I was then undaunted in my faith, children"—he had gone to offer his help in exorcising this demon from the "poor sinner." But rather than finding a "miserable soul" contrite about his wrongdoings, he said, he had found a virtual "den of iniquity"—the professor was "living in sin" with a "poor, helpless strip of a girl."

If Alan Bosnan's concentration, never too keen, wandered back to the Parchesi board at this point, Reverend Smith now had Arnold Davies's attention.

"A child molester?" Davies asked. His face darkened as painful memories pushed their way through his thoughts.

"I'm afraid so, Arnold," the reverend said wearily. "But that's not the worst of it. The professor wanted nothing to do with me, of course, but being concerned about the child, I inquired about him among a few of his neighbors. And one of them, a fine woman, told me she had been concerned about goings-on there as well. The things she saw and heard—but never mind, it's not important. She told me she'd reported him to the county. And only today they sent a woman out to investigate but"—and at this point Smith bowed his head—"he

. . . he succeeded in fobbing her off. It appears nothing can be done.''

"The *bastards!* Excuse my language, Reverend," Arnold said, "but they're *always* able to do that. No one will ever believe—" He broke off. Tears were brimming in Arnold's eyes.

"There, there," Susan said, patting his shoulder, "there, there."

"That's not the whole of it, either," Smith went on. "I went straight to the university myself, to tell them what I'd heard—but I was shown the door. I'm not certain whether it's just that they don't believe me or that they know about it and don't care. Although, if you must know, I'm half convinced it's the latter."

"We *can* do something about it," Simon insisted. "We . . . we can hold a rally—a protest rally. At the university."

Relaxing a bit, Smith let himself be "comforted" by his Chosen Few and finally allowed as how his faith had been restored by them.

He told them he had to rest, however, and after a little consultation with each other, the three of them—Alan Bosnan had wandered out of the room while Smith was talking—decided to adjourn to the Student Union to do their planning. They hoped, with such an issue, to get more than the twenty-five members of his little "flock" to participate—and possibly get some beneficial publicity for the RotL from it besides.

Wrap that around your cigar and smoke it, Smith thought at President Mellon as they left.

He was taking off his socks when Alan Bosnan wandered back from the john. "Sorry," he said. "Where'd everyone go?"

"The Student Union, Alan. To plan the protest rally."

"What's it about, Reverend? I tried to listen, honest, but it's easy to forget."

"Just remember what I said about Professor Baxter, Alan."

"Who?"

"Write it down, Alan." Deciding to keep it as simple as possible for the giant, he added, "The man whose demon I wanted to exorcise, only he wouldn't let me."

*   *   *

Alan Bosnan, leaving Reverend Smith to his rest, licked his lips and concentrated hard.

If Smith wanted him to remember what he had said about Professor Baxter, Alan was willing to make the effort—even to the extent of taking his suggestion and writing it down in big block letters. He wrote:

1. Profesor posses by demon.
2. Get profesor for Rev. Smith.
3. Exercise demon.

Alan, looking at what he had written, decided that while there might have been more, he at least had the major points down. He folded the paper and put it in his pocket.

32

Although his name was involved, at first Willis was only amused by the pitifully small demonstration—or at least one aspect of it: When the campus police came on the scene, and the demonstrators decided to leave peacefully, a slim female student with glasses seemed almost disappointed when the tall young security man had to let go of her.

Rawlins, the grizzled Chief of Campus Security, asked Willis if he wanted to press charges; Willis said no, and Rawlins said this was just as well, since then the newspapers probably would not carry anything about it. Or, if they did, not anything to be bothered about.

Although Willis was not altogether certain about this, he felt curiously detached until he got into his office, opened his desk drawer, pulled out a bottle, and shakily poured himself a drink.

For the past three months he had lived in fear that something like this could happen, but now that it had, he decided it was nothing he couldn't bear. The timing was somewhat puzzling—he'd half expected something like this to happen when Anathae had first started to live with him, but when it hadn't he had grown to think perhaps it never would. How these students had gotten wind of it, he did not know. But he hoped Rawlins would prove to be right and, if the papers did pick it up, this would not start people talking.

At the end of the day he fortified himself with another drink and walked home. It was cold and windy, with the threat of more snow hanging over him all the way; his fingers had grown stiff by the time he got to the apartment, so he could hardly turn the key in the lock. But at last he did, went in, dropped his briefcase, pulled off his muffler and coat and tossed them on the couch. "Anathae!" he called.

She came out of the bedroom, dressed in pale blue. "I have dinner for you," she said. She pointed her dainty finger at the dining-room table, where a steak dinner appeared, complete with lace tablecloth and three-tiered candelabra.

"Well," Willis said, "it's certainly an advantage to have you around."

She smiled and touched his cheek. "You seem in a better mood, at least."

"Appearances can be deceiving," he said. Willis saw her smile fade. He had been trying to work himself up to the point where he could confront his problem with her. He couldn't quite do it yet but he still wanted to avoid unnecessary and pointless arguments.

"Sorry," he mumbled, sinking into his purple chair. "I didn't mean that. It's just . . . well, there was a demonstration at the university today—against me. Only twenty or thirty students were involved. Some of them were carrying signs accusing me of immorality, although fortunately it wasn't specific enough to mention you. I can only shudder to think what might happen if it got into the papers that students thought I was living with an underage girl and that lady from Social Services saw it. She'd probably begin her investigation all over again, for starters."

"They were here, too."

"Who?"

"A couple of demonstrators."

"*What?* Tell me about it."

Anathae bent over him, took hold of his arm, and gave him a gentle tug away from his seat. "Over dinner," she said. "I won't let them spoil dinner."

So they went to the table, and Anathea slipped smoothly onto her chair; as she did so, her dress changed to a low-cut black satin gown which clung hungrily to her supple body.

"It was nothing, really," she said, poking a fork into her Caesar salad. "Four guys came and beat on the door, yelling about a Reverend Smith who could save your soul. It was almost amusing.''

"What, exactly, did they say?"

"They didn't *say*—they yelled. But as you might expect people to yell if they're really not sure anyone can hear—your know? They thought you might be here but were pretty sure you weren't. Anyway, they said you were endangering your immortal soul, that you'd end up in some special level of purgatory before you broiled in Hell. That was when I started to get annoyed.''

"Annoyed?"

Anathae nodded. "Nothing annoys me quite so much as people pretending to expertise when they really don't know what they're talking about. Maybe they really believed that nonsense, but it was the fact that they were so *self-righteous* about it that bothered me. That's when I turned all the water to ice.''

"Water? Ice?"

"Out in front of the apartment, around the steps where it's been shoveled,'' she explained. "They started slipping and sliding and grabbing hold of each other for support. Then, after they'd fallen down two or three times each, they started to get angry at each other. To hear them tell it, there's also a special level of purgatory where people get broiled for not keeping their damned hands to themselves when they can see the other fellow's slipping.''

Willis laughed at the picture Anathae painted, despite himself, feeling mirth for the first time in several days. He forced himself to be serious. "We do have a problem, though, if this goes on much longer.''

"If it comes to that, Will, I do have documents—they'd stand up in court—to prove I'm your ward. And the boy who delivers your newspaper knows you sleep in the living room—he's 'seen' you there and heard you snoring.'' Seeing the inquiring look in Willis's eyes, she said, "I've been aware of this problem for some time and I've been working on it.''

"And come up with part of the solution, if not all of it,'' Willis said. "Is there any wine?''

She gestured and spoke a few words, and a bottle of

Château Ausone and two crystal wineglasses appeared. Willis poured.

"What I'd really like to know," he said, "is how they got a line on us."

Anathae took a sip of her wine. "It seems their 'Reverend Smith'—whoever he is—heard about us somehow. The kids, at least, are in deadly earnest—they're horrified that you're 'risking your immortal soul,' as they put it."

Willis shrugged. "So what do they know?"

Anathae savored the last few drops of wine from her glass, then said, "You don't sound very convinced."

"It's not that," Willis said quickly. "It's just," he went on, "that no one knows what happens—after death. By what standards are we judged? Is there a feather of truth against which our souls are weighed? You're older than you look, so I haven't 'contributed to the delinquency of a minor'—although, on some grander scale, I might be guilty of contributing to the delinquency of a minor demon."

Anathae laughed at the notion.

Willis went on, "But the thing is, does our relationship, yours and mine, fall into the category of 'consorting with demons'—and, if so, do I automatically go to Hell?"

Anathae laughed again—it was a tiny tinkling bell. "Would you believe me if I answered your questions? After all, Will, I *am* part demon."

Willis smiled too, then looked earnestly into Anathae's dark green eyes. "You wouldn't lie to me, Ana. We know each other—I think we're coming to understand each other—but *I* have a problem that affects us both, and we need to talk about it. Let's start here—if you know the truth, tell me."

"All right," she said, "I'll tell you whatever you want to know—but I don't expect you'll believe me. Anyway, I'm not altogether certain that what knowledge I have could be labeled Truth with a capital T." Her eyes got a faraway look as her pink tongue darted over her lips. "Let me give you an example. You go off to some primitive country and meet a bunch of natives who assume, because you can kill a wild beast with a noisy stick from some distance, that you have the inside track on the Truth. If one of them asked you whether the idols they worshiped were really gods, what would you say? How would you explain the universe to them—and would you introduce them to the more sophisticated 'gods' of your culture? Your cosmology is more complete than theirs—but what elements of it are you certain of and what things do you accept on faith? Do *you* know the difference between the two, and, if you do, how do you make the savage understand that difference?''

"You're saying I'm the equivalent of a backward native?''

"Not at all,'' Anathae said. "Humans have a number of things which make them superior to demons, not the least of which are their potential to choose to be for good or evil and their quest for knowledge. But particularly because of the latter, they have a lot of preconceptions. There are a lot of things I'm really not any more sure of than you are, although I have a few more certainties.''

"Well, try me with a few of those,'' Willis suggested.

"I've lived through a number of civilizations here, Will, and each of them had a whole system worked out about what happened after death. Back in Egypt, they thought a person's *ka*, the vital force, rejoined the Life Force when they died. That was close—sort of an 'oversoul' idea.

"The specifics—like the *ka* crossing the water and a field of rushes to find an existence just like the one they'd left, or the Greeks' idea of crossing the Styx to find a gem-lit underworld, or the Hebrews' of a great chasm between Heaven and Hell—they were all wrong. But the underlying *idea* was sound.''

Anathae paused to eat a bit of steak and a bite of bread, then went on: "So what, you want to know, are Heaven and Hell? They're all one place. Dying brings your force back to the oversoul—but does it have anything to do with the kind of life you led? You'll end up the same, born blank as any baby. Heredity and environment will shape you, although you can carry your basic goodness or badness with you too. So look at it this way—you're basically a good person, Will. Sometimes your confidence falls and you think of yourself as a nebbish, at which point you start losing your temper over nothing and become a bit of a bastard. But usually you don't deliberately hurt people. You have intellectual curiosity, honesty, and integrity going for you. I'd say that's a good underthought to bequeath yourself.''

Willis stared into the candle flame, which had grown brighter as the daylight outside the apartment dwindled. "It sounds good," he said, looking back at Anathae, "except . . . you're a demon, so there must be a Hell."

Her eyes glittered. "I told you you had preconceptions, Will. What you call Hell and Heaven are just an alternate dimension which touches this dimension on the two sides where they match—a triangle and a tetrahedron. It's possible for inhabitants of that dimension to cross over, or be barred from crossing over, to this one by means of the proper incantation.''

Anathae frowned. "I don't know about humans going the other way. I think for someone totally human to get there, it would require making a machine of some sort on the other side—although don't ask me what kind because I haven't got the slightest idea.

"Anyway, gods, devils, angels, demons—they're just words humans have used to describe inhabitants of that dimension. Magic is my dimension's way of creating balance in its portion of the multiuniverse. 'Balance' is the operative word— the multiuniversal constant. I know magic must seem like robbing Peter to pay Paul—but it's actually taking what Peter owes you, so you can pay Paul, who owes the same amount to Peter. Or, actually, the ability to perceive and utilize these balancing circumstances. So there are even limits to magic. But in my dimension, Will, there's a tremendous battle going on—always has been—the nature of which even *I* don't fully understand. Except that neither side wants to win it totally, because that would topple the balance. If what you would call the 'bad' side loses a particular battle, the 'good' side waits until the bad recovers to continue the fight. And vice versa.''

"What about," Willis asked, his forehead creased in concentration, "making deals with the Devil for one's soul?"

"Ah," Anathae said. "You know what I am—half human, half demon. In that dimension, I'm on what you would call the 'bad' side—but I'm very minor, as you know, as demons go. My training was in making mischief, not in inflicting real harm. But there are major demons, Will, and they'd gladly make deals for your soul for a little simple balance shifting—were all but One not permanently locked into that dimension now. But the souls they collected were never tormented—that's propaganda, fostered by the major demons to give humans a little torment over on *this* side.''

"What happens to the souls they bargain for, then?"

"Your essence is your own—but you can give it up. If you make a magic bond with a demon for your soul, your essence, the demon can claim it after you die. They merely clean your personality out of it, so that it can be brought into their dimension, and then they use it."

"They 'use' it? Whatever for? Do they wear it, pretend to be human or something?"

"No."

"Then what *do* they use it for?"

Anathae's voice was almost a whisper: "Wallpaper."

"You wouldn't kid me, would you, Ana? I mean, this isn't the stock joke demons tell when someone asks about Hell?"

Anathae shook her head from side to side. "I said you might not believe me, Will. But think about it. It's either the truth or a riddle—mortals never could tell one from the other. But don't let thoughts of retribution in the Netherworld or those kids with their half-baked dogma bother you—your soul is in no danger from me."

Willis looked into her youthful face—a face which all logic told him was thousands of years old and yet which did not look a day over sixteen. The breasts which peeked from her satin gown, indeed the line of her slim graceful body where it curved in and out, broadcast adolescence. And that was it, the basis of his Problem—if only he could bring it up with her. It was not something, he knew, which could be improved by the new positions she had suggested. The problem he was having with this child-woman was deeper, interwoven with her slender, almost childish figure and a resemblance he had come to note, of late, between her and his niece, Maribelle, who was just fifteen and who lived with his sister in Elkridge.

Anathae had even, in this conversation, complimented him for his honesty—yet still he could not bring the topic up. *It's not her fault*, he told himself. So he smiled at her, and after they finished their meal, they went to bed. And this time, because he wanted so much to make love to her, he almost made it. Almost—but not quite.

"Perhaps," he said to her in the darkness, unable to keep the frustration out of his voice, "we're seeing too much of each other."

33

John Smith glanced nervously out past the flowered sheet that served as curtain for the front window of the Holy Tabernacle of the Receivers of the Lord, a.k.a. his basement flat. Outside it was dismally cold, and the only people he saw were some well-jacketed girls walking briskly in the direction of the university campus. The wind was blowing, and piles of dirty snow mounded the sidewalks.

"Must have given him the slip," he muttered and went to the folding table that served as a desk as well as a dining table. Smith shivered and sat down, and almost jumped when a key clicked in the front lock.

But he recognized the three bundled figures who came in. Simon was recognizable by his Navy peajacket, although his face was bound by a bright plaid scarf. Susan, by the glint of her smudged glasses beneath her hood; she came in, stamped around the floor to clear her Adidas, and took off her jacket to reveal her jeans and waffle-weave undershirt. And the large bundle of clothes about the size of a small sail which moved in after them and easily closed the door which was forever jamming with a gentle push of his giant paw would have to be Alan Bosnan.

"Did you see anyone outside?" Smith asked.

Susan rubbed her hands briskly and glanced at Simon, who sat on the floor to unlace his boots. "That guy who was asking questions about you? No."

Smith got up and began to pace. It had been a long time since he had been within such easy reach of the law. That the man was a plainclothes cop he had no doubt, just as he was certain that this occasion was not brought on by ordinary coincidence.

Never one to admit his own mistakes, even to himself, the idea that he had overstepped his bounds in trying to blackmail the university—sown the wind to reap the whirlwind, as it were—simply did not occur to him. He saw himself as someone's victim—*some*one who had sold him down the river. Not any of his flock, although he had considered that as a possibility. He'd gone out to make a buck-and-run into misfortune in the form of the man in the black coat who seemed to track him everywhere. The reverend did not have enough money to effect a hasty exit from the Commonwealth, so he couldn't even run. And *who* was really at fault here?

"Willis Baxter!" Smith growled. His voice was so gruff that the three others turned to look at him. "He took no heed of your demonstration. And I must say you botched the publicity by leaving too early."

The *Herald* had run nothing at all, the *Post* only fifteen lines next to a girdle advertisement—and the thrust of that had been that a bunch of religious nuts was attempting to harass a university professor who was too good-natured even to press charges.

Simon hung his head. "We tried," he said, "but most of the girls we tried to convince thought it was too cold to hold a demonstration, whereas the guys thought it was 'cool' of the professor to live with that sixteen-year-old—most of 'em had seen her around and said *they'd* be glad live with her, if they could."

When Arnold Davies was around, Smith tended to use the child-molester angle, but with these three he knew it was better to stress a more religious aspect. Ignoring the fact that he'd overheard Baxter saying he'd felt "possessed," Smith inwardly congratulated himself on his sudden inspiration to change course: "If you must know, when I first heard that that professor might be possessed, I was disbelieving. I, who have never doubted the Great Spirit, doubted His Adversary. The more I think about it, though, the more convinced I become that this Baxter is evil incarnate, a dealer in damned souls, a veritable Priest of the Devil Himself!"

When he spoke like this, the three got a glazed look in their eyes. He turned his eyes upward imploringly and said, "I'm trying to do Good and he's using his devilish influence to try to have me run out of town. He's a Priest of Satan, I say!"

He sat down wearily on the couch and put his face into his hands. "Who will rid me of this troublesome priest?"

Willis brushed snowflakes off his coat, stamped his feet on the welcome mat in front of his door, and walked into his apartment. "Anathae!" he shouted.

The professor went into the living room, the study, the bedroom, the bathroom, and the kitchen—she was not in the apartment.

"Ana!" he called halfheartedly. "I'm sorry," he said to the empty apartment. Then he found the note in the bedroom, on his folded trousers.

Dear Will, it read. *Maybe you're right that we're seeing too much of each other. I hope you don't mind if I say, even though I'll only be gone for a little while, that I already miss you terribly! Anathae.*

Just that morning, a Saturday, he had awakened to find her sleeping peacefully beside him. He'd wanted to wake her, unsay what he'd said the night before out of frustration at his own failure—but he had to go back to the campus to bring home some files for review, some papers to grade. He had to busy himself with something because tonight he had to go to that faculty party over in the new Blakely Memorial Building at the edge of the campus.

And now she was not here.

Willis glanced at his watch. He dreaded going to the party, yet dared not be late. He did not feel he could put up with the gossip he was always subjected to, the kow-towing and jock-eying for position and prominence among the professors and their wives and their pitiful attempts to make the proper impression. Worst of all, there would be plenty to drink.

It was not that he considered the idea of his being an alcoholic any more seriously, but Willis had begun to realize that he drank too often and too much, and that his becoming drunk often had less-than-desirable consequences.

He moped around the apartment for a couple of hours, not finishing the meager amount of work he had assigned himself. By seven o'clock, Anathae still had not returned.

There was no point in worrying. Besides, he decided, if she didn't want to be with him, she didn't have to be.

Now there, he thought, *is the true illogic of my position. First I tell her we're seeing too much of each other—then I feel rejected because she takes me at my word. Oh, my Ana!*

Willis somberly dressed himself in a dark suit and went to the Blakely Memorial Building alone.

"Oh, Professor Baxter, do come in. Everyone else seems to have arrived already." Dean Cromwell Smith's rotund wife, Olivia, took Willis's hand and drew him into the sparkling chandelier-lit room. "Have an hors d'oeuvre," she said, adjusting her silver-gray wig.

Willis obediently took a tiny hotdog in a bun from a large pewter tray along the wall. He sought desperately for some ploy to escape Olivia Smith, who had a habit of grabbing unattached professors and cementing herself to them.

"That's a lovely green pantsuit," he said, watching her eyes shine with the compliment. "And what a novel idea— you and Gertrude Twill wearing practically the same thing."

Mrs. Smith peered into the crowd of men which had formed, as it always did of late, around Trudy Twill. "Why, so we are," Mrs. Smith said faintly. "Of course, she's much too thin these days—poor girl. Another twenty or twenty-five pounds and her clothes wouldn't hang so. Of course, that lean, half-starved look seems to be 'in' these days."

Willis looked at Gertrude to assure himself that she had not been wasting away; most men would call her figure voluptuous, but he had to concede she might look thin alongside Mrs. Smith.

"You go and enjoy yourself, Professor Baxter—but please do me a favor. I seem to have spilled something on my jacket. If you see Cromwell, assure him I've not snuck off with the new biology professor but have only run home to change."

Willis nodded as Mrs. Smith hurried toward the cloakroom, then ambled forward looking for a friendly face. At

last in his wanderings he came upon the corpulent person of
Larry Hawthorne, talking with Peregrin Forsythe (Mathematics), Frank Petruccio (Chemistry), and David Rosenheim (Economics). The wives of the three latter gentlemen—all full
professors save Petruccio, who was an associate professor—
were glittering in chiffon-and-sequin evening attire.

"Glad to see you," Hawthorne said, looking uncomfortable in the jacket and tie he wore. "You know Professor and
Mrs. Forsythe—we were just discussing the importance of
mathematics to the general-diploma student."

"You alone tonight?" Perry Forsythe asked. "I've heard
you have a lovely . . . ward." He smoothed back his thinning hair as though he thought that Anathae might somehow
appear from the woodwork. To himself, Willis had to concede this was possible if unlikely.

"That girl's a bit *young*," Mrs. Forsythe muttered to Mrs.
Rosenheim. The three women sipped from stemmed glasses,
then began to talk in low voices to each other.

Willis, who had intended not to drink tonight, snared a
glass of whiskey from a passing tray and tossed it off. He felt
an anger so cold that it burned his cheek.

Mrs. Forsythe snickered; Mrs. Petruccio sneered; Mrs.
Rosenheim laughed.

Willis took a second glass and, as he felt its contents
entering his stomach, was able to nod at what the professors
were saying to Hawthorne, just as though Mrs. Forsythe's
remark had not been heard and the conversation and laughter
which followed had not been about himself and Anathae.

The three professors and their wives moved off just the
slightest bit, and Willis was effectively alone with Hawthorne.

"Easy, Willis," Hawthorne said, observing that Willis was
downing his third drink in quick succession. "You don't
want to get as blitzed as the last time I saw you, at O'Leary's.
If my memory serves, you were three sheets to the wind at
the time."

Willis felt himself relax. "I suppose that's about as close
as one could come to a quick summation—and even there you
might be a sheet short."

The other professors and their wives turned back to Willis

and Hawthorne in time to hear Hawthorne asking, 'So what have you been up to lately?"

"The usual humdrum stuff," Willis answered, considering taking another drink from the liveried waiter who paused nearby with a heavily laden tray. But he had himself calmed down and decided against easing the waiter's burden. "Everything's so under control at the university, I could take a sabbatical and there'd be no ripples in the water."

"Didn't know you had any research projects under way," Professor Rosenheim said conversationally. He held his wife's arm rather tightly, Willis noted; she seemed about to say something, but a frown from her husband had frozen her lips shut. Willis was simultaneously saddened and amused; he realized Rosenheim was holding her in check. It was both funny and sad because it was the sort of truth one does not care to look straight in the eye: Even a full Professor of Economics does not want his wife insulting the Chairman of the Arts and Sciences Division—and the reason had nothing to do with whether the professor might agree or disagree with the insults his wife might mouth.

"Actually," Willis said, more to cover the silence than because the conversation interested him, "it's been one of my lifetime desires to travel, see in person some of the German and Balkan manuscripts. Unfortunately, a lot of things have kept me from that."

"*A lot of things,*" Mrs. Petruccio whispered under her breath to Mrs. Forsythe, "*or a pair?*" Mrs. Forsythe reddened.

Willis managed to keep his own features under control and, after a few minutes, to excuse himself. He made his way toward the exit and along the way got another large glass of amber liquid, which he quickly downed without tasting.

34

Willis hardly noticed the cold as he staggered through the snow; he was too busy imagining all the things he thought he should have done and said. Like, "And what the hell is *that* supposed to mean, Mrs. Petruccio?" for starters.

He could almost see her turning to smile sweetly and say, "Beg your pardon? Are you addressing me?" and his quick retort that he had not been aware of any *other* Mrs. Petruccio in the room.

And then a lecture on how those who talked behind other people's backs did so in an attempt to make themselves feel superior—but that the very act was a revelation of their own pettiness. He could have told her to replace jealousy, spite, and maliciousness with grace, humor, and goodwill toward one's fellow human beings.

Almost satisfied with that, he might well have added that his relationship with Anathae was none of her goddam business, condemned her for a malicious gossip, and even pointed out that since he had survived for thirty-seven years without her approval or good opinion it was unlikely he would need either in his lifetime.

He was within a few blocks of his apartment before he thought of another good one. He could refer to the Biblical Book of Numbers—which was filled with phrases like "And Ezekiel *knew* his wife, Rebecca, and she bore unto him a son Almitar, and *Almitar* became of age and he *knew* Samantha, who bore him a son," etc.—and then offer her some advice from one of the great philosophers. To the harsh icy wind, Willis said, "Mrs. Petruccio—*know thyself*."

But by that point the coldness had at least sobered him a bit and he was just as glad he'd had enough control to say none of these things. "Because, Mrs. Petruccio," he whispered, "that would bring me down to your level—and I find it hard to imagine anything more pitiful than that."

While Willis Baxter was trudging ever homeward, Alan Bosnan studied a little list.

You *do* recall Alan Bosnan, do you not, dear reader?

Alan Bosnan was no Albert Einstein, nor Manny Schwartz for that matter, but he had heard the reverend say the demonstration run by Simon and Susan had been a failure. Alan, studying his list, made a huge intellectual leap and felt he understood why this was so. It had not succeeded in getting the professor for Reverend Smith. It had not succeeded in getting the professor to exercise.

Deep down inside, Alan Bosnan wanted very much to make a good impression on Smith. All his life, Alan had tried very hard to do things for people he considered his friends—only to have them backfire, usually because he had not quite understood what the friend wanted. This frequently resulted in "instant former friend"—no water need be added.

For example, the friend who had unthinkingly expressed the desire to be able to fly without an airplane. Alan had picked him up and tossed him thirty feet and could not understand why, thereafter, he avoided Alan's company.

Or the football coaches at Powhattan. Alan's size and strength had not gone unnoticed. Although he'd never played in high school, the coaches were certain he could be turned into a holy terror on the football field.

And, indeed, they were partly right—he *was* a holy terror on the field. The coaches had been his friends and he had tried to do what they wanted. What they wanted, they explained, was for him to tackle the man carrying the ball. Which he did. Regardless of which team had the ball. Regardless of whether the person carrying the ball had on a football uniform or was wearing a black-and-white-striped shirt.

Which discouraged his coaches no end.

Alan sat considering the list he had written in large block letters. He did not want to make another, similar mistake again.

"Will?" Anathae's voice drifted toward him on waves of perfume as he opened the door. He peered through the soft light that seemed to emanate from their bedroom, then pushed the door shut behind him.

"Ana!" he said brightly as the grandfather clock struck a single *ding*, indicating eight-thirty. "You in bed already?" Willis came into the bedroom, staggered only slightly, to see Anathae arranged in the enticing altogether.

"You can't say we've seen too much of each other today! Did you miss me as much as I missed you, Will?"

Willis sighed, sank down onto the bed, patted the green coverlet. "Yes, I missed you—very much. Jus' foun' out tonight—I just found out. Don't *care*—this is what I jus' found out—don't care what those nincompoops think. Think you're a child. Think I'm screwing a minor—an immoral, lecherous cad. Got some satisfaction—told 'em off. Well, almost tol' 'em off but decided I was better'n that—'cause, pish, talkin' to them, tryin' to talk to 'em, it's like trying to explain how to drive a stick shift—to a cranberry."

Anathae rose to press her body against his; her creamy face brushed his stubbled chin. "Forget them, Will," she said "Let me help you forget."

She began to unbutton his shirt.

"Them 'n' their catty remarks. So I just walked out. Because I spent *years*—you hear me, Ana?—*years* caring What People Thought. Suddenly, tonight, wham, it hit me— what do they matter? Do I kick up my heels and die if I don't have their good opinion?

"Freedom like that—realizin' I had freedom like that— could make me a hero. I could be one, y'know. Most people, they just won't let the hero outa theirselves. Just don't believe it's there, is what."

Willis rambled on while Anathae slipped his shirt off, struggled with his belt, then pulled his zipper.

"Let 'em bite! I don't care. Let 'em bite all they want.

They wanna be snakes instead of heroes, let 'em—I'm immune to their venom!''

Willis got an angry frown on his face. "Only thing bothers me's when they talk about you."

Anathae sat up from the job she had undertaken. "About me? What about me?"

Willis said, "Too young for me an' followin' me down the path of sin."

Anathae laughed merrily. "Four thousand years doesn't make me a spring chicken, Will. As for sin—well, sex has gotten a lot of bad press but so has almost everything else that's enjoyable."

"So true," Willis said and sighed. "And here we are, steeped in meddlers, waist-deep in gossips. On one level it doesn't matter, but on the other han' it's like spending eternity sloshing around in sewage. There's gotta be something better. Got to!"

Willis managed to keep one eye open as Anathae began to untie his shoelaces. "Hey, something I been meanin' to ask you for a long time."

"What?"

"How come you—I mean, how come you look as young? As you do? I've always wondered. Fifteen or sixteen or seventeen or so."

Anathae dropped one of Willis's shoes to the floor and began untying the other. "I decided on that a long time back," she said with a smile. "I could use illusion to look any way I wanted, of course, but that's a strain. So, I decided when I reached sixteen human years that I liked the way I looked and put a stop to it there."

Willis closed both eyes again, nodded, lifted his foot. *Plop*, went the other shoe.

Anathae tugged and his trousers came down. She gave him a gentle push and he fell back onto the bed. She folded his trousers with care, placed them on a chair by the bed, covered Willis, and climbed in beside him, twining her arms around him. "Don't worry, Will. Things will get better—perhaps tomorrow. You just wait and see." She waited for Willis to reply.

A few minutes passed and then Willis, ever so gently, began to snore.

It should perhaps be noted in passing that the faculty party went on without Willis. But if his early departure provoked a few comments, it was as nothing compared to the gossip which was circulating on the Powhattan campus by the following morning about a few others who had been in attendance.

It seems Mrs. Forsythe had gone home with Associate Professor Petruccio, Mrs. Petruccio with Professor Rosenheim, and Mrs. Rosenheim with Professor Forsythe. Indeed, this was nothing new to them; they had been engaged in this "modern" activity with each other for close to a year.

But heretofore their nonmarried pairings had always been conducted with some measure of discretion—and two of the three wives had been so quick to pass on tidbits of gossip about others because they wanted to divert any suspicions about improper behavior away from themselves.

They might flirt with one another at parties, and indeed the wife of one professor might sit on the lap of another professor on such an occasion without anyone necessarily being the wiser. As proof of this, they had done so many times before.

But beginning about nine in the evening at this particular faculty party, something even they could not later explain to themselves had seemed to make them throw all caution to the winds. All three of the wives were seen to be giving much too passionate kisses to entirely the "wrong" professor, while the professors were observed being much too familiar with their hands on the bodies of entirely the "wrong" wives. As if this were not enough, Mrs. Forsythe had made it quite plain, within the hearing of others, what she intended to do with Professor Petruccio when she led him from the party, while Mrs. Petruccio and Rosey had been found totally compromised by the Rosenheim's baby-sitter—the daughter of Powhattan's Assistant Dean for Planning and Research.

What was it that made them behave in this way? What, indeed?

There is an old saying: "Those who mess with the bull may get the horns."

Could it be, dear reader, that the same might be said of demons?

There is an old saying, "Those who mess with the bull may get the horns."

It be, dear reader, that the same might be said of

35

Don't worry, Will. Things will get better—perhaps tomorrow. You just wait and see, she had said to him the night before. It had come to him as from a great distance.

Sunday morning, through nothing Anathae had done, turned out to be warm. Gone was the threat of more snow, and replacing it were blue skies and puffy cottonball clouds. Although the morning paper forecast a 50 percent chance of rain, nowhere was there even a hint of precipitation. So to that extent, at least, the day was better.

Willis stooped to pick up the paper and immediately regretted the action—the movement started his head throbbing again. *That settles it,* he thought. *No more booze for me.* He closed the door—*very* gently—and moved as slowly and soundlessly as he could back into the lonely apartment. He was frowning, partly because of his hangover and partly because he realized that Anathae was, for the second time in as many days, nowhere to be found. He could not recall any other morning in the past three months when he had not awakened to find her in bed beside him.

He was angry at himself. He *should* have told her, the night before, that he did not really feel they were spending too much time together, instead of falling asleep on her. He now realized how much a part of him she was, how he had grown used to her company and conversation—and how he had dreaded the possibility of losing her.

He made a slow turn through the apartment, as if he might

have overlooked her on his first creep through. He found the note in the bedroom:

Dear Will, it read. *Guess I'd best be away again today. Why don't you relax? Watch a little TV*—Willis would have snorted had he not been convinced this would be disastrous in his present condition; he didn't want to hear someone chewing chicken with rubber teeth, much less a noisy Sunday TV program—*or read a book? Just forget about the university for a while and maybe things will be better for us tonight. Ana.*

Willis put the note aside and sighed.

Getting dressed took more effort and concentration than usual, and when he finally got out to the kitchen there was no hot breakfast waiting in the usual place. "Damned Cheerios," Willis muttered, picking them up individually as he spilled them over the rim of his bowl. After searching through the drawers, he came up with a clean spoon; then, after another expedition, he located the sugar bowl in the back of the cupboard; there was no regular milk, so he combined half-and-half with skim milk. His solitary breakfast was not equal to the sum of its parts.

I'd make it up to Ana if she were here, he thought. By "it" he actually meant several things—his foul humor of the past few weeks, his behavior the previous night, and all the things he'd done in between which had served to keep them apart.

At this moment the doorbell chimed, and Willis smiled through the pain this caused him. She's back! Their life together could begin anew, on a sweeter note than it had ever been before. "Ana!" he said on his way to the door. Willis was surprised, when he threw open the door, to behold not Anathae but someone he did not know at all. It was a student. A very *large* student—at least 350 pounds of muscle on a seven-foot frame.

Surely, dear reader, you've not once again forgotten Alan Bosnan?

"Yes?" Willis said uneasily.

"Professor Baxter," Alan said. "I come here to pick you up for a little exercise." The gargantuan student picked his knuckles up off the floor of the porch and laid a hand the size of a breadbox on Willis's shoulder. "You don't want to come," he said, "I'll just have to pick you up and carry you."

"Exercise?" Willis said incredulously. "Carry me? What are you talking about?"

"I never could explain things too good," Alan said apologetically. "I didn't want to, I never done nothing like it before, but I guess I gotta do this."

Before Willis could speak or move, Alan tapped him lightly on the jaw, using just the smallest part of his strength.

Willis spun around three times, careened off a wall that had been ten feet behind him, tripped over a stool, his easy chair, the couch, brought down a lamp and a picture when he bounced off the other wall, slipped on the rug, and finally slid under the coffee table.

Needless to say, he remembered none of this—he had been unconscious throughout the whole trip.

Willis swam about in celestial ether for an eternity or two, playing kickball with the stars, chatting up a pretty planet, riding comets; he knew everything of space but nothing of time.

When he awoke, the first thing he noticed was that he was on his feet—a truly extraordinary experience after all that swimming about in outer space. Woozily, he attempted to lie down—but a large set of hands, he suddenly noticed, was gripping him firmly. Furthermore, he realized he had a burlap bag over his head, and it smelled *awful*.

"Deep knee bends, Professor," a voice he recognized as the overlarge student's said to him. "You do some deep knee bends for me now."

Willis's knees buckled as the large set of hands pushed down on his shoulders, then his legs straightened out again as the hands tightened to pull him up again. He got the idea; he did a few deep knee bends.

"Five, uh, uh, six, uh, uh," Willis said, "I don't, uh, uh, uh, think I, uhn, ungh, argh, can do, ungh, argh, blurgh, any more."

"Reverend Smith said you got a demon in you and it should be exercised."

Willis, panting heavily, asked, "You sure, hunh, hunh, hungh, he didn't, hoog, hooog, ahuga, say ex*orc*ise?"

Willis did two more deep knee bends before the hulk he sensed beside him said, "Maybe. What's the difference?"

"When you, uh, uh, ex*orc*ise, ungh, ungh, hoog, you, ah, uh, I can't—I gotta stop. Phew!" Willis panted, gasped, sweated, choked, and rasped until he caught his breath. "Perhaps," he said at last, "you should take me to Reverend Smith—to see if this is *really* what he wants."

"Okay," Alan said cheerfully enough.

He grabbed Willis by the arm, forcing him to run—which he did until, exhausted, his legs gave out.

He felt himself being hoisted into the air and draped over the monster's shoulder.

The fellow carrying him opened a door as Willis returned to his senses, wondering whether he had passed out or had just fallen into an exhausted slumber. The burlap bag was still over his head, and it smelled, if anything, worse.

He heard Alan exclaim, "Reverend Smith!" followed by a rustling sound as someone in the room apparently jumped up. It might have been more than one someone—but a man's voice said, "This, uh, this is not, er, what it looks like."

Willis was set down, none too gently, onto a chair. Yes, there were definitely two people here. It sounded as if they were busy doing something with belts and snaps and zippers.

The man's voice continued, "This is our latest convert— her experience was so, so, well, so intense that she, uh, like the Biblical men of the Old Testament, rent her clothing— and mine as well . . ."

"That's right," a curiously familiar female voice said.

". . . and then—and then she had, uh, a *stroke*, yes, a stroke, and I was giving her artificial respiration. However, Alan, I don't think you should mention this to anyone—I may be a hero but I'm only a humble preacher, as you know, and I don't want to brag. Even though, as you can plainly see, I've saved her life."

"Yes," Alan said.

"Would you mind telling me," the man's voice continued, gaining in authority now that it was no longer making explanations, "who this person with the bag over his head is and why you've brought him here?"

"It's Professor Baxter," Alan said, removing the burlap bag from Willis's head. "I brung him for you."

"Henrietta Bradmorton!" Willis exclaimed. There she sat, on a dingy mattress, still putting a T-shirt on over her bare front. Her eyes widened in surprise.

"John," she said, "what's going on? Why has Professor Baxter been brought here in this way?"

"Ah, just a little overenthusiasm, Henny, I'm sure. These things happen." He stepped toward Alan and pulled him aside; thinking of the plainclothes man who had been following him, Smith's whisper to the large student was harsh. "You know they can throw away the key on you? Even if he were a kid, we'd need a relative's *permission* to kidnap Baxter, *written consent* to assault him. Now you go off half-cocked—"

Alan began to burble—which is to say, tears came to his eyes and he beat his large hands on his chest and made a mournful wailing sound. No sense could be made from what he was trying to say.

"Never mind," Smith said. "There, there, I shouldn't have been angry. I'm sorry, Alan."

"Would you mind telling me," Willis asked, "what's going on here? I'd like to know, too."

Reverend Smith sighed, looked at Miss Bradmorton and at Alan, and said, "We're going to try to rid you of your demon, Professor."

Willis eyed Smith dubiously. "You're not going to jump on me and tear my clothes off, are you?"

"No," Smith said. "Different strokes for different folks. Alan, make yourself useful—tie Baxter to the chair he's sitting in."

Dutifully, Alan tied Willis to the chair.

"Henrietta," Willis pleaded, "have you gone mad? I know we're not exactly the best of neighbors, but how can you permit this?"

Miss Bradmorton looked at Smith. Even though this was entirely unexpected, and despite the fact that it seemed wrong to her, she realized Smith was her Man and that she must stick with him, right or wrong. "Do what Reverend Smith wants, Professor. I'm sure he means no harm. If he says he can rid you of your demon, I'm certain he can do it."

"I assure you, Henrietta, and you too, Reverend Smith—I am *not* possessed by a demon." As he spoke, Willis tested his bonds. Quite tight. He could turn his chair over with no trouble anytime he decided that the best place for him to be was on his nose on cold concrete. In the meantime . . . "Now, come on—no harm's been done. My jaw's a little sore, but I'll forget about it—untie me and we'll pretend this never happened. I won't even call the police."

Smith looked at him furiously—Willis had not the slightest idea why. Then the reverend turned, rummaged about in a pile of knickknacks by the toilet, and, grunting with satisfaction, pulled out a dull and tarnished cross and thrust it in Willis's face. "Depart, demon, the body of this poor wretch—depart, servant of Satan!"

Willis clenched his teeth. This was ridiculous and intolerable. He needed a drink. This whole situation was beyond belief.

The fact that he had forbade Anathae to read his mind now entered his mind. Which meant *she* couldn't save him.

But that was all right too, he decided. He would get out of this ludicrous mess on his own hook. He wouldn't call for help from her even if he could.

Which only proves, gentle reader, that pride goeth *after* a fall as well.

36

"So after I damn near ran him down," the cab driver was saying, "he runs around to the other side and hops in—with, s'help me, a pig in a pearl-gray suit!"

But the driver's favorite anecdote was totally lost on Anathae, daughter of Ptenagh, who was consulting a mirror in her purse in disbelief. Coursing down her freckled cheeks from misty eyes were genuine saltwater tears.

Baelzebub! Demons weren't supposed to cry!

She wanted to grab something—anything—and hurl it out the window. She knuckled her eyes dry, tried to review some of her favorite forms of mischief, and then looked in her mirror again. The tears were fresh.

As the driver rambled on about some ventriloquist who used a pig, Anathae buried her head in her arms and sobbed quietly. How ironic—and all this time she had been the cool one, always under control, always having the upper hand. She had known she'd had some fond feeling for the lovable klutz—but now she had played in the quicksand too long and it was sucking her under.

It had hit her while she had been shopping at the Outlet in Falmouth; she'd been in the perfume department jockeying for position among several ordinary humans when the realization came to her. Here she was in a suburban shopping center, being so disgustingly human—and loving it because it was what that absentminded, alcoholic, bookish boob with chalk dust on his hands wanted of her.

So she forgot about the perfume—she wanted to rush back

to Willis, hold him in her arms, and make him understand. She had been on the verge of transporting herself back to the apartment when she felt the wetness coursing down her cheeks and, on impulse, had hailed the cab instead. She wanted to tell Willis about these things but she didn't want to do it with tears in her eyes; she would need time to regain control of herself.

For four millennia she had thought she had been happy at this point in her development. Willis, however, for all his faults and problems, was making her grow up. She had been called to Earth many times by many magicians—always to be used for their greedy ends. She had not minded this—indeed, she had come to expect it of humans and had always had her own fun, granting each of them his wishes while ofttimes playing tricks on them in the process.

With Willis, though, it was different. She had known that practically from the start, of course—it was the extent of the difference, her lack of control over the situation, which bothered her now. *If only,* she thought, *he'd confide in me. If only he'd tell me what is bothering him. If only . . .*

But that was what the tears had been about—that, and how glad she was that she had a human side. She wanted to reach out to Willis, to tell him how her relationship with him was throwing new light into her darkness—but he wouldn't let her touch his mind. And she had reluctantly agreed to keep her distance.

Anathae put her head back against the seat of the cab, tuned out the driver, and let the tears course down her cheeks.

And I thought Hell could be hell, she thought.

Previously, John Smith's method of deprogramming had been simplicity itself. He stashed his kidnapped victim—usually a boy or girl of about college age—in a hotel room and, before their parents arrived, made a deal with them.

He always painted a graphic picture of how it could be done the "hard" way and then went on to tell them that *he* did not care what they wanted to believe—only their parents wanted to change them. He just wanted to make money. If they would go along with him, spend a few days in the hotel, watch some nice programs on TV, go to their parents and spout a little antireligious propaganda, he would give them 25 percent of his fee. They could clock some hours in their beds, get some of mom's apple pie in their stomachs, and, as soon as their parents dropped their guard, *they* could split—with a few bucks in their pockets.

Most of them, outraged at their parents' attempt to change them, made the deal; the ones who didn't, shrugging off outrage and materialistic gain lest they have even a small setback in their spiritual development, he gave up on and let their parents have, taking only part of the money.

His entire career in religious deprogramming lasted only a bit more than six months. His recidivism rate did nothing to enhance his reputation, and he was undone when the inevitable happened—a few of the young men and women with whom he had cut a deal found their parents to be, if perhaps misguided, nonetheless acting out of love and broke down and told them the truth.

But as he had delved deeper into these religious cults which were scraping the flotsam off the vast ocean of American adolescent discontent, he discovered how much these charlatans and shysters were raking in with a few glib words about God and Love.

Which convinced him to purchase a divinity degree and go into the religion business himself.

Only now he was back—involuntarily, to be sure—into something like deprogramming. He decided to try his old tack, or at least a slight variation. He got Henrietta to go to the Catholic church for some holy water and Alan to scout around for other RotL members and then began his pitch to Willis.

"I'm not enjoying this, Professor. What I really want is to make you a well man. But you won't even admit you're sick—when only the other day I overheard you saying you felt you were 'possessed.' Still, I'm willing to concede that you're not possessed by a demon."

Willis's eyebrows shot up in surprise.

"Let's make a deal, Professor. I'm sure you want to get out of here—and I'd like to let you go. I don't even care if you go back to that young girl you're living with. The thing is, I've told my followers—some of them, anyway—that I believe you've been possessed by a demon. If you'll give that a little lip service, let me perform a ritual exorcism, then jump up and renounce your demon, maybe even call me a great man of religion and healing, I'd be able to attract more followers. Once I started showing a decent profit, I'd cut you in for 25 percent. I'm a reasonable man, Professor, no crazy Charlie Manson. I just want to make a buck—and I do it by making people feel happy and fulfilled and giving them something to believe in. That's not such a bad thing, is it?''

Willis looked at him wide-eyed. "You—you mean you're not a fanatic?''

Smiling down at him in a friendly fashion, Smith confessed, "Gracious, no. I just get more attention if I act that way.''

"You're not going to fall on me and tear off all my clothes?''

"No.''

"Then we can talk reasonably?''

"Most certainly.''

"I can't talk, tied up like this.''

"Sorry,'' Smith said. "We have to make our agreement first.''

"I need a drink.''

"Wish I were in a position to offer you something besides water.''

"Never mind, then.'' Willis was quiet for a while. "Listen, I couldn't do what you want—because I really *do* have a demon—''

"Don't be ridiculous.''

"—and if I go about 'renouncing' her, I'd hate to think what might happen. My demon, you see, is half human, and I'm not possessed by her.''

"First you say you *are* possessed by a demon, then you say you're *not*. Would you make up your—''

"No,'' Willis said patiently. "At no point did I say I was 'possessed' by a demon—*you* said that. I said I *had* a demon, and that's a different matter. And I think, I really think, that being the case, you should start considering the possible consequences of your actions. Because if *she* gets ticked off at you—"

Smith sighed and held up his hand, indicating that Willis might just as well stop talking—and so Willis did.

"I was afraid of something like this," Smith said. "My course is set. I'd like to let you go, but I'm afraid I'm going to have to make a show of it. Just keep babbling like you were and maybe I can convince you you're not really possessed."

"I *know* I'm not possessed—"

"Yet you say you have a demon—"

"That's right. *I* have a demon, the demon doesn't have *me*. And if my demon gets angry with you—"

They were interrupted by Alan, who led Simon and Susan into the room. Simon, who had heard the last part of the conversation, was saying in his zealous way, "You cannot threaten us, Professor. We're not afraid because the Lord is on our side."

"I have to admit I admire your bravery," Willis said to them all. "You do seem like the sort who might rush in where even an angel might fear to tread."

"Thank you," Simon said smugly.

Susan said, "Don't thank him—he's insulting us, Simon. Haven't you ever heard the phrase 'Fools rush in where angels fear to tread'?"

Alan picked Willis up, chair and all, and shook him. "Don't do that no more," he said to Willis, whose brains felt scrambled in the shaking process.

"Sure, fine, anything you say," Willis said. And even though he knew that, having asked Anathae not to read his thoughts, it was unlikely she would hear him, inside he was screaming, *Anathae! I need you! Help me! Anathae!*

37

In all her four thousand years Anathae had never, until now, known either helplessness or fear. She had paid the cab driver in the middle of his anecdote, somewhat to his annoyance, finally gotten her tears under control, and made her way up the walk to the apartment.

The door was standing ajar.

Willis *never* left the door open. Not even when he was blind drunk.

She walked inside.

The living room was a mess, with clear signs of a struggle. Various pieces of furniture had been overturned, a picture had fallen to the floor, and broken glass had scattered where it fell. The lamp, too, had been knocked over.

A violent struggle.

"Willis?" she said and got no answer. "Willis?" she said again, tears once more coming unbidden to her eyes.

Anathae reached out with her mind—but even her magic had its limitations. At his request, she had not entered Willis's thoughts for many weeks. If he were in some familiar place—say, the university or Larry Hawthorne's or O'Leary's—she might have been able to reach him. But he was, obviously, somewhere else. And she, who could go anywhere she cared to in an instant, could not go to Willis if she did not know where he was.

Against her will, the thought entered her mind that Willis might even be dead. That, too, her magic would be unable to deal with—she might reanimate his corpse but the thing which lived inside his body would not *be* Willis. Not even demon magic could reach into the oversoul and withdraw the essence which had once been Willis Baxter.

Anathae bit her lip. She might have made a foolish mistake. Like Willis, she had never considered Reverend Smith or any of his followers to be any kind of a real threat. They had, both of them, almost laughingly dismissed those "fanatics" out of hand.

But now, with Willis missing and the signs of a violent struggle all around her, Anathae was not so sure. There was such a thing as a dangerous religious fanatic—some even had delusions about being God's avenging angels. If such a one thought God had told him Willis should be destroyed . . .

It was hard to put thoughts like this out of her mind. For the time being, however, she told herself she might still hope Willis was alive. Anathae sat down on the floor, in the middle of the mess, muttered a few words, and made a complex gesture.

Before her appeared a ghostlike figure of her lover. It made no sound; it came from the kitchen, a frown turning to the smile she knew so well as it mouthed her name. *Her* name . . . ! She saw the ghost reach the front door and open it; outside was a similar phantom, a human of massive proportions. The two ghosts exchanged a few words, then the larger one dealt the Willis-figure a blow that sent him careening through the living room, doing all the damage she saw about her. The large one came in cautiously, shaking its head sadly, put a ghost burlap bag over her ghost lover, picked him up, and carried him with no effort out the door. The "act of violence" having been recreated, the ghosts faded into nothingness.

But that had been what had happened—for all the good it might do her.

Arnold Davies, his fists clenched angrily at his sides, made his way up the walk in front of Willis Baxter's apartment. Seeing the door opened, he walked a little faster and then broke into a run when he heard a girl's sobs from inside.

He hit the door so hard it slammed against the inside wall, almost coming off its hinges.

As he glanced wildly around, he took in the girl—older

than he'd expected, but still quite young—sitting on the floor in the middle of overturned furniture.

"My God!" he said, with a combination of pity and disgust. Seeing no one else in the room, his anger quickly focused on what he saw, interpreted it, and turned to rage. Between clenched teeth, Arnold asked, "Where is the stinking sonofabitch who did this to you? I'll take him apart—I swear to God, I'll kill the lousy bum with my bare hands!"

Anathae looked up at the stranger and almost started a spell, but some instinct made her reach into his mind to discover what his intent had been in barging in. She came up with an image of herself at twelve or thirteen, another of Arnold's strong desire to give Willis a sound thrashing in "defense" of herself.

"Do you think you know me?" she asked, braced to meet anything his confused thoughts might show her.

Arnold looked at her with concern. "I thought you were younger. But still, I was on my way here to tell you you don't have to put up with this sort of thing. I didn't know you'd been assaulted—but you don't have to worry about that anymore. I'll protect you. Is he here?"

Anathae saw some of the conflict in his mind—the desire to give Willis the kind of beating he imagined Willis had given her cooling to the more sensible wish to get her out of the apartment for her own protection. A proviso to this was the intent to return and "have it out" with the professor. Then her probe reached through to the hidden chapters of his childhood, and suddenly Anathae was confirmed in what her instinct told her.

"No," she said, "Willis isn't here."

The young man relaxed a little but said, "I'm taking you away from this. Reverend Smith will help you."

She pushed a little further into his mind, discovered where Smith's apartment-cum-Tabernacle was located. Anathae quickly stretched her thoughts in that direction.

. . . *Anathae!* . . .

It was Will! He was alive, but in trouble!

"I'm sorry, Arnold," she said. "I know it's wrong to do this, but I'm going to make a few quick changes in you. I hope they'll be for the best, because I owe you something for your concern. If I'm doing a wrong to you, I apologize, but I have several pressing matters I must attend to. It's the best I can do."

"Huh? Hey, how do you know my name?"

But Anathae answered in a strange language and a few curious gestures.

"The people at Social Welfare *did* believe you, Arnold," she said. "They took you away from the father who beat you and the mother who never had anything good to say about you and put you in a foster home. That might not have been the best possible life for you, but things could have been worse, and at least your foster parents didn't beat you. Your foster parents are dead now, but you remember them with love and respect. They taught you how to care for others, and in doing that, you learned not to fear people or to react to them with violence."

"I understand," Arnold Davies said.

"Forget you came here. Make friends. Love life itself."

"I will," Arnold Davies said as he turned and walked out the door.

. . . Help me, somebody! . . .

Her attention now focused on Willis, she turned even as Arnold was walking away, her pity for him replaced with a boiling anger.

"I'm coming, Will," she cried. She gestured and muttered; her words echoed in an empty apartment.

Alan set Willis, chair and all, back down on the floor. Simon, however, was still angry, so he walked over to the bound Willis and pulled back a balled-up fist to hit him.

The lights suddenly went out.

"Hey!" said Simon.

"Hey!" said Smith.

"Hey!" said Susan and Alan.

Hey? thought Willis. *Ana?*

That's right, sweetheart, returned the demon-girl's familiar voice in his mind.

Just get me out of here, Ana.

Sorry, lover, she said back to him, *but there's an old saying—"Those who mess with the bull may get the horns."*

I'm just going to show Reverend Smith that demons have horns as well.

Willis, chair and all, began to levitate. He snapped his bonds effortlessly and snorted flames out his nose. His mouth opened and closed, not under his power, and a voice issued from him that sounded like a penny being eaten by a garbage disposal.

"*Smith—ye who do not believe in demons, behold! I am the demon you seek.*"

Susan fainted. Simon began to whimper. Alan stood nonplussed.

Smith ran to the door and pulled desperately at the knob—which came off, sending him sprawling onto the hard floor. He got back up again, but Willis pointed a finger, and although the charlatan tried to keep moving, his feet seemed to be frozen where he stood.

"*You said you wanted to do battle with me, Smith,*" Willis said in the voice which was sending chills running up and down *his* spine. "*You must face me now for that challenge—and should you fail, I will claim your immortal soul.*"

Smith reached inside his jacket and pulled out the cross he had kept there. Pointing it at Willis—and Willis could not help but muse how people who may scoff at an idea one minute can take it quite seriously the next—the reverend said, "Begone, demon!"

"*False is your belief in that symbol, and thus it will not serve you!*" The finger Willis was pointing crackled with static, and a jagged blue-white light leapt from it to hit Smith in the nose.

"Yeeeeeeeeeeeeeeeeeeeeeeeeeeeeeeeoooooooooooooooooooooooo-wwwwwwwwwwwwwww!!!!" was about the way Smith put his feelings on the matter.

Willis brought his hand down to his side and said, "*Now, Reverend, perhaps you should tell your friends here—the ones who are still conscious, anyway—the real truth about yourself.*"

Smith licked his lips. Willis started to lift his hand again.

"My real name is Duncan Hodgkins I'm a fake a charlatan I'm just after money I've never had a decent motive in my life I know perfectly well everything I have ever said is false

I spend our collections at O'Leary's Bar and Restaurant I'm sorry now PLEASE LET ME OUT OF HERE!''

"There's the matter of possession of your soul."

John Smith giggled in hysterical fright.

"No please anything I mean hahaha my soul's worth nothing and wouldn't you rather have my baseball-card collection instead?"

"You have the Willy Mays 1961 and the Mickey Mantle 1959?"

"Yes! Yes!" cried Smith hopefully, and he added jubilantly, "Yes!"

"Too bad. So do I."

Smith began to grovel. He pleaded. He begged. He implored. Such gnashing and grinding of teeth, such whimpering and whining confessions and beggings for forgiveness would have put all the denizens of the seventh level of the inferno to shame.

"I claim your soul, Duncan Hodgkins! I will drag it kicking and screaming back into Hell with me to consume at my leisure!"

"Noooooooo!"

"A scrap of flesh a year, a finger a century, to skewer and roast—"

Willis found himself pausing, turning his head a little as if in thought. *"You wouldn't have the Crackerjack card of Frank 'Homerun' Baker, would you?"*

"I have it! I have it!"

"How about Honus Wagner?"

"I've got that too! Over there by the cot in the shoebox." He pointed a trembling, hopeful finger.

"I'll take your entire collection. And you will get out of town!"

"I will! I will!"

Willis picked up the shoebox and disappeared in a cloud of smoke.

38

Let us follow a sleek train leaving the Commonwealth and entering a neighboring state. It is a long train, a passenger train. This particular passenger train is equipped with berths, and in one of the uppers are Mr. and Mrs. Duncan Hodgkins.

"Good works, Henny," Mr. Hodgkins is saying to his new wife. "The only way I can see to do it is with good works. I know I haven't been a good person up to now and the honest life may be a little hard for me to adjust to, but just because I'm not a real reverend doesn't mean I can't do a little good in the world."

Henrietta Hodgkins, née Bradmorton—who would have Followed Her Man Anywhere and even played Bonnie to his Clyde (although she is frankly just as glad she does not have to)—is ensconced in the pillows beside him. She shakes her head at him fondly and smiles. "And all because you *think* you saw a demon."

"I *did*, it came and possessed Professor Baxter, I tell you!" the man who had once been known as the Rev. John Smith says defensively.

He pulls the sheet up over his hairy chest and sulks—after so many years of making people believe whatever ridiculous or impossible notion he could think of, he is now finding it hard to be believed by his own wife when telling her the solemn truth.

"Anyway," he says after a while, "that's not the only reason."

His wife moves a little closer to him. "What else?"

His eyes glint slightly as he speaks. "I know it's a base and selfish motivation, and that might work against me—but I really hope it doesn't. The way I look at it, if I can *try* to help people, if I can be humble, if I can strive to help my fellow man, and if I'm actually successful in doing what I strive to do, maybe if I'm lucky I can get my baseball cards back."

He reaches up and turns off the light.

But who knows, dear reader—maybe, for once in his life, Duncan Hodgkins is right.

Willis was so relieved to be back in his own apartment that at first he did not notice the change. Most of all, he felt dizzy and strange and elated.

Anathae asked, "Do you notice anything different, Will?"

Willis looked around. The damage that had been done to the living room had been repaired, but he suspected this was not what Anathae meant. He looked at the old dining set and the couch and his old purple easy chair but could detect nothing different about them or, indeed, anything else.

He turned to Anathae. "I guess you've got me. What—" He stopped.

It was Anathae who was somehow different. She had grown a bit taller, her hair was longer, her face fuller with not quite so many freckles, her breasts were rounder and even more firm. She was—or seemed—older.

"Somewhere between eighteen and twenty, wouldn't you say, Will?" Anathae asked, turning slowly so he could take her in with his eyes.

Willis said, "You read my mind."

"Couldn't help it, Will—we were as one. There was no way I couldn't know your deepest thoughts."

"You're twice as beautiful as before, of course," he said, shaking his head. "But, damm it, you shouldn't have to change for my sake."

"Will, if you'd only *told* me. My 'being' sixteen was all vanity—*my* vanity."

Willis lowered himself into his easy chair. "You don't mind?"

"No. Because you've helped me grow." She grew more

serious. "Will. About your fourth question. Do you recall it?"

"Yeah," he said with a touch of a smile. "Wasn't it ridiculous?"

"No, Will. No, it wasn't ridiculous."

He tried to maintain his smile. "I'm not sure what you mean, Ana."

"You're a fine man, Willis Baxter. A good man and a kind man. You're noble and brave and honest. You're loving and giving and caring. You are by far one of the finest human beings I've ever known. And you're an alcoholic."

Willis ran his tongue over his lips. This was ludicrous, absolutely ridiculous. Too absurd for words. All he needed to set things right now, he thought, was a good, stiff—

—drink?

"Will, are you listening to me?"

"Yes," he said. "I am. And, you know, although it really comes as something of a surprise . . . I just had this funny/not-so-funny idea that you could be right."

"I'm not telling you this to make you change for my sake, Willis," Anathae said. "But you *must* change for your own. You tell yourself you're not an alcoholic because you have a notion that alcoholics are all drunken bums. That's just not so. But the thing is, if you don't give it up and give it up soon, that's just what you'll become."

"You're wrong, Ana. I could never—"

"*No*, Will—*you're* wrong. Think about it. It's been bad before, but now it's getting worse. All your adult life, whenever you've had a problem you couldn't solve immediately, your response has been to take a drink. It doesn't help solve them—it just lets you escape them for a while. You used to be a social drinker—but of late you've been drinking frequently when you're alone. You've got several bottles stashed around here for what you think of as 'emergencies.' You've even got one locked in your desk drawer at the university—"

"But Ana," Willis tried to protest, "almost *every*one—"

"Not true!" she interrupted. "Stop and listen to yourself, Willis, and try to *think!* That's the excuse you offer yourself—that 'everyone' does it. But they don't, Willis. Or the few who do, you don't respect at all. And deep down, you realize it. That's partly why you've been thinking of taking a sabbatical.''

"I've been planning to take a sabbatical," he contradicted, "because I'm not really needed. My programs are going forward and there are just a few minor details to be attended to—details a good secretary could handle just as well. And Gertrude's a *very* good secretary."

"I said 'partly,' Will. You've also had a few occasions where you knew something was affecting your judgment. You just never put two and two together to realize that the 'something' was the booze."

Willis sat frowning, trying to get everything Anathae was saying to make sense. That he felt a drink would help him to accomplish this only seemed to underscore the fact that what she was saying was correct.

After a moment he looked back at her and asked, "Isn't there something you could do—with your magic?"

"Yes," she said, "but I'll only do it if that's what you really want. But do you recall, Will, I once told you there were things my magic could do to change you but it would really be much better if you made those changes yourself? It was this I had in mind."

"I don't understand."

Anathae sighed. "It's usually wrong to use magic to force *inward* changes on any human being. I did it to one of Reverend Smith's followers—a very troubled boy who nonetheless felt concern for me in what he mistakenly believed to be my sorry plight. I really thought he needed it, so I changed him. But even with what I've learned in my four thousand years, I have no idea if the change will *really* be good for him, though I still hope it will be. My good intentions are no excuse if I'm wrong, nor is the fact that I really didn't have time to deal with his problem in any other way."

She shook her head to throw off her unintended digression and went on, "And in your case, Will, with your particular problem, it would be a temporary solution at best. I could cast a spell to free you of your physical need—but it wouldn't do you any good. Sooner or later a problem would crop up, you'd want to take a drink, and you'd take it because you'd know I could always cast that spell again. This is something *you* must deal with—although not without support. But unless you force me to do otherwise, I'll only help you in any *human* way I can.''

Willis took in a deep breath and let it out. He said at last, "Well, I went against your advice on using magic once before, and the result was barely short of disastrous. But I'll need your human help."

Anathae sat down on the arm of his chair and took his hand in hers. "You'll have it."

"And what about . . . my other problem?"

The demon-girl dimpled. "Well, while your drinking has contributed, you were mostly right about that. You couldn't cope with making love to someone who looked so much like a 'little girl.' But as you can see," she said, rising, "I'm a woman now. I'm going to take a shower—give me twenty minutes, okay?"

Willis acknowledged her with a nod. When he heard the shower running, he got up and went to his study, opened the drawer to his desk, and pulled out the letter he had drafted to Dean Smith—the application to go on sabbatical. He still felt as he had when he'd first written it, that he wanted to see Europe and possibly South America, but he also realized this would give him the time he would need to come to grips with his drinking problem. And by the time they got back, he reflected, the change in Anathae would probably go unnoticed.

He signed the letter and put it in his briefcase so he would not forget it the next morning; it would take about a week to process, but it was time for a new beginning. The longest journey always begins with the first step.

Willis turned from his desk and walked into the bedroom while unbuttoning the sleeves to his shirt. Raising his voice over that of the water running in the bathroom, he asked, "Did I understand you correctly to say that you read *everything* in my mind?"

The water stopped. "Everything," Anathae replied. She came into the bedroom still drying herself. "You believe you're in love with me and wonder if I feel the same for you."

"And do you?" he asked as he unbuttoned the front of his shirt.

'Love you?'' she asked, dropping the towel over the back of a chair and climbing into bed. "As alien as it seems to me, I'm begining to think I may. But would it upset you too much, Will, if I said I'm still not certain?''

Dropping his shirt on the seat of the same chair, Willis smiled. "I guess not," he said, remembering what he'd felt in her mind not a half hour before.

"What do humans mean by 'love,' Will? I read your mind but I'm still not sure. If you mean do I really care for you as a person, the answer's definitely yes. Yes, Will I *care* for you so much it sometimes hurts, because I know you care for me—not just the demon part which can perform magic at your bidding but the human part. The human part, for which *you*'ve performed a kind of magic. I've known numerous human men, Will, but you're the first who kept in mind that I'm half human as well as half demon. The human part of me is still quite young—and, until I met you, untouched.''

"You've come of age, Ana," Willis said. He had finished disrobing and now lay down beside her, kissing her warm moist mouth. "We both have.''

"Make me feel human, Will.''

Willis caressed her side, her knee, the inside of her thigh.

"Feels nice," she said, her eyes almost closing.

"Yes," he said. His mind was unable to think of anything at all now except how much he desired her. "Oops. Your tail.''

"Um. Yes.''

"If you don't cut that out, I'm going to mush your mouth.''

"And you expect me to cut it out?''

Willis kissed her. Gone forever was the trembling fear he had once felt—gone all feelings of ineptitude, unsureness, unworthiness. He knew he could make love to her and that it would give equal joy to both of them; he knew he should make love to her so that they could share this joy; he knew he could make love to her—and so he did.

It was a step. But every journey must begin with one, dear reader, and end with one as well.

AFTERWORD

by Ted White

Michael F. X. Milhaus made his first appearance in print with a letter published in the December 1975 issue of *Fantastic*. In that letter he complained that the stories in that magazine weren't what they had been twenty-five years earlier: "It used to be that the prose in *Fantastic* (and *Fantastic Adventures* before it) wasn't as polished, but the authors had *stories to tell*. You know: stories with beginnings, middles and ends— real plots. A guy would have a problem and he'd solve it. Those were really satisfying stories for me to read.

"Now at this point you're probably shaking your head and saying to yourself, 'This guy's got a case of nostalgia.' And I thought maybe you'd be right, so I pulled out some old (1948 and 1949) issues of *FA*. Remember them? Raggedy pulp edges you couldn't thumb through and shedding dandruff all over your lap? Real colorful covers? Big, double-page illos— even a double-page contents page! Of course the paper's getting yellow and brittle now—mine are, anyway, but they've been up in the attic for twenty-five years—and I had to be careful turning the pages, but I read some of those issues, Ted, and even though I didn't remember the stories at all, and some of the writing was a bit crude by present-day standards, *I really enjoyed them*.

"Well, sitting down and spending a couple of evenings reading those old pulp issues really inspired me, and I wrote a story of my own, 'A Personal Demon,' which, it seems to me, has a lot of the flavor of the stories I enjoyed. Now I know this whole letter sounds like a buildup to my trying to sell you this story, but that's not the point. The point is that I had to write this story in order to be able to read the kind of story I enjoy. Maybe it's a lousy story by your professional standards, but I'm enclosing it just so you can see what I'm talking about. Who knows—maybe you could get stories like this from your present authors too, if they knew anyone wanted to read them.''

Milhaus's letter was followed by this editorial response:

''I get letters more or less like this one from time to time, in which would-be authors point out to me how much better their stories are than the stories we print. However, Mr. Milhaus's story is the first to favorably impress me. It's not the greatest piece of fiction I've ever read, but it is what he claims it to be: refreshingly old-fashioned. You'll see it here soon, perhaps even next issue.''

And sure enough, ''A Personal Demon'' did appear in the February 1976 *Fantastic*.

It was generally well received. One reader wrote (in the letters column of the August 1976 issue), ''Mr. Milhaus is right. 'A Personal Demon' is just the kind of story that can pick you up after a long day of hard work and frustration, instead of pushing you over the edge like a lot of the new wave crap does. It's hard to believe this is his first story; his style is so smooth. What I liked most was the fact that, while the style is old-fashioned, the plot is not. There was no mention whatsoever of a pact with the Devil, our hero being tricked into immediate payment, or our hero tricking the Devil, etc. Thank heaven! (Better make that, 'Thank Michael Milhaus!') I wonder if he can do it again.''

By then he already had; ''In a Pig's Eye'' had appeared in the May 1976 issue. But aside from a letter of his own in the August *Fantastic*, Milhaus did not appear again in the magazine until more than a year later, when ''With Good Intentions'' was published in the September 1977 issue.

An editorial blurb hinted at problems behind the scenes: ''Michael Milhaus was lucky. With a letter accusing us of not publishing enough of the 'good old-fashioned' stories here anymore, he sent us a story to show what he meant: 'A Personal Demon.' Flushed with success, he quickly sent us a second, 'In a Pig's Eye.' Then things bogged down. A draft of his third story was not acceptable. Back-and-forth correspondence ensued, during which Milhaus came to realize that 'good old-fashioned' stories require more than just the desire for them to occur; they demand good old-fashioned craft and work—lots of work. Out of that realization comes the New Milhaus: no longer dilettante, but working writer. . . .''

After that the New Milhaus was back in the December 1977 issue with "A Trick of the Tail," this time the subject of the cover painting, and in the April 1978 issue with "Where Angels Fear to Tread." And that, as it turned out, was his last published appearance, although he was rumored to be "working on a novel."

Michael F. X. Milhaus was not, as you must already realize, an actual person. He was instead the "house name" or pseudonym for Dave Bischoff, Rich Brown, and Linda Richardson (who was then writing under the name of Linda Isaacs) under my editorial direction. I was *Fantastic*'s editor.

Milhaus's was a long-delayed birth. Conception occurred on election night, November 1964.

In 1964 I was a young up-and-coming science fiction writer, and many of my friends held similar aspirations. We had formed an informal writers' group that met on Tuesday nights each week. Our purpose was not only to critique each other's stories, which we did, but to talk shop and to develop ideas in collaboration. (The group produced two books, the pseudonymously authored *Invasion from 2500*, and my collaboration with Dave Van Arnam, *Sideslip*.)

On the first Tuesday of November 1964, we alternated shoptalk with election returns on the TV: LBJ soundly defeated Goldwater. In the course of the evening Rich Brown, Dave Van Arnam, and I discussed an idea that John Boardman had suggested to us. Boardman, a physics professor at Brooklyn College, was fascinated by the trappings of the occult, and had at someone's urging drawn a pentagram on an apartment floor and spoken the Latin incantations which were supposed to summon up a demon. Naturally no demon appeared, so John followed through with the rest of the incantation, which summarily consigned the laggard demon to hell. Then Rich pointed out that if there were in fact demons, they were probably all irretrievably consigned to hell by now, since that was the customary thing to do when one of them failed to answer a summons—so it was no wonder none appeared anymore.

This suggested a story to us, and my contribution at that point was to suggest that in the story the demon who finally answered the summons should be female and cute. I was thinking specifically of Charles Myers's "Toffee" stories, which had appeared in the late-forties *Fantastic Adventures* and the early-fifties *Imagination* and *Imaginative Tales*. These stories (which I regret to say have failed to live up to my youthful memories of them) were in turn loosely modeled on Thorne Smith (some people called them "swipes," but that was unfair), evoking a little of the mood of *Topper* and Smith's other sophisticated whimsical fantasies.

It was my idea to create a modern "Toffee"—a cute female demon who would wreak inadvertent havoc upon some poor male.

Nothing came of it. We kicked the idea around and built up a fairly good story, but no one actually sat down and *wrote* it.

Years passed. In late 1968, I was offered the job of editing two magazines, *Amazing Stories* and *Fantastic*. Two years later I moved from New York City to the Washington, D.C., area. In 1971, I took part in a series of Guilford Writers' Conferences held in Baltimore. And a year or two after the last Guilford Conference a couple of its alumni, Tom Monteleone and Grant Carrington, suggested we form a local writers' group, to meet weekly, on Wednesday nights.

Thus was born the Vicious Circle, a group of professional and semiprofessional writers who got together to critique stories, talk shop, and develop collaborative ideas.

My own place in this group was unique, since I was its resident editor and constantly looking for good stories to publish in my two magazines. I have no doubt that the contributions of the Vicious Circle enriched my magazines, and the encouragement I was able to provide as an instant market for the group's stories undoubtedly kept enthusiasms high.

In 1975, it occurred to me to trot out the idea which had been conceived eleven years earlier. I was fortunate that Rich

Brown had also moved to the D.C. area and had joined the group. He was able to supplement what I remembered with additional details, and between us we described to the others in the group all that we could recall of our original story.

Several members of the group liked the basic idea and were eager to work on it. After details had been settled, Rich, Dave Bischoff, and Linda Richardson emerged as the actual authors, but the rest of the group made many critical contributions.

After Rich and I had described our basic ideas, we began as a group to kick around plot ideas. From these came a first draft of the first story, "A Personal Demon," which was closely critiqued at a subsequent meeting.

When we criticize a story in the Vicious Circle we operate on several assumptions, one of which is that the author is professional enough to divorce his or her ego from the story in question, and that criticisms will be fair, but merciless. Stories are stripped to their skeletons and examined closely for structural defects. Then both their conceptualization and their prose are put under the microscope. Few stories emerge from this process unscathed; all are improved by it.

That first draft of "A Personal Demon" was demolished. I had loaned copies of my Thorne Smith, Charles Myers, and P.G. Wodehouse books to the putative authors of the story, hoping that the light breezy style would rub off on them. It hadn't. The tone of the story was wrong, and the plot didn't entirely work. But from that session emerged what would be the modus operandi for the production of all of Michael F. X. Milhaus's work.

First one of the three collaborators would bring in a draft based on the previous week's plotting session. The draft would be pulled apart and criticized by the group as a whole. As the editor and original conceptualizer, I would distill the criticisms into a coherent form and suggest the course for the next draft. The second draft would be written by another of the collaborators, and would undergo the same process from the group. Sometimes the second draft would be an almost wholly different story, and sometimes it would go too far in the opposite direction from the first. The third collaborator would take both drafts and their resulting criticisms and reconcile them in a third draft. Sometimes the third time was the charm; sometimes yet another draft would be necessary.

There was no set pattern that determined which of the three collaborators would write which draft; it depended on enthusiasm, time, and ability. Each author had his or her strengths and weaknesses; together Bischoff, Brown, and Richardson developed a complementary strength.

What emerged from these sessions was a series of stories which were unique in tone and flavor. The "Milhaus" style was unlike that employed by Bischoff, Brown, or Richardson in their solo stories; it was like musical collaboration in which members of a band jointly create works with a distinct collaborative identity. What I noticed early on was that the Milhaus stories had a particular *moral* tone. This, more than anything else, defined the "old-fashioned" quality of the stories.

Here was this guy, Willis Baxter, who had fallen into a comfortable and unchallenging niche as a college professor. And then—bang!—everything changes with the advent of Anathae. It would have been easy to follow the "Toffee" route—mishaps and pratfalls, cheap laughs and embarrassing complications, all leaving the protagonist unchanged by the end of each story so that each story can be seen as parallel to the others, and stories can be read in any order—but we could do better than that.

Thus Anathae poses a challenge to Baxter, providing him with a situational problem (or two) to be solved in each story. Baxter's challenge is to grow. From his growth as a human being comes the solution to each of his problems.

And although in apparently lightweight stories like these supporting characters are usually made of the thinnest cardboard—existing largely to strike the proper attitude, especially the antagonists—in *these* stories the supporting characters also develop in response to their problems, and the best solution to a problem is seen to be that which benefits everyone, at no one's expense.

Thus, the Milhaus stories are *sequential*: Each follows and depends upon its predecessors; each takes Willis Baxter's growth a step further. As Baxter grows, so does his appreciation for the people around him, who are also growing, each in his or her own way.

That's old-fashioned.

"Where Angels Fear to Tread" wrapped up one phase in Willis Baxter's life, but the story was not intended to wrap up Milhaus's writing career.

We started planning the novel in 1977, and Linda wrote its opening chapters. But the momentum wasn't there. The novel evaporated. Rich's marriage was coming to an end. Dave was enjoying increasing success on his own (after collaborating with Dennis Bailey on *Tin Woodman* and with me on *Forbidden World*) and was undertaking an ambitious book-writing schedule. Linda, after a notable career writing short stories for a variety of markets, was having problems with her marriage and turning away for the time from writing.

And I was about to leave *Fantastic*.

I'd been editing *Fantastic* and its sister magazine, *Amazing SF*, for ten years. For ten years I had accepted the lowest salary and smallest editorial budget in the field simply because I loved the magazines and I wanted to do all that I could for them. (*Amazing* was the world's oldest sf magazine, having launched the whole sf field with its first issue in 1926.) But after ten years I had done about as much as I could do, and when the magazines changed owners in the fall of 1978 I decided after a brief try that working for the new owner would be intolerable (he wanted to pay even *less*).

Suddenly the conditions that had created Milhaus weren't there any longer. And then neither was he.

I'm sorry about that. I wanted to read the novel.

I'd still like to.

Do you think there's any chance, Ana . . . ?

—Ted White

About the Authors

DAVID F. BISCHOFF was born in 1951 and grew up carousing with Air Force brats near Andrews A.F.B. He graduated from the University of Maryland in 1973 with a B.A. in TV and Film and worked for six years with NBC Washington, then became a full-time freelance writer.

He has written a number of novels, including *Nightworld, Star Fall, Mandala, Day of the Dragonstar* (with Thomas F. Monteleone), *The Selkie* (with Charles Sheffield), available in a Signet edition, and the upcoming *Infinite Battle* and *Cosmos Computer*. *The Destiny Dice* and *Wraith Board,* Books One and Two of *The Gaming Magi,* are also available in Signet editions.

His short work has appeared in such magazines as *Omni, Analog, Magazine of Fantasy and Science Fiction,* and *Amazing,* as well as a number of original anthologies.

He has served as both secretary and vice-president of the Science Fiction Writers of America.

Bischoff loves movies, rock and British folk, and other things too humorous to mention. He now lives in Silver Spring, Maryland.

RICH BROWN, 42, has been a cab driver, multilithographer, temporary typist, and editor and/or reporter (as the occasion warranted) for several newspapers, from some "shoppers" on Staten Island to a daily Wall Street trade paper, as well as a financial writer for Reuters. He is divorced and presently lives in Washington, D.C., where he is an editor for a trade association. Besides the collaborations upon which this novel is based, he has sold stories to *Amazing, Fantastic,* and *Vertex.* A former member of the SFWA, he nonetheless cherishes his status as a fan. He has been an active participant in sf fandom since 1956, attending conventions and club meetings and publishing fanzines; he currently edits *beard-*

mutterings, which, often as not, has nothing whatsoever to do with sf or fantasy.

LINDA RICHARDSON was born in 1944 and grew up through all those now-exalted eras of postwar reconstruction, the 1950s, hippiedom, and the Vietnam War. A graduate of the University of Maryland, she sold her first story to *Galaxy* in 1973, and thereafter sold a number of other science fiction tales.

Currently, Linda lives and works in the Washington, D.C., area, and her greatest interests are natural science, medicine, philology, hiking—and learning to ski.

More SIGNET Books by Robert A. Heinlein